Cat's Crossing

BILL CAMERON

Vintage Canada

VINTAGE CANADA EDITION, 2004

Copyright © 2003 Bill Cameron

www.randomhouse.ca

NATIONAL LIBRARY OF CANADA CATALOGUING IN PUBLICATION

Cameron, Bill, 1943–
Cat's crossing / Bill Cameron.

ISBN 0-679-31169-6

I. Title.

PS8555.A51872C28 2004   C813'.6   C2003-905680-5

BOOK DESIGN BY CS RICHARDSON

Printed and bound in Canada

10 9 8 7 6 5 4 3 2 1

For my wife, Cheryl
With love and thanks

One

THE BLACK CAT woke in the late afternoon and felt something wrong with his right hind leg. There was a new presence, a strange thin layer between the flesh and the muscle. He stretched. This film in his body tightened and loosened and followed him as he moved.

He jumped down onto the big room's carpet and felt pain in his leg when he landed. It set him slightly off balance. The leg didn't hurt, but it felt numb and only half connected, as though the muscles had pulled and then gone slack and weak.

The sun had begun to move toward the horizon, and the light in the room was beginning to fade. He had a few minutes before the person came. She'd arrive in a billow of sweet scent, and he'd arch his back and bump against her, waiting for the rattle of dry food into his bowl. She always fed him and stroked him at this time of day, but now he felt an impulse to avoid her, even if that meant missing his food. He wasn't hungry.

There was a loose screen in the window at the top of the landing. He had noticed it a few weeks ago and marked it with the scent from the side of his mouth. He moved into the hall and up the stairs. The presence in his haunch was constant. He sat on the smooth wood floor of the hallway and stared at the glowing window and then gathered himself and jumped up onto the sill, nudged the screen aside and squeezed onto the ledge.

The outside world was endless. He was used to the

bounce of sound off the hard walls and the slur of voices from the floor below, but here in the open air the noises came clearly: below a sweep of water on grass, voices and the hammering of metal, the scrape of claws against bark and a rubbing of leaves, and smudges of noise from above, a faint pulse of wings. He felt dizzy. He knew contained life, the spaces inside the house. The longest distance he remembered was the hallway that ran along the second floor. Now he was in an enormous nothing-filled quarter-dome, the wall at his back, the ground running far underneath him away to the distant trees. He was frightened by the size of the empty air. From inside the house he could sometimes hear bird calls through the glass, and he'd sit and listen and growl, but those sounds were tiny and this place was rumpled and alive with wind, with thin shifting smells, and with the faint sounds of creatures breathing and moving on and below the surface. The air swept over him and against him.

His bad leg pulsed. He sensed something far away, even farther than the forest, something so distant he couldn't settle on its exact direction, but he knew what it was. There was a tree limb that ended about three feet from the window and the healing would be somewhere beyond that, in the direction the wind was coming from, far off beside some water. It would be a plant, maybe some kind of grass. He would know it when he reached it. He felt a moment of weariness. It was very far away, but the signal was very clear, unmistakable, reliable.

The black cat jumped, slipped, clung, swayed and worked his way along the limb to the trunk of the tree. He saw the ground far below and stopped, feeling the distance and the possibility of falling, landing hard, hurting himself, damaging his body further. He thought of turning to back down the shaft of the tree, digging with his claws into its seams and skin, but that would mean moving into an unseen space, ending up maybe in the mouth of some undetected hunter. He shuffled, mewed, hunched and finally half jumped and half ran down the tree head first, his claws shifting and scrabbling on the bark, his eyes narrowing, and as the earth came closer he pushed off from the rough surface and landed on the gravel of the driveway.

Straight-edged shadows from the house fell across the failing light. He heard human sounds, footsteps and words. He was hungry and his hip was annoying. The crushed stone pushed against the pads of his feet. He moved along the line of the outer buildings, flowing like oil away from the big house.

The cat was beginning a journey into a city built on a lake at the convergence of two rivers. The city had grown inland along the rivers, climbed a line of hills and descended into a bowl of pasture and plain, scraping them flat, cutting them with sewers and paving them over. The rutted, piled-up, shoved-aside land smelled of nails, dust and new sod.

There were three million people in the city now. Along the lakefront the concrete, glass, metal and flesh were crowded so closely together that they seemed to press the air between them into dense blocks filled with soot and fumes. The birds that flew in from the lake found their wings labouring, and at night when they knocked into the towers that reared into their airways they fell straight down to the street. The paths through the air were stitched with power lines and saturated with the phantom crosstalk of wireless telephones, broadcast signals and magnetic fields that blossomed out from the pylons. The birds flew above the malls, their bodies glowing with signals from the earth.

A mile north of the lake, the city rolled up a long line of bluffs and onto a fertile plain. The earth here was sealed under a jumble of concrete, tar, lawn, gravel, oil and steel, plaited below the surface with plastic tubes for sewage, water, power and communication lines. There was a constant moving weight of trucks and vans carrying meat, bread and processed vegetables for the doughnut shops, burger palaces, falafel stands, sausage vendors, chip wagons, curry, roti, Chinese, Korean and Thai outlets that sustained the suburbanites and the office workers. The buildings in this outer arc of the city were smaller than the ones downtown and were filled with local branches of the big downtown banks, the offices of lawyers who had not been asked to join the noted firms by the water, and suites of accountants who processed the unremarkable tax returns of middle-income salary workers who lived in the housing developments nearby.

Beyond this band of medium-level life was a wide highway that funnelled traffic through and past the city, a chute of moving lights and drifting fumes, streaks of rubber pasted on concrete and peels of tire tread on the shoulder, and then abruptly just beyond the roar of the road a sudden flush of trees and a sweetening of the air, and then large estates laid out beside new lakes. Some streets had houses that were built to resemble columned Southern manors with white statues beside neat vineyards; they belonged to grocery and wine kings, recent money, immigrants. People with old English money lived on other streets, nearby but separate, in houses with timbered stables, mud rooms and leaded windows.

The cat was beginning his journey from a mansion with long lawns and clipped hedges. The automatic sprinklers had come to life for their evening cycle, the water falling on the outer leaves of the oak trees with a sound like tearing paper. There was a tuft of dog hair and a tang of dog piss on the corner of the last building and then a gap, a belt of churned earth and a tiny opening in the shrub where the rabbits had chewed out a passage to a vegetable garden. It was late April, the ground was freshly turned over and the seeds just buried, but the rabbits had been here already, moving along their track from the field beyond the hedge. The cat wound his way into the hedge and along the rabbit trail, the hairs on his neck prickling upright at the half-familiar scent.

In the air above, the sudden slight hiss of an owl's wing. It was almost night now. He'd been moving quickly to get away from the house, but now he slowed, and at the bottom of his hearing range, where the sound turned into vibration, he picked up a low, surging roar from the highway. He would have to get past that barrier; he could sense his cure was far beyond it. He could almost feel the rough rasp of the grass in his mouth and the tenderness of the shoots after he pulled them from the earth, the crushed green and the juices beginning to dissolve this thing in his hip.

Julia Will came into the drawing room and turned on the light, looking for her cat. He usually slept here in the late afternoon and woke when she came in, stretching and yawning, his ridged salmon-coloured mouth showing behind the row of little white teeth. Usually he would purr and nudge at her hand; she could feel the little thud and swipe of his muzzle on her fingers. He wasn't here now.

Julia always fed the cat. She told the housekeeper she wanted to keep an eye on his weight, but in fact she liked his calling, back-arching ingratiation when she pulled his box of dry food down from the shelf in the pantry. He seemed to live for the twice-a-day rattle of pressed dried pellets into the white china bowl. Julia had put one on her tongue once and found it sour and grainy, but the cat liked it. She knew a little bit about this, since her husband's money came from meat-packing. She'd been to his sausage plant and come away amazed at the scrimping and saving, the effort to use every part of the carcass—the steel rakes gathered the bones for the button makers, the slimy wagons bore piles of sodden hides off to the tanneries and the pet food machine took in the leftovers, minced and baked them and extruded them in tiny blunt brown discs.

He had to be sleeping somewhere else.

She looked around at the big room, half pleased with it. She liked the symmetry of the big space, with its great square mirror and the parallel lines of the books and shelves behind the glass, but there were unpleasant curves and yielding shapes in the furniture. Her husband had wanted comfort, confining, consoling soft surfaces. She looked at herself in the mirror, approving of the straight angles of her arms, neck, shoulders and jaw, ignoring the rest.

Her husband had ordered the oval pool with the absurd weak fountain, its water curving hopelessly upward, failing and falling back. She'd commissioned the straight-edged stairways and the high broad rectangular doors with brass handles instead of knobs. It had gone on like that as the house grew, his taste for soft and round contradicting her taste for straight and clean, and in the end the whole place was zoned into hard areas, aligned and controlled, and soft, full of ellipses and fussy curls. The only curves and arches she liked were those of her cat, his rounded sleeping back, his tail curled around his feet, the tip at his nose.

François the meat packer had a shaved head with a smooth crown and when he came into the room the dome of his scalp reflected moving panes of light from the great south windows.

"Have you see Jones?" she asked.

"No," he said, and turned on the television set. He sat down in the deep soft chair.

"He's always here this time of day. And it's almost time for his dinner. He likes his dinner."

"Oh, well," he said. "Just out hunting. Out looking around. Looking for birds."

"But you know he doesn't go out. He's not an outdoor cat."

"Oh," said her husband. "Well."

Julia left the room to go looking for Jones.

With a sudden thump and broken squeak, the owl found a mouse, pierced its twisting body with its claw and flapped upward again toward the high branches of a beech tree. A tiny drop of salt-sweet blood hit the earth in front of the cat, and his mouth began to water.

There was a slight pounding of padded feet and then again silence. He turned his head and caught a little swish of tall grass springing back. The flow of saliva increased. He crept to the screen of reeds and looked through. His ears flattened. The rabbit had her young out, maybe their first trip from the nest—there she was, just a little way beyond, two bounds or a quick rush over the grass—and she was stalled in confusion, sensing him, trying to decide whether to risk the noise that would come with a rush to safety. The breeze shifted a little. She caught his smell, jumped and began to scramble back toward the hole where the nest was, driving some of her young ahead of her. He leapt through the gap in the reeds. She turned and kicked and missed. He dipped his head and bit, his teeth closing on the head and ear of one of the little rabbits. She kicked again, her foot thudding onto his snout, the claw scratching his eye. He held tight and backed away, growling, the little body jerking in his mouth, biting down harder, feeling a rush of warm blood, backing into the tall grass, the mother turning again to try to rush the rest of the litter back into the hole. The body hung slack in his mouth now, its weight pulling on the muscles in his neck. It had a firm, rubbery feel, overlaid with the softness of the fur on his tongue. He dropped his meal on the grass and began to tear at its stomach.

Two

SERGEANT JUDD WAS screening. He'd started doing it when he was twelve. He'd read about screening in a detective magazine article called *Stay Awake—Stay Alive—Stay Aware*. Be a camera, said the article. Take your surroundings and scan them for objects or people that don't fit, and when you find them zoom in with your mind as though you were looking through a telescopic lens. At the same time, visualize a group of little secondary lenses and post them at the edges of the zone like sentinels, ready to pick up new targets as they move into the surveillance. Judd found it hard to look at the street now the way a civilian would. He had a cop's eye.

He was on the edge of the big downtown park, the Southern Gardens by the lake. He sat in his brown car and blanked his mind, waited for the odd and unexplained to flow toward him through the windshield. It was a late April dawn, and the sleeping-baggers were starting to poke their noses out, last night's Chinese cooking wine, souped-up sherry and Lysol hammering in their heads. Dogs patrolled the lawns, sniffing hamburger wrappings. The night gardener in the greenhouse switched off the fluorescent lights that forced the seedlings on the bench to grow without sleep. A jogger with cups of music on his ears trotted past on the wet gravel.

Judd could change filters in his mind. He'd scan the scene for anything red and draw everything red into a pattern, switch the detector to blue, then green. The rising sun was bringing up the colours and washing out the hiding places in the park. The junkies would be stumbling off now to their dirty little rooms or cardboard forts under the bridges.

He loved this moment at the end of his shift. He'd crossed the city through the night, alert for novelties and exceptions, drifting down alleys and shining his floodlight into crannies, holes and alcoves. Sometimes there was a sudden startle and scurry at his light, a hooker and a john detaching quickly. Or a half-known figure crouching beside an open garage door, an addict looking for power tools or a radio, anything for the hock shop; Judd would take him in and drive him downtown, watching him tremble and sweat in the mirror.

Sometimes there'd be a scramble, an all-cars gun call, with Judd and the others squatting beside their bumpers with their pistols drawn while the emergency task force officers strapped on their armour and pumped rounds into the chambers of their shotguns. Usually the white-faced bandit finally stepped into the hot lights, obeyed the harsh electric voice and dropped to the ground. Three times Judd had joined in an endgame, firing into the air for diversion as the cowboys went in and ended it. Judd would come away from this trembling and jangled and exhilarated.

This morning was quiet after a quiet night. Two whores had gotten into an argument and gone after each other on the street, one with a razor, the other with a knife, but the fight was half-hearted, more yowling than anything else, and stopped when the razor girl had opened a little gash on the back of the other's right hand. He'd hauled them both downtown, hissing at each other behind the wire mesh that sealed off the back seat. That was it. Their scent still hung in the car like fog.

Judd watched the light from the east seep over the buildings. He could hear the city breathing and turning in its sleep. He could even sense its dreams, of angry bosses and bogeymen, filtering out of the city's windows. He heard the thumps, groans and flushes as ten thousand people rose in the dark and stumbled to the bathroom.

He loved the city for its noise, its bounding energy and the blood on its dark streets. He knew its secrets. He saw it with its pants down.

The city ate, and its waste flowed down concrete pipes that lay beneath the streets, gathering with other debris, slick paper packaging, half-eaten bread, torn newspaper, insects, paint, blood, sliding through pipes of increasing diameter on the way to the lake. Just as nobody thought much about where the food came from, nobody thought much about where it went. It came to momentary rest in huge tanks, where it was stirred, diluted, blasted with violet purifying light, measured and tested. Then it passed on down a huge winding culvert to a gushing mouth six miles out across the lake bed and was finally released six hundred feet below the surface of the water.

Once, Sergeant Judd had gone to the tanks, the stinking way station, to look at the body of a city worker who'd slipped in a sewer far up the hill and ridden the slick, as the sewer technicians called it, all the way down to the lake. The worker had tried to hold his breath in the rushing scraping dark, but the stuff blocked his nose, he gasped and choked and then it filled his lungs. His body was bounced around on the trip downstream so that his bones broke one by one, unlinked and turned to jelly, and he became a flexible tube of used-up matter, filled with garbage, following the growing course of effluent in the black interior of the pipes. When the worker's body popped up on the surface of the tank beside the lake it was ten feet long.

The body bobbed against the slimy concrete of the holding pool, wrapped in a coat of sludge, the bones of the head squeezed into a smooth cylinder like a newborn's, the closed eyes ovals. Judd stared at it. It seemed the city was a shit producer, one mass of waste sliding toward the future. You could ride the slick for years but not forever; you had to find a refuge from the rush of waste and protect it, no matter what. And anyway it was life, just life, brainless and innocent. He spent his nights shoving and shovelling human trash that was as natural and blameless as the waste paper and dog crap in the litter bins and the stinking flow in the underground pipes. As long as he had his little alcove of safety, his harbour to share with his wife and daughters, he could move through the garbage world untouched, even loving its sins, its stupidity and its occasional surprise. He was a sergeant, a manager of trash, a wiper-in-chief.

He usually liked to end his shift with a sausage bought from the early-shift vendor at the park, the only place in the city you could get a Friendly Pig Bavarian or a Sweet Italian as the sun rose. Judd liked mustard, ketchup and pickled sliced hot peppers on his sausage. He carried little sealed packages of wet paper towel to clean his fingers when he was done. He drank from his can of cola. Sometimes when he ate in a restaurant he drank beer, but when he was on duty he preferred cola. It seemed right for a working man, a man in uniform, with the greasy metal feel of the can and the sugary bite of the liquid as it flowed from the slick, cold oval perforation.

Judd was tall, thin and pot-bellied. He looked as though he'd swallowed a globe, with the equator pushing his shirt out over his leather belt. He was always patting and stroking his sharp face, tapping and pulling his lip, as though he was reminding himself of his position in time and space. His beat took him up, down and around 17 Division, the police district that reached from the waterfront north to the projects and east and west along the crossed arms of the shopping blocks. Mostly the work was predictable. He knew when he shone his flashlight into the side windows of parked cars on Long Drive that he'd see hunched shoulders and a suddenly still head with two yearning legs beneath. Sometimes there was a surprise, a safecracker keeping strange company with a booster or a pimp, and then he'd jump on the mystery and pester it until he understood.

He started the car and headed out on the final patrol of the morning, going home, feeling the strange contradictions of life in that other world coming over him with successive waves of love and desperation. He took his time, drifting along the streets, stopping briefly at one of the big intersections near the lake highway. It was almost bare. The street people avoided the spaces where the streets converged. They preferred the hidden bays below the windows of St. Jude's Cathedral and the concrete and brick recesses at the centre of the block, pawnbrokers' storefront windows with old saxophones, broken record players, dusty watches and faded cameo brooches with profiles of delicate ladies, next to greasy spoons puffing out mists of fried potatoes and onions, and brightly lit chambers where social workers and uniformed missionaries waited for the tides of the street to wash up souls so wretched they'd accept salvation.

Judd's thin nose twitched and pointed. He saw Wally the mooch limping, one leg whole and the other swollen like a soft log under his pant leg, a condition Wally maintained every day by running a ballpoint pen along an open channel of flesh above his knee. He kept little packages filled with old meat in his pockets. He'd hobble along outside a grocery store and the customers would think they were smelling his decomposing body; he'd leave with a heavy palmful of change. On the street beside Wally were two bill collectors watching each other's back, a drunken stranger, necktie crooked, heading for some showdown, a young whore with her wig on sideways, teetering on her new shoes, and Lukey.

Lukey. One of Judd's people, reliable, clear as glass, every twist and sin displayed, guilty before charged, shuffling down the street. When new talent came on the scene, Judd filed their images and records in the humming lobe of his brain and there they remained forever. He'd known Lukey for years. This morning there was something new to the cast of his back. Lukey was cradling something.

Lukey was the worst shoplifter in the city. He was

short, hunched and scrawny, and he looked like a thief, with a narrow face and eyes that scuttled away from contact, always with a heavy coat that anyone could tell was rich inside with pockets and loops. Security guards with two hours on the job figured Lukey out as soon as they spotted him.

Lukey saw the car too late to turn away, felt Sergeant Judd's gaze enveloping his body, the sad little shoplifter pale in the early light with a pouch strapped to his stomach. Lukey straightened his shoulders, signalling unconcern, his lips in a little O that stood for a carefree whistle. Judd rolled down the window, put the car in gear, drifting alongside. Lukey, with his stuttering step, tried to ignore him. He tapped the siren once: a short steely blat. He could see Lukey looking at him sideways, but he didn't stop.

He was carrying something.

"Whatcha got there, Luke?"

Lukey's voice was low, shaky. "Nothing."

"Put your hands down, Lukey." Lukey brought his hands down, and Judd put on the brakes.

A snake's head was rearing up from Lukey's belt buckle. Judd could see about a foot of it, shiny brown with black diamonds, the body so proud and rigid that for a moment Judd thought he had a new and completely unexpected flasher beside his cruiser here in broad daylight on 17's main street. Then he saw the snake's flat face tilted forward, one tiny button brown eye staring at him. Its stare was steady and indifferent, as though there was nothing special in front of it but looking away was too much trouble.

"Where the fuck did you get that?" Judd imagined Lukey inside a pet store, lifting the screen from the snake's cage and grabbing it with both hands, wrapping it around his waist inside the booster's coat and then walking rigidly past the pet store owner out onto the street, the puzzled animal beginning to squeeze his skinny ribs.

"I bought him."

Judd leaned over the shotgun rack, wound the window down all the way, looked at the snake straight on.

"You're on probation, Lukey. You're not supposed to have anything dangerous like that."

"He's not dangerous."

Judd couldn't tell how long the snake was, but the part he could see broadened to the thickness of an arm. "That thing's not poisonous?"

"Naw. He's a squeezer."

Beautiful, cross-hatched skin layered with smooth pebbles, lines along the mouth giving it the look of an old wise man with his teeth out. No flickering tongue, just that brown estimating eye, intelligent, skeptical.

"What does he eat?"

Lukey looked down at the snake. "Lettuce."

Judd was pretty sure that wasn't right. He couldn't tell from the snake's seamed mouth if it had fangs in there. He imagined the mouth opening almost to a straight line, the sharp-ended tubes flying out, dripping poison, the jaws clamping down on him, the muscles under the chin pumping the stuff into his blood, his heart racing, numbing, shutting down, burning out, his wife and daughters left alone, walking behind the cheap coffin hand in hand, weeping, nobody to protect them. It could be worse, meeting a cobra or a rattlesnake—you could have a hero's death if you went down to something like that. But if it turned out this was some kind of garter snake, there would be jokey announcements on the station's public-address system and all the desk stooges and radio guys and lowlifes in the front room would bust their guts laughing.

God knows what else Lukey had in there. Sometimes he'd go for a week without being picked up, and then a search of his coat would turn up the usual shoplifter's haul of watches, compact discs, portable television sets, along with half-eaten candy bars, fishing line, shoelaces, doilies, vegetable peelers. It was the act of taking that turned Lukey on as much as the take itself. If Lukey had been trawling pet stores he probably had rats, ferrets and owls in his pockets. Too late in the shift to get involved in that.

Judd wound the car window up again, nodding, dismissing Lukey and the snake, which continued to watch him, its head craning out from Lukey's stomach as he drove away, glancing back in the mirror, the snake's gaze following him to the corner.

Three

WHEN IVAN TEUTI was little, he played after school behind the counter in his father's pharmacy. He built palaces of empty cylindrical pill bottles on the floor, elaborate transparent structures that housed kings, chamberlains, servants, knights on horseback and ranks of fighting men. He was safe behind the tall counter next to the locked glass cabinets with boxes and tall vials. He was curious sometimes about the stuff inside these cabinets, and his father explained that they were like the dials on a television set: they made little adjustments to the world so people could bring it in tune. He wondered if the things in the bottles had little hands that reached out and made the adjustments, and who told them to do it, and who told them to stop.

When Ivan was ten, he started delivering packages to the pharmacy's customers on his bicycle, his jade green three-speed Raleigh with the beaded spokes. Between trips he returned to the wooden crate his father placed for him beside the glass cabinets that protected the bottles of pills, liquids and powders. He knew now that there were drugs inside the cabinets and that some people would do anything to sit where he was sitting and rest their cheeks against the cool clear glass and be close to the boxes and bottles. He pretended sometimes he was an armed guard set below the counter to protect his father: if a junkie came in, he'd spring up, take aim, bam!

He liked making deliveries, the quick looks into strange interiors—women in bathrobes coming to the door, once a girl two grades ahead of him dressed in a skirt and a bra, the tops of her little breasts swelling out lightly, taking the package from him coolly, tipping him a quarter like a duchess. The package was tampons, but she didn't know he knew that, and that was the kind of little secret that put him one up on the world. But he liked being at the store as well, watching his father's smooth hands as they poured liquids into brown vials and tapped grains of medicine into jelly to make healing salves. The colours of the medicines were almost magically blue, red, green—circus colours—powerful, glowing with strength and health.

On the wall there was a picture of a man with his skin peeled away to show his striped scarlet muscles, yellow tendons and blue branches of veins. The man stared calmly toward the bathroom tissue and headache pills, one eyeball flayed open, the size of a golf ball, the other still with its lid in place. Ivan Teuti tried to imagine all these ducts, tubes and fluids inside his own body. He thought he could feel the blood rushing in its channels up and down his arms and legs. But when it came to his father, the image failed. It seemed to Ivan that his father must be all one substance, one strong white solid tight-packed mass with black hair on the knuckles and curling out from the cuffs. The floor behind the pharmacist's counter was raised. When you brought your prescription to the back of the store, you'd look up past four shelves of medicines and vitamins and see only his head and shoulders far above you.

Sometimes when Ivan came into the store he'd stop at the front counter, where Mrs. Godwin ran the cash, and smell the candy kept well behind her, out of reach. The scent came through the slick wrapping, and as you moved past the cash desk you detected variations. Small yellow cubes of cardboard held maraschino cherries bathed in pink syrup and cased in a shell of nuts and chocolate, then wrapped in tinfoil, the aroma sickly sweet. The plain bars smelled more forthright and masculine. One was chocolate with square pockets of strawberry, caramel, dark oozing fudge and almond. At the end of a night his father might hand him one of these—just take it from the shelf, without paying, and Ivan would marvel at the careless power of this, proof his father owned the whole store and everything in it.

Mrs. Godwin was a small tanned woman who kept herself in a kind of continuous confinement, her hair in a tight bun and big breasts bound snugly under a crisp white blouse. She knew what everything cost, the state of the customers' accounts, who could be trusted for goods on credit. His father controlled the potions and medical creams at the back of the store, but she had dominion over the front shelves, which held cigarettes in smooth cellophane and tobacco in round hollow-sounding tins, compresses and salves, oval medicated patches for sore feet, tiny bottles of eyedrops, tinctures, essences, sprays and hoses. Cod-liver oil in small hard capsules, the same kind Ivan had to swallow every morning, the waxy pebble slowly progressing down his throat and finally falling away into his stomach. Mustard plasters, pink thick chalky syrup for upset stomachs, strong black dress socks that would squeeze varicose veins back into their allotted places under an old man's pale grey skin.

Ivan's parents came from Eastern Europe, and so did many of the customers, old people who smelled of soap and talked to his father in the home language, full of deep, spitting gutturals. His father said they liked the cures they knew, and sometimes Ivan tried to imagine what those might be—a goat's eye in vinegar or pieces of bats. The traditional cures were kept in the same kinds of bottles, tubes and vials as the ones made today, so they had a kind of modern authority. Ivan could see flashes of pale hope in the old eyes as his father passed the medicines packaged in crisp white paper bags over the counter.

"You know this is the right one?" an old man would say, peering at a little bag as though it had a whole new life in it. Maybe a life as a laughing, brazen soldier, sweeping farm girls off their feet, or, with bad luck, long years as a bent-over beggar palm up in the rain outside the dusty cathedral door.

"That'll fix you right up," his father would reply, and the old man would shuffle off past the belts and splints, heading home.

The pharmacy was the intersection of Ivan's world and the adult one, where the new country touched the old one with its gnarled mountains and flat, dull plains of wheat, riffled in moving lines by summer wind. The old people still seemed to have the dirt of that world on their swollen fingers. The wheat-field wind had plucked them up there and put them down here, but they hadn't changed their clothes or their smells of woodsmoke, garlic and the grainy, slippery fumes of plum brandy.

His mother cooked in the European way, boiling potatoes

and grilling rabbit with onions. The food reminded Ivan of his foreignness. He'd brush his teeth furiously before he went to school, but afterwards he could still taste the food from the night before, the cabbage and tripe, and he thought a smell of it hung around him and told everyone in the class what he was. He always made his own lunch, peanut butter between slices of dark bread, to make sure nobody would ever smell alien food in his lunchbox.

Ivan spoke the old language when he was a baby but came home from the first grade one day with his memory apparently wiped clean of everything but English. His mother spoke slowly and distinctly, trying to force the words into his ears, but he didn't respond. He crowded the old language into a separate place in his mind and spent hours trying to tamp it down and strip it away. In bed at night he'd practice relinquishing words, letting them drift out of his mind and away into the darkness. He made his mother speak to him in her simple, heavy English.

His father had picked up the language effortlessly, as though he'd breathed it in like a scent from the air of the new country. His mother tried to settle into English by watching television dramas in the afternoon, but she was upset by the clothes and the flexible moral standards, and she covered the dialogue with a complaining commentary in her own language and learned almost nothing.

She chased God. She was always out at the cathedral, lighting candles to guide Him like a descending spacecraft when He finally agreed to come down to heal her. So far He was keeping His distance, only coating her mouth and gullet with green phlegm, which she coughed up into a

Kleenex. At the end of the night the garbage pail was full of sticky tissues. On work nights Ivan's father ate his solitary mid-evening dinner in silence and retreated to the television set afterwards, looking shrunken in his checkered shirt.

Ivan couldn't put the two fathers together. The bright, bluff man on his raised, closed platform, pouring and measuring, bantering with his customers and his son, and the small, curled-up, tired, silent man at home, keeping a room away from his angry semi-crazy wife. The two men lived in the same body but seemed to have nothing to do with each other.

At the store once or twice his father had to come off his platform and out through the swinging gate to deal with a troublesome customer, and then he seemed black and loud and mighty like a thunderstorm rushing off the lake. One fat untidy man with brandy on his breath wouldn't pay for a shower curtain and wouldn't give it back, said it was a fair exchange for the one he had bought here before that tore away from its rings the second goddamn time he pulled it. He tried to crowd past the blocking bosom of Mrs. Godwin, shouting in some old language. Then Ivan's father came running, caught the man and pushed him out of the store with one hand on his neck and the other on his back, both of them bellowing and threatening. As the untidy man banged through the front door, he fell on one knee and howled. Ivan's father reached down, picked up the bent box with the shower curtain inside and walked back into the store, breathing hard, his eyes wide, telling Mrs. Godwin in a voice loud enough to be heard outside that if that crazy trash ever came into the store again she should call the police at once.

That night Ivan's father was transformed. The hearty drugstore father overthrew the sour small home father. He drank a beer at the kitchen table and told Ivan's mother about it, acting out the bum's rush like a movie. Ivan's mother didn't seem to recognize her husband in this high and masterful mood. She went to the bathroom and stayed there for two hours, speaking in a low drone that sometimes grew to a wail, as though a sudden wind were sweeping through her.

Life in the drugstore changed too. Ivan's father was suddenly spending more time away from his bottles and tubes, down on the packaged-goods floor, arranging boxes on the shelves and helping Mrs. Godwin reconcile her cash. She leaned into his father sometimes so that her bound-up breast squashed against his arm. She'd do that even when Ivan was around. He couldn't picture what might happen in the storeroom at the back when he was at school. He thought of big soft bodies bumping together on wrapped stacks of toilet paper.

Two weeks later it all changed again. It was a dark October night with wet leaves smashed on the pavement. Ivan leaned his bike against the wall in the laneway and turned the corner to walk into the store when he saw his father, once again out from behind the pharmacy counter, but this time on his toes, standing tall and rigid. A small man with a scarf tied around his face was holding a pistol to his father's jaw. The gun looked absurd, shiny and light as a toy, but Ivan's father was terrified, his eye bulging as big as the flayed man's. He was reaching back past Mrs. Godwin's desk, his hands scrabbling in the cash drawer, pulling out bills and stuffing them in a white plastic shop-ping bag. It was already jammed full and bulging, with the white lids and brown necks of drug bottles poking over the top; his father had to look down, pressing the flesh beneath his chin against the barrel of the pistol, to force the bills past the drugs and into the bag. Mrs. Godwin was standing very still beside the rows of chocolate.

The small man took the bag from him, backed toward the front of the store and then dropped the hand with the gun as though disgusted, turned and walked slowly to the door, putting the pistol casually into his pocket like a work-man returning a hammer to his toolbox. As he passed Ivan he pulled the scarf down and away from his face, bunching it in his hand like an actor leaving a stage, staring at Ivan, giving him a clear look at his little blunt nose and misty eyes. Then he rounded the corner.

Ivan looked into the store again and saw a dark patch on his father's tan pants where the white jacket fell open.

Ivan's father stood still, as though the small man had driven a stake through him. Ivan felt fear coming at him from every direction, fear of the robber, fear that his father would ask him to help, fear that his father would break down and weep, fear of behaving badly, even fear that somehow his father would turn on him in anger—all those years you sat behind the counter with your little toy gun, where were you when the real thing came along?

In the end Ivan just stood outside in the damp wind watching through the glass while his father and Mrs. Godwin moved slowly inside the store, murmuring and tidying. He waited for one of them to pick up the phone and call for the police, but neither did. They seemed ashamed, as though they had robbed themselves, neither looking at the other, neither looking toward the door for him, finally beginning to turn out the lights in what seemed to be a kind of moving sleep.

When the last light went out, Ivan got on his bike and rode home through the cold. His father followed a few minutes later, wearing a new pair of pants. He said nothing to anyone, ate his late dinner and went to bed.

The fight with the fat man had lifted him up, but the robbery had jerked him down again. He was silent at home and short-tempered with his son at work. Ivan couldn't figure it out, and it seemed his mother was puzzled too. She spent hours on her knees scolding Jesus, reproaching Him for ignoring her—what kind of Man are You, after all? Then she started writing Him long notes and burning them at the front altar of the cathedral, the paper curling black over the dollar candles, the sexton complaining at the fire. Nothing brought her husband back.

It wasn't that the druggist had lost his tongue. He was hearty with the customers. He stepped up his output of jokes, swapping raw stories with the men. From his box Ivan heard about the minister, the priest and the rabbi on the falling plane with only two parachutes and about the French father who took his son to the whorehouse. The men threw back their heads and hooted at the ceiling while Mrs. Godwin tidied the shelves in the front of the store. Ivan on his box laughed along. But when he was alone with his father, there was nothing but short-tempered orders and scorn. And from what he could tell, his father and Mrs. Godwin were avoiding each other—no more brushing and pressing, just short formal exchanges on questions of business.

"Will we be having a delivery of facial tissues this week, Mr. Teuti?"

"I believe it is on the order paper, Mrs. Godwin. Give me a minute and I will check." Ivan had seen a television show about a department store in London fifty years ago. The managers and the clerks spoke to each other clearly and slowly, with painful good manners that covered molten layers of emotion. It seemed like that in the pharmacy now.

"Are the cash receipts completely reconciled, Mrs. Godwin?"

"It all seems to be in order, Mr. Teuti, although perhaps you would care to check the calculations yourself." Out his father would come, pluck the paper from her like a half-tame squirrel snatching a piece of food from someone's hand and return behind the counter to his maze of shelves and potions. Even his typing became more deliberate, click, clack, as he filled in the labels—take with food, one refill.

Ivan felt he'd been shown half of a mystery. The little man had skipped away from the store like a goblin with a pocketful of cash and a bagful of drugs and on his way he had pulled down his scarf to show Ivan his face, bringing him in on it—I know your kind; you won't turn me in. He had reached into their lives, taken what he wanted and gotten away clean.

Ivan began to look for small opportunities to experiment with defiance and bad ways. He no longer asked for candy at the store; he just took it. Once he saw Mrs. Godwin watching him. His stomach tensed a little, but he looked straight at her, tore the wrapper off the bar, stuck it in his mouth and smiled. She looked away. Then a week later he stole a can of soda from a corner store a block away, the crazy Swede's place. He could have taken it from his father's shelf, and he knew the Swede would love to double-lock his front door and take Ivan by the shirt and drag him back to the pharmacy, shouting about this kind of kid you're bringing up, but that was the point, the test. There was a giggling pleasure in sneaking it out past the creepy, dingy old man, paying for a bag of jelly beans and walking away with something extra. The dark soda prickled against the inside of his mouth.

One day almost a year after the little man robbed the pharmacy, Ivan saw a group of kids on the edge of the schoolyard and heard yelling and weeping. The older boys had Phyllis by the shoulders and around the neck and were doing a check on her. This meant holding her while someone reached down her pants and felt between her legs for hair. Most of the boys thought Phyllis was stuck up, and there were quite a few of them in the checking circle. Ivan moved in behind Harry Domm, who had her by the elbows, and reached around him, his hand brushing down Phyllis's twisting body, along her side, under her grey sweatpants, down her stomach to the naked cloven space. There were two hands there already. He pulled away, ran away before the circle broke up, the feel of her skin on his fingers. Phyllis was away from school for two weeks afterwards, and the principal put out a call for those who had insulted her, as he put it, to come forward. Ivan kept silent, contented and proud. When Phyllis came back he passed her once or twice in the hallway and looked down at her crotch briefly, even absently, just to put it in her mind that he might have been one of them.

Ivan knew that criminals returned to the scenes of their crimes, and he expected the little man to come back to the drugstore any day. Maybe not to rob it again but just to swish in with a babe on his arm, buy some chocolates, laugh at Ivan's father, reach over to squeeze Mrs. Godwin's chest. Maybe he'd claim Ivan and welcome him into the back of his stolen limousine with a television set and a rattling bar full of tiny glass bottles.

Ivan's father was watching more television now. He sat in his leather chair, slack and reduced, and stared through the pictures of adultery, amazing good luck, sudden death and sparkling cleanliness as though they were just part of the air. Maybe he was looking through them at the old country with its turnips and cows or maybe at Mrs. Godwin's tits flapping against his chest months ago when he was still a young man.

"Be all you can be," said a deep-voiced choir in the television set, and Ivan thought his father was all his father could ever be, pressed down into the apartment like a potato in the earth. The little man had broken him. Ivan would never break.

Four

By morning the cat had reached the highway. He crouched in the grassy trench beside it. The road was louder than anything he had ever heard. The roaring ran above his head, a varying chord of sound, low grumbles, higher bee noises, travelling past from right to left, and beyond that a fainter reciprocal roar of something travelling left to right. The place had an artificial burnt smell. In front of him lay the corpse of a brown dog, its hair clotted with dark oil.

The cat raised himself cautiously to try to look at the furious metal river and the sound increased until it hurt. There was a burst of wind, and the air pressed down on him hard and forced him back into the trench, his ears flattening, his eyes closed.

There was a sighing, bubbling sound beside him. The corpse had opened its eyes. There were flecks of blood on its lips. It was a farm dog, smelling of grass and manure. It showed its teeth and moved its front legs, but a tire had flattened a band across its belly; it had crawled off the highway into the grass and then collapsed. Its head wanted to get at the cat, but its body could do nothing.

The cat was curious about whatever was pinning this dog to the ground, and he moved closer to its jaws. The dog seemed furious, desperate and ashamed. The cat was almost close enough now to taste the flecks of spit and blood on the dog's muzzle. The dog suddenly twisted its shoulders and snapped, brushing the cat's right ear with its teeth. Then there was a gush of blood from the dog's mouth.

The cat jumped back and ran down into the ditch, where there was a stand of reeds that was tall enough to hide him if the dog managed to lift up and start chasing him. He jumped for the reeds, closed his eyes as the tall stalks slapped his head, felt them yield under his stomach and then fell through into a sudden nothing.

He opened his eyes. It was almost black. The reeds hid a culvert, two feet in diameter, that stretched underneath the highway. It smelled of steel, dirty water and the scat of some animal he didn't recognize. His pupils widened. He could see down the tube to a bend, then nothing.

There was a sudden thump from the highway above him and a rustle from the reeds. He bounded into the black tube.

When he got to the turn in the culvert the glow from the ditch fell away. He could sense the space stretching ahead in a straight line. The slight wind was from behind him, a mild presence on his fur; he'd have no scent of anything ahead of him. He turned to go back but the twisting motion disturbed his hip and it burned, so he turned again and set out along the slippery channel under the road.

It took him half an hour to pick his way along the tube, feeling a route around clumps of mud and dead branches and at one point the bodies of three pigeons decaying together in a puddle. There was a constant flow of water, sometimes slow, sometimes a quick spray as it forced its way around a barrier. He kept shaking his feet to get the water off them, jumping from place to place, the odour contaminating him.

Another bend and an opening to the light again, a hundred feet away.

There was a grinding roar from the highway over his head and the fall of something inside the tube behind him. He ran forward to the light. There was a sour stink in the air, a smoke that burned his eyes. He stopped at the edge of the culvert; the rough grass sloped down in front of him and ended in a line of low trees.

There was a splintering bang above him, a grinding squeal and hard sounds of yielding metal, then loud voices and an oily smoke rolling down the grass.

He ran down the slope, then stopped and looked back into the morning sun. The roaring had stopped, and there was fire along the line of stationary metal and a high trembling wail in the distance.

He went into the trees and felt the shadows close around him. The earth and grass under his feet gave way to dry leaves, moss and soft shards of rotting wood. There were sharp, sour odours rising from markings from strange animals, strips of pale wood on the trees where the sheaths of bark had been torn away from the trunks. It was suddenly cold. Then there was a shaking in the leaves and the thump of something quick on the ground; he jumped, and the fox missed his hold, his shoulder pitching the cat sideways onto his back; the cat smelled the fox's musky scent and felt the hard round shapes of acorns under his body. He rolled and sprang away as the fox turned back toward him, running beyond a screen of branches. He sensed the fox behind him slow and stop.

A high voice, a soft and rhythmic chant: "Hi-yuh, hi-yuh, hi-yuh."

The cat ran out of the bush onto a ragged lawn. There

was a rusting swing set on it; one of the spikes holding it down had come out of the ground and it was tilting to the left. A little girl was swaying back and forth on the swing, shifting her weight, trying to pull the structure over. The cat moved along the small line of shadow where the trees met the earth. The chains of the swing scraped on the rod. The little girl called out to him listlessly and kept swinging.

He could feel the fatigue creeping along his muscles, the loss of the energy he'd spent in the crossing and the chase. He needed someplace dark and protected to sleep. He could smell dogs around. He needed to be safe from foxes and dogs.

He jumped onto a wooden table and down again, checking underneath for a pocket of space where he could sleep with his back protected. He could still smell the fox and the salty breath of the dying dog. He saw darkness between two rectangles of lattice that closed in the underside of a back porch.

He squeezed inside. There was a smell of decaying cardboard boxes and rotting wood and rust from a broken bicycle lying in the dirt. He was so tired now that weakness was coming over him in waves. There was a sudden stamping sound beyond the cardboard and a burst of stink.

A raccoon poked her pointed muzzle over the yellow cardboard flap, showed her teeth and hissed. Pain moved up the cat's hip. The raccoon hissed again and blinked. The cat sank to the ground. The raccoon's face disappeared, returned; she started at the cat again, twitching her lip, and then withdrew into the space on the other side of the cardboard. A fight would draw in dogs or people. She wouldn't attack him unless he came over the cardboard barrier. She flexed her small black hands. The two animals slept.

The day dragged on in the suburb. The sun blasted the bare streets. Television sets radiated music and voices: hottest springtime ever. Birds sat stunned in the trees. There was talk of restrictions on water, but for now the children could run under the sprinklers, the light searing their legs and shoulders. Parked cars became furnace-hot, belching blistering air when the doors opened. The tar on the roads turned into sludge. The little girl swayed on the swing set, loosening the steel leg.

A mile away on the other side of the highway, Julia's driver, Kessler, was trying to think like a cat. He was a short, squat, sallow man with a big round face that was pocked like the moon. He was a driver now, just a chauffeur, but he thought if he played his cards right he could parlay himself into a big job with these rich people. Better than ferrying drunks around in somebody else's cab. The boss's wife was weeping in her bathroom for her lost cat. When he brought it back he'd be able to write his own ticket.

Where would he go if he were a cat?

He crouched on the gravel driveway, pointed his stubby olive-coloured nose toward the fence and tried to imagine the black cat's travels. He'd watched a lot of television. He knew Indians could track fleeing horses through the desert from faint hoofmarks and bent branches, and could hear them fifty miles away by picking up vibrations through the dry packed sand. He looked around and then laid his big head on the gravel, listening for light cat steps.

"Kowabunga." The gardener in his stained brown over-alls, yukking at him.

"Fuck off." Kessler stood up and brushed the dust off his knees.

"Booga booga, kemo sabe," said the gardener, and walked on, laughing, toward the greenhouse.

"Well, shit," said Kessler to himself, and thought about the stupid cat, and thought about the cat's owner with tears in her eyes, naked in her long, smooth bathtub.

Julia Will's bathroom was built of marble from Italy. The bathtub had brass fittings and small hidden motors to churn the water around her. Beside it were shelves of fine treated wood to hold her glass, thick towels and sweet soaps from France, clear oils and lotions from Japan and Portugal, a little rasp for her feet, bottles of mud masks and cream for blemishes, a hundred pots, tubes and bottles in a tray at her left hand.

Her straw hair floated in the scented water; her knees emerged from the surface like twin islands; her breasts were two more, sleek and shining through the swirling froth of the bath; her eyes were misted. The cat liked the heat of the bath and usually joined her, lying on a towel and stretching in the moist air. When she'd moved into her husband's new house she'd brought some clothes with her, some books and music and a sparse box of inexpensive jewellery, but nothing she cared about except her cat. He was one of the lines back to her previous life. Now she felt as though an anchor had disengaged and left her drifting in the big damp room.

Julia's mother was the other constant she'd brought

along to the butcher's big house. Her mother had been widowed early, after four retrospectively perfect years of marriage. She carried her tragedy openly, keeping it out in front of her at all times like a corsage—everything in her life was dated before or after the fatal, wretched, always-to-be-regretted night.

Julia was tall, with high blunt cheekbones and a wide jaw that was her mother's target of choice. She was always at it with shading brushes, trying to wipe it narrower like a painter working on a landscape.

Julia was conceived on a boat that cruised the lake. Her parents found a dark corner behind a tall coil of rope on the service deck, beyond a chain with a sign that said "Crew Only." Julia's mother still remembered the rub of the rope through her dress, the nudging-aside of the underwear and the feel of the slick iron wall against her back in the dark. Julia was born in the spring, a beautiful baby, and three years later Julia's parents left her with a girl who worked in her father's office and took the cruise ship again.

The ship ran to a little town on the southern corner of the lake, a toy village, an image of the way people thought towns might have looked a hundred years before, with groomed horses pulling leather-seated wagons. Behind the counter at the drugstore, university boys with pasted-on moustachios swirled milkshakes and poured lemonade.

The cruiser cast off under a clear sky at midnight for the voyage back with its jazz band playing hot notes under the new moon. Julia's parents were embracing again on the crew deck when a siren sounded and there was a grinding thud along the ship's port side. A steel-hulled police corvette, searching for smugglers and running without lights, had cut a ten-foot gash in the cruiser's hull.

The passengers jammed the deck, making jokes about great liners sinking with losses of a thousand souls. The corvette was buckled and smashed.

Julia's father took command of the forward half of the deck. He ordered the passengers into life jackets and arranged them in groups. "Women and children here to the port side!" he shouted, waving his arms. "All men to starboard. Mind how you go!" He was a dentist and worked quietly in small rooms but had always dreamed of taking charge in a crowd. The crewmen pulled and swore at the lashings that held the boats in place. Some of the chains were rusted to the davits. Julia's father strode from the rail to the lifesaving stations, calming the fearful and lending his strength to the boat crews, feeling his young wife's gaze, conscious of his own strong body moving. "All together! One, two, three!" Children wailed, and a bank of cloud cut off the little moon. The banjo rang out in the dark.

The corvette kicked up at the stern and began to slide below the surface. The police commander made a jump for the cruiser and caught hold of an open porthole. A wave washed the sinking corvette against the ship, and the commander's leg was caught between the wood and the metal. He screamed and fell into the water. Julia's father sprang toward the rail, looked back at his wife, grinned and dove into the dark water. The two men disappeared under the churning surface, the police commander trying to climb up the dentist's back to safety.

Julia's mother embraced and rocked her little girl all the next day. In the office below, the dentist's partner worked a double shift, the whine of the drill filling the child's room. Julia's mother held her tightly. Later she'd tell her the story over and over: "His beautiful smile, you could see it for miles; he did it himself with a mirror in his office, grinding and polishing. . . . It was the last thing I saw as he went over the side, such a beautiful sweet smile. . . ."

Julia imagined a picture of it, almost remembering the round life rings flying over the water, the curves of the sinking boat and the shining moon. The image left a gap inside her that she could almost visualize—rectangular, small, strong and empty, a vacancy reserved for something that might happen in the course of time or might not. From time to time she felt happiness or grief, but thinly, she thought, without the fullness of other people's emotions. She read about girls who were obsessed with horses or Jesus. She thought her inner space suppressed any chance that she could feel like that.

The daughter and the mother lived on in the little apartment over the dentist's office, getting by on the rent and the settlement from the marine insurance company, which sent its cheque once a month in an envelope marked with a crown and anchor. Julia came to think of the crown and anchor as a token of her father, a message from him from under the water. Once a month Julia was taken downstairs to have her teeth examined. The dentist, her father's partner, tapped her molars and incisors with his mirrored wand and never found a blemish. "Beautiful, beautiful teeth," he'd say to Julia's mother, who always sat right next to the big chair, mindful of anaesthetics and the tricks some dentists got up to with unconscious female patients.

"You must never," she told Julia, "never ever go into a room alone with another person unless it is a member of your family."

"You are the only other person in my family."

"You are my own most precious love," said Julia's mother, "and I am worried about other people touching you. Not touching you like just touching you but touching you in a bad manner."

Her mother's moods shifted constantly from love to anger to curiosity to dread. Sometimes she'd remember she was a parent and hurtle into an educational phase. One night when Julia was nine, her mother called her to the kitchen, opened the door of the refrigerator and began to describe the rules and uses of milk, faded vegetables, ground meat and cheese. "You need to know these things. These are the things every woman knows."

"Do you know them?"

Her mother's face was half lit against the white rubber-edged door. "I know enough to help you know. Tell me now what baking soda does."

Julia looked down at the folds of her red bathrobe in the yellow-white refrigerator light. It felt like a spelling or arithmetic test but more urgent. Her mother sniffed and swallowed.

"I don't know. Why should I know?"

"What do you mean why?"

"Why should I tell you what baking soda does?"

Her mother stood up suddenly, with two sharp clicks from her knee joints, grunting, then shouting, "You tell me because you tell me!"

"But that's—" She was silent now.

Her mother's face was very close. Long brown curls bending from the sides of her head. Sweet lemon-lavender perfume in the dark kitchen.

"Tell me."

Julia said nothing. Her mother said clearly, slowly, "Always remember when you are angry or hurtful to a person, the person could die. If I died tonight, how would you feel? How would you feel?"

Julia dreamed about being invisible. Her body would disappear, and she could see people as they really were. She imagined finding secret places where people took off their flesh like clothes, laid it in piles on the floor and sat around in steaming piles of bones. There were other dreams deep in the night when the space inside her opened and filled. She dreamed of swimming, the lake water burning her eyes, turning on her side, seeing a line of fishermen with reels that whirled in lines from the lake and her father's smiling face rising and breaking through the surface.

When she was ten the girls at school started trading information about boys in the cafeteria at lunchtime. "Never sleep with a man before you marry him," said Willa Walker, "because then he'll change his mind. That's if you even want to marry him, of course. If it's just fucking for fun, then it's just fucking for fun."

Willa was twelve and well informed and maybe even

experienced, and Julia was still trying to bring together the "Fuck you" of the playground and the mysterious action Willa was talking about. There was something about bodies merging. She had an image of a man crawling all over her and absorbing her like a jellyfish sucking up some tiny shred of food at the bottom of the lake. But little by little the new world of blood and knowledge came out of the air somehow and gradually entered her. One day she realized she knew about cocks, tampons, new curling hair and how a baby might one day push her legs apart and come lunging down her into life.

She liked little jobs, housework that her mother left undone for weeks. She liked cleaning the bathroom. Even years after her father died she'd find short, thick, dark hairs in the cracks behind the sink, straight black military lines he'd scraped from his face. She liked the feeling of cloth on smooth glass and porcelain. She liked the sudden swipes of cleanliness through the thin film of dust and stain.

Once when she was cleaning the bathroom at night she became aware of another presence in the house, in her mother's room; there were low, blurry tones from beyond the tiled wall, creaks and rattles, a gasp and laughter. She was afraid to open the door. She was caught on the floor next to the toilet with a full bucket of water whose surface seemed to ripple.

The movement eased and stopped. She waited, then poured the water out of the bucket loudly into the toilet. The bowl flushed. She dropped the bucket onto the hard floor, then opened the door and walked down the hall to her room. As she passed her mother's room, there was a sudden long crack of light and a man's eye, neck and naked shoulder. It was the dentist from downstairs. His delicate hand gripped the door frame. Her mother made a little complaining sound from inside the room, and the door closed again.

Julia dreamed through school. She liked history and art, subjects with stories she could study by herself. In sex education classes she contemplated the academic accounts of intercourse, pregnancy and childbirth. It all seemed unsatisfactory and unsanitary—the idea of a meaty cylinder pushing into her, thrusting, leaving someone else's sticky fluids that merged into bubbling cells and then an entirely new creature growing within her. She thought of a baby eating away at her like an embryonic spider devouring a captive slug that in the end was hollowed out into an empty dead container.

Her looks changed. Her face lost its skinny fat-jawed cartoon appearance and became strong enough to support the large wide-set green eyes.

One day Willa Walker's brother Matthew fell into step beside her after school. He kept in step, as though the two of them were a tiny army.

"What you said in art class. Is that right?"

"What did I say?"

"I don't know." His plodding feet made heavy noises on the sidewalk. She had a sudden image of the health textbook and tried to imagine his cock, tucked up in a little white cloth basket or swaying down the loose leg of his boxer shorts. Willa said he had a big one, a trouser snake, some lucky girl's friend. He was breathing heavily through his nose. The autumn sun glowed behind the warm turning leaves. She suddenly caught her own scent, clear and floral with sweat underneath and some deeper musk.

Her mother was waiting for her at the top of the narrow stairs. "Who was that?"

"Willa's brother."

"Do I know him?" Her mother knew no one, since she never went out except to buy food or cosmetics or press a battle with the neighbours.

"No."

"Who's Willa?"

"Just this girl."

"I don't want you talking to people's brothers when I don't know who they are. You don't know what could happen to you."

"Oh, shit."

"What did you say?"

"Nothing." She pushed past her mother, shoving with her shoulder so her mother thumped into the wooden door frame. She stamped down the hallway, her mother following, shouting.

"What have you been doing? Where have you been going?"

"At least I don't bring them home like some people I know!" She caught a glimpse of her mother's face as she slammed the door.

Two hours later she knocked on the door of her mother's room. "Mum?"

Silence inside.

"I'm—"

A rustle as her mother's body moved on the bed, then silence again.

I'm a virgin, she wanted to say, but the word sounded foolish in her mouth and might somehow be offensive, condescending, to a woman who'd had a strange man in her husband's bed.

"I'm going out."

Through the door: "Where?"

"Just to the library."

Two soft steps and the door opened. "I love you."

"I know, Mum."

"Don't be late. Dinner at six, semi-formal attire!"

An old joke. They'd made peace and established a new balance. Two women in the same small divided protected space.

On her eighteenth birthday Julia took a job as a junior administrator in a stock-trading company. It suited her. She liked the hallways, elevators and desks and the flat grey-green computer screens. She liked having a regular time for lunch in the company cafeteria with five rotating specials, one for each day of the week. She checked and filed insurance claims, vacation requests and overtime payments. Sometimes there would be an abrupt letter from a lawyer or creditor with a garnishee for a worker's wages, or forms to cover an injury or illness, perhaps a shrivelling case of lung cancer or a foot crushed beneath an overturned filing cabinet. This was as close as the job got

to real life, although sometimes Julia's mother stood outside the building wringing her hands at the thought of her
daughter spread-eagled on the photocopier with a line of
men stretching into the corridor.

One winter afternoon Julia stopped at the window of a
pet store, her eye caught by a small shape leaping in the
artificial light. It was a black kitten with a streak of white
on its left front paw, bounding stiff-legged behind the
glass, spinning and dancing.

"Hybrid vigour," said the pet store owner, looking at her
breasts. The cat was a mixed breed, with none of the
overdeveloped needs and weaknesses of the aristocracy. A
strong peasant cat.

Jones was already gelded and was missing a tiny part of his
left ear, nobody knew how. He settled into her life quickly.
He thought Julia was warm and reliable. When she came
home at night and found him archbacked and stamping or
when he jumped on her in bed and kneaded her like a
baker, her heart opened.

Five

SERGEANT JUDD ALWAYS spent an hour or so in his daughters' room after they went to sleep, listening to the whisper of their breathing and smelling their soft powdery scent. Eight and six, one blond, one dark, one charging into life, hugging it, one hanging back to be protected from it. He thought he could already see a little coarsening of the eight-year-old, picked up from television or her friends. They lived in a tough part of 17 and they went to a tough school. Every morning the teachers walked the playground looking for condoms and needles.

"Are you going to work?"

His wife standing in the dim doorway.

"In just a minute."

He usually spent the time before his midnight shift in this room, searching his mind for an escape for his girls. Sometimes he tried to imagine a perfect robbery, but he knew from experience that almost every robber turned suddenly, amazingly stupid right in the middle of the crime or right afterwards. He pictured himself in a high-ceilinged bank with a hood over his head and a note in his hand. He was pretty smart, but some of the men he arrested were pretty smart too. He'd screw it up, leave something behind—his wallet, his police badge—and then they'd come and pick him up like a little piece of crap in a plastic bag, drag him past the cameras and throw him down the toilet while his little girls watched. His face went hot in the dark.

He thought about private schools, modelling courses, tennis lessons, instruction in Irish dance, his daughters rolling safely from place to place in large dark cars. He lost himself for a while in thinking about how happy they would be and what it would be like to find against all the odds that he could build that life for them: a lottery win, some sweepstakes office calling with news about a ticket he didn't even remember buying, the father of an old school friend who'd kept a secret eye on him and left him a bundle.

Her voice came from the hallway. "I worry about you. The lunches, I found two of them in the back of the car, you didn't touch them, and you're putting on weight, eating junk."

"I know. I'm sorry."

"And the veins on your legs. Are you going to get the doctor to look at those?"

"Yes. I will. I know."

He loved her, but he was at the bottom of the well trying to climb up the slippery sides, and she was hugging him and her weight was holding him down with the two girls clinging to her and crying. He needed someone up top with a rope. It would curl down through the darkness, thrown by someone he couldn't see, strong enough to pull them all up into the clear air.

Of course he wasn't the only one looking for guidance. His crazy aunt lived by the lake, her brain shot through with holes, dribbling and raving. "The moon, the moons of Jupiter, gaseous giants, the planet Europa . . ." She was depending on the stars for directions. When he came by with a box of groceries, he could smell animals through the walls. She had dozens of cats in there, maybe a hundred; every ragged stray from miles around had found a home with Aunt Donalda. She was his only relative and his only real shot at a way out of the well, but sometimes he couldn't face the black stink and he left the food and went away without knocking.

His older girl breathed in sharply and turned. His wife was still watching from the door. Goddamn his life: six loving arms around his neck and the water already up to his collarbones.

Aunt Donalda's neighbours complained to the city, and the city came to him as the responsible relative. He remembered standing on the sidewalk, listening to the old Ukrainian from next door roaring about the goddamn cats, the man's breath battering his nose. Once he'd gone in with the inspectors and helped haul a truckload of yowling cats out of the place. Donalda looked on, offended, cold, mad. An educated woman, a teacher, a valuable house, rooms strewn with cat shit, furniture all torn up and stained, family keepsakes that might yet come to his daughters, remnants of a respectable, cultured past, all smelly and wrecked. She was crazy and stubborn too, wilful, sinking herself in cat-filled solitude, crazy but not crazy enough to be put away, crazy enough to find a hundred new cats to replace the ones they'd taken.

There was a bubble at the edge of his older daughter's lip; it ebbed and grew as she breathed. Her skin was lovely, pure paleness except for a single freckle under her left ear. On the wall above her were pictures of cartoon bears and boy singers.

The city's great sludge river seemed to divide at this room, and somehow sweep around it, leaving his girls alone. There might be other spaces of purity, but this was the only one he knew. There were no grimy gum-stamped sidewalks here and no tattered bushes hiding blood-crusted syringes. The dirty sun and the cynical moon were shut out, the shit ran to either side and he would keep them from it.

The boy singer above his girl's bed touched his crotch and grinned at Sergeant Judd. Just lightly, nothing obvious, a reminder of something that was going to happen for sure sometime.

He thought about Donalda's face with folds hanging down under her chin, the loose meat of her upper arms and the spotted, cold hands, the sound of her cats eating, like big ants chewing away at a South American jungle.

He could eat the lunches his wife made and save a few dollars a day, and he could put in for weekend time doing crowd control at concerts and parades and make maybe a hundred dollars a shift. But she wanted a new kitchen. She hated the gummy old artificial cork floor and the press-board cabinets. He didn't like it much either, but she loathed every minute she spent in the room. A new floor was four thousand dollars: not out of the question in the long run all by itself, but running pipe underneath for a new dishwasher, laying supports for new counters and cabinets, call it twenty thousand—new refrigerator, stove, dishes, a mountain of money.

They were in the hole already. Neither of them liked to open the mailbox. Sometimes after a week he'd reach in and take out the sheaf of bills and demands, sort them into standard forms and sinister thin notices marked Urgent and the high-quality envelopes that contained lawyers' letters.

They'd been okay when she was working for the bus company. She was a clerk in the chief accountant's office. She'd move papers and run for coffee and never complain, and almost as a joke the president gave her a little assignment, choosing one poem every month to be printed on rectangular placards and displayed above the heads of the passengers. It wasn't expensive, and many people seemed to like it. She loved the job. One way or another she'd always move a conversation, even with the butcher or the postman, around to the arts and literature and the finer things in life, and then, modestly, she'd reveal her calling: editor of poetry placards for the largest public-transit company in the country.

One day, completely out of the blue, the president turned on her, shouting that she'd gotten a big head, Mrs. Poetry Expert, what she chose was crap, and she was getting way beyond herself. He was famous for unmotivated tantrums, but she felt as though someone had hit her hard on the top of her head. She picked up her purse and left the office and spent a week in bed weeping while Judd tried to get the story out of her. Well, life was coarse and people were shits and he had this kind of thing happen to him all the time, but she wasn't built for it and this stupid craziness broke her in half. He promised himself that he would dent that president's head for him if he ever got a chance, but she was out of work and too sick and sad to look for another job. He knew she loved him, but sometimes her sorrow and humiliation made her angry at everyone, at him and even their girls.

His older daughter's eyes fluttered, her mouth moved, she fell deeper into sleep. He kissed his wife before he left the house.

An hour later he parked his cruiser for a while in one of his sanctuaries, at the edge of a parking lot behind a big industrial laundry. He smelled the starch in the air and watched the workers smoking on the loading dock. He could feel the heat from the dryers riding on top of the heat of the night air. The workers were skinny, broiled on the job. The foreman shouted at them, his uniform soaked in sweat. Pigeons crooned and rustled in the factory eaves, the aluminum sliding under their feet.

Judd looked out into the night. He could sense 17 crawling with life. By the railway tracks that ran past the laundry, runaways camped in the scrub under garbage-bag canopies, piling wood in firepits scooped out of the sand. To the north, ravines ran up to high steel fences that protected the estates. On High Street, half a mile away, there were jugglers, squeegee squads, chalk artists, quick-stepping pickpockets casting stolen wallets into mailboxes, wads of cash in their underwear. And all around him, the straight citizens who plodded through their days and nights, wives and husbands grinding on each other.

He reached down and felt his burgeoning belly, the basin of lard attached below his chest and above his groin, all his sins, laziness and weakness laid down in layers of fat. He could still move when he had to. He could take his club by the little handle that poked out of its side, whip it through the air and land the end on someone's head precisely hard enough to stun him and get the cuffs on him, and ten minutes later there would be nothing on the guy but a headache. But the mound of fat was slowing him down. It was like carrying a medicine ball in a sling twenty-four hours a day.

A worker flipped his cigarette out into the night and went back into the laundry. Two minutes later there was a glow from a pile of plastic film lying on the ground beside the dock, then a flash and flame shot high as the door, ripping along the pools of dirty oil left by the delivery trucks. Judd sat up straight, suddenly filled with sharp excitement, grabbed the radio mike and called it in. The foreman was standing on the dock with an extinguisher in his hands, spraying the flames. There was a puff of grey smoke from a pile of wooden pallets in the brush beside the dock and a sudden burst of yellow light from the bushes by the fence.

Judd got out of the cruiser and walked over to the fire, the smoke clogging his nose and the heat pricking his face. His cap slipped on his sweaty hair. His skin was wet under his shirt.

Five minutes after the first glow of flame, a fire supervisor's van wheeled into the laundry parking lot, and thirty seconds after that a hook and ladder. The first team of firefighters ran for the loading dock with canisters of foam, and the second team ran hoses to a hydrant. The fire had caught the dry weeds beside the dock and the flames were reaching out toward the building. Little patches of fire detached themselves from the burning mass and snapped up into the darkness. There was a tart dark oily smell and then a choking chemical odour as the fire retardant from the hose hit the base of the flame. The fire squads swept the line of chemical back and forth and pressed the flame back into itself.

Nine minutes later the fire was out. There was a stench of burnt wood and the clanging sound of the laundry alarm. The workers stood in the parking lot and watched the firefighters dragging their gear back to the truck while the supervisor poked through the scorching ash.

"Shit careless," said the supervisor to the laundry foreman, who turned and swore at his workers. A charred bin of dirty clothes was sending greasy smoke into the air. The ugly ragged brush at the side of the loading dock was gone.

Judd walked back to his cruiser, looked at the police equipment he loved, the little on-board computer, the billy club with the side prong, the dark red and clear white glass of the lights on the roof rack. The scent of the fire was in his clothes, and he could feel a thin layer of grime on his sweaty skin. He sat down on the front seat of the dark car and watched the fire cars move out of the parking lot.

Six

WHEN IVAN WAS thirteen a pet store opened down the block from the pharmacy. He used to stop in to look at the puppies squirming and yawning in the cages and the cold-eyed, stupid fish in the tanks with their tiny sunken skulls and plastic treasure chests. Guppies and neons and black mollies, even a saltwater blue ribbon eel that rose toward the surface of the water whenever anyone came near, nosing for food. The eel was from Indonesia. The owner of the pet store said that fishermen there threw poison into the water above the reef, pulled out the fish as they came to the surface and sold the ones that lived.

The pet store owner patrolled the streets at night in his old van, scooping up stray cats and untethered dogs. He answered classified advertisements offering free puppies to good homes, and sometimes he took Ivan along to help pick up what he found. The animals went to wholesalers and research laboratories and trainers who hung them from ropes for their fighting dogs to practice on. The pet shop man paid Ivan five dollars a trip because a boy on the scene made the deal smoother. Even if most people knew what the score was, it was nice to have a child along to look happy at the handover.

Along the back wall of the store there were cages of bait and prey animals, crickets for the frogs and spiders and white mice for the snakes. Ivan liked to feel the mice running over his skin. He'd turn his hand palm side up and then over and the mouse would scramble for a safe place, revolving three feet above the floor. Then Ivan would close his hand on the mouse and feel its heart pounding through its soft sides.

One afternoon when the owner was busy stacking a shipment of dog food, Ivan took a mouse from one of the cages and carried it out into the laneway behind the pet store.

For a while he played with it on the ground, letting it run, catching it by the tail when it had almost gotten away. It was a white mouse with pink eyes.

He wondered where the little robber was now. It had been a year since he'd seen him in the store. He dreamed about him sometimes, the two of them riding in a limousine, on their way to a job or from a job, the little silver pistol lying on the floor of the car.

The mouse scrambled on his hand, clinging and dangling when he turned it over. Its pink tail whipped in the sun.

"Eye-van," said the pet store man from the door behind him. Ivan almost liked the sound of it. Different from his mother's strange breathy Ee-von. Eye-van was stronger, a name for a Cossack on horseback. He held the mouse in his closed hand against his pant leg.

"Eye-van, you want to make some money, working around the place, or maybe you're too busy with your dad?"

"I'm not busy."

"Just helping out Saturdays, carrying stuff around, you know, maybe after school a couple of times, and maybe Sunday come in and feed them and clean up. Could you handle that?"

He'd have a key. He'd be alone in the place sometimes, with hundreds of lives under his command.

"I guess. You want me to start now?"

"Saturday. Ten o'clock. You could go at four."

"Okay."

The pet store man went back into the dark storage room.

Ivan took a pencil from his pocket, held the mouse in his left hand and put the point of the pencil to the mouse's jaw. He tapped the tiny teeth with the point of the pencil. He forced the mouse's lips back.

The mouse's pink eye rolled and his tail lashed.

It was very interesting. He was watching himself as much as the mouse, imagining what he might do if he was brave enough. Suddenly he shoved the pencil down the mouse's throat, into its body. The mouse twisted and thrashed against his hand. The pencil came out the mouse's stomach and stabbed deep into the flesh at the base of his thumb. The mouse's blood mixed with his own. He felt a lance of pain, grabbed and squeezed the spitted mouse, feeling the blood run down his wrist and arm.

Ivan pulled out the pencil and threw the mouse into a corner of the alley, then sat down on an overturned garbage can. He'd crossed a channel, the one that separated those who knew the score from those who did not. He'd tested himself. He found he could do something like that. He hadn't enjoyed it particularly, but he had been able to make himself do it. That was good information. He knew life on this side of the channel would be dangerous and full of surprises, but he was ready for it. He was a free agent.

He walked back two blocks along the main street to the pharmacy. Mrs. Godwin was stacking tubes of headache remedy on the shelves.

"Could I have a bandage, please, Mrs. Godwin?"

His punctured hand was still bleeding a little. He wondered if she could see anything unusual about the wound or about him. She didn't fuss or treat him like a child; she swabbed salve on the cut skin and wrapped gauze and tape around it as though he'd cut himself working, threshing or sawing. It was a worker's wound. He was a different kind of person now. He remembered the mouse struggling in his hand, going rigid, going soft. He still had the pencil in his pocket.

The cat had been sleeping under the porch for three hours. The little girl had been swinging steadily. For the past half-hour the swing set had bumped as it rose with her weight, the spike in the ground heaving upward and then plunging down again. The other backyards were empty in the afternoon heat. The little girl's shoulders were red. She sang to herself as she worked on the swing. The cat and the raccoon dozed in the darkness under the porch, hearing her, smelling the dogs, listening for the scrape of feet or the mumble of human voices.

Finally the swing set came loose like a tooth wrenched out of its socket, and the top bar came down on the girl with a hard crack. She sat on the ground silently with her eyes closed looking at flashes of light, listening to her breath and feeling the place where the bar had hit her. Her eyes opened. A woman came out the back door of the house, looked at the girl and the overturned swing set and went back in.

The girl got up and went into the house, coming back

after a minute with a bowl of milk. She raised the lattice under the porch and put the bowl down near the cat. He looked at the saucer, felt the sour taste of old blood in his mouth, rose and began to drink. There was a sound from behind him. He stopped and looked back over his shoulder.

The woman's voice called from inside the house. The girl rose and went up the back steps. The cat moved aside, lay down and watched as the raccoon waddled out of her hiding place over to the bowl.

It was hotter all around the world than it had ever been, ever in history. There had been a drought in the thirties and a dry time in the fifties, but this was beyond those, way over the red line; the sun seemed to move closer to the city and press down on it like an incandescent iron. Children and the elderly were warned to stay inside and avoid exercise.

The wind died. The highways were jammed with cars headed out of the city. The exhaust from the engines rose, paused, mixed and rose again and then stopped and gathered in the shape of an inverted bowl over the line of cliffs set back from the lake. Airplanes cut white streamers through the dingy sky. The bacterial count in the lake rose, and lifeguards shouted down from their white wooden towers at people preparing to go into the water. The sewage moving through the pipes slowed to walking pace and heated to body temperature.

Miles upstream in the flat-topped hills, a farmer who was expecting a visit from a government inspector filled his truck with cattle manure and drove it ten miles down the highway to a little stream. He stopped his truck and listened. No traffic either way. He backed the truck down the boat launch ramp so that the back tires and the edge of the gate were in the water, climbed up into the muck, his boots sliding on the slick metal beneath the manure, slammed the gate down and began to fork the stuff into the moving stream. When the load was completely over the side, he put the gate back up and drove away. It was against the law but so was having too much cow shit around.

When the germs in the manure hit the water, they spread downstream, multiplying and dying, a busy froth of life that seeped down through the rock to the aquifer that supplied the city's water. The germs could bind themselves to organs and intestinal linings in vertebrates. It was a chance evolution that did neither the germs nor their hosts much good.

In the morning the woman started shouting inside the house. The cat heard the noise and decided to get moving. The raccoon was still sleeping, her light breath whistling between her teeth. The light was beginning to build toward whiteness.

He moved along a row of fences, jumped up and prowled along the tops of the fences that separated the backyards. Other cats had left their marks on the edges of their territories, but the fence seemed to be a thoroughfare. Once or twice he caught a sense of another cat watching him or making a point of ignoring him.

There was a broad boulevard at the end of the fence, with a line of bushes down the middle. On the far side were more bushes and then a strong storm fence, the bottom buried in the ground. He put his muzzle to the air and tasted the wind. The plant signal was still coming from the south, far beyond the fence. Somewhere in between was a confusing braid of smells—new and old meat, dusty grass, the metal from the fence, dogs, smoke and cat, but strange cat, concentrated, acid.

Fifty feet down the fenceline behind a tree and some sheltering scrub he found a scoop in the earth where a dog had gone to work on the barrier. The dog had cleared just enough to get his big shoulders through and given up. The cat shook his head at the sharp dog stink and pressed himself underneath the fence.

More trees, big ones, and then another high barrier. The plant smell from far beyond it. Smooth fence, too slick and tall to climb. The twinge in his hip again.

A bird fluttered high in the tree, looked down, saw the cat, shot away into the air.

Trees again. He leapt and clung to a trunk, began to move upward, pushing hard with his back feet, releasing and grasping with his front claws. White bird stain on a crotch of a branch. Faint airborne trails of squirrel scent. He looked left, beyond the fence. A great plain, the grass brown in the sun, rolled up to the crest of a hill far away. He turned and landed awkwardly on the top of the fence, felt a stab of sharp wire, screeched, felt the rebounding wire throw him upward and beyond the rest of the barrier. He fell eight feet down onto a slack heap of dead grass.

Seven

IVAN TEUTI WAS SMALL and fair with regular features and large blue eyes, the irises so pale they seemed almost without colour. In some lights he looked like something blind that had evolved without sun, deep underground. By the time he got to the first year of high school, the year after he'd killed the mouse, he had two nicknames.

Some of the girls found it unsettling to look into these eyes, and they called him Mandrake after a comic-strip magician who could stun people with a glance. Some of them thought he was creepy, but one or two thought he was cute.

He had a strong sense of privacy and was easily humiliated. He feared and hated the locker room where bigger boys snapped towels at smaller ones, the fabric making a cracking sound as it bounced off the flesh. The jocks called him Tootsie. They mostly left him alone since he wasn't quite small enough to be obvious prey or big enough to be a challenge. He hated the name, although he kept his face still and blank and acted as though he hadn't heard.

Bill Grant sometimes caught him in a headlock and rubbed or scraped his scalp with a knuckle. Ivan struggled but did not fight or cry, and Bill usually went on to someone else. Bill was a year older than the others, a class behind, dark, his top lip shadowed with black hair, strong, sullen, resenting his own lumbering meaty body.

One afternoon in October, Bill caught him in the locker room, held his left arm behind his back and started to croon his nickname. When Bill forced his naked body forward, Ivan stepped back to keep his balance. His right foot landed on the damp floor near Bill's heel. Without thinking he leaned to his left and brought his bare right foot back against Bill's leg. Bill let go of Ivan's arm, wobbled, threw his hands in the air and crashed hard on his left side. His body made a dull full sound as it hit the concrete, and he started to yell.

The gym teacher got Bill to the principal's office, Ivan following, looking serious, struggling to keep from laughing. It was funny to see Bill twisted and limping, lurching and whining down the smooth linoleum hallway. After he was taken to the hospital, the principal called Ivan in for a talk.

"It was an accident. I didn't mean it—he just caught me and I was off balance." The blue-white eyes looked at the principal candidly.

The principal had never seen Ivan Teuti before; he was a new boy in the lowest grade, but sometimes the bad ones gave you warning. Ivan had thrust himself out of the moving, shuffling crowd, so he'd bear watching. His public school file showed fair marks, no serious discipline record, nothing out of the ordinary.

"Do you understand you may have hurt Bill seriously? Could be a couple of ribs broken. You can't meet violence with violence, you know."

"I really didn't mean to hurt him at all. He just caught me."

"Just think about it. You can go."

Six months later, with holidays eight weeks away and the spring light glowing in the tall classroom windows, Ivan's

science teacher, Miss Donalda Massie, began to talk about
pre-Columbian civilization and the life of the highly cultured Olmecs, Aztecs and Mayans of Central America. She
pulled the long green curtains shut, pulled down a portable
screen and turned out the lights. Glowing images from a
projector appeared on the screen: the steps of a giant
ragged pyramid covered with tourists and guides, green
sway-backed jungle ruins, paintings of religious ceremonies
on great ziggurats, lines of sweating captives dragged up the
stone steps and wrenched down into the stone crib at the
top of the Pyramid of the Sun. The teacher's dry little voice
scraped away at the story. Two old men would hold each
prisoner down while another cut his chest open with a
crystal knife and another seized the beating heart, twisted
and yanked it out and held it up to the sky.

Miss Massie went on about maize, beans, crop rotation,
trade lines that ran along the coast as far north as Alaska,
dried squid found in packsacks dug up from graves deep in
the Yucatán and in the cold forests above the American
plains. Something about all this caught Ivan like a hook. He
dreamed of the sun-blasted ziggurat, each tier lined with
fewer and more powerful people, and finally one great
king at the top. He dreamed of himself standing in the sun
looking out over the jungle, beside the huge stone frog
faces, one of the four old men who performed the sacrifice, a holder-down, cutter or extractor. The captives' eyes
were resigned and willing.

That was the really compelling part. The victims pre-
sented themselves for sacrifice. They wished it and longed
for it. The teacher's chalk rasped, the clock hands clicked,

the bell clanged the end of the period, but his interest continued, certain, strong and permanent.

Donalda Massie was a short middle-aged woman with thick legs and flabby arms, a woman who had watched her history and science classes for signs of real perception for years and found little of it, just the occasional obedient girl angling for extra marks. Suddenly one of the blanks, little Ivan Teuti, was coming up to her at the end of the day and asking for the names of books on Central American civilization. Years ago she would have been excited, and even now she took notice.

"What in particular interests you about this place and period?"

"I don't know. It just kind of jumped out at me."

"A very violent civilization, but very carefully arranged."

"They played a ball game?"

"They killed the losers," she said. "Beheaded them."

"They had calendars?"

Why would he be interested in that? "Very complicated ways to measure time based on the movements of the stars. They built special towers for observatories." She had been to Mexico and spent days and nights in the old stone chambers gazing upward, and she'd read everything she could find on ancient Mayan astronomy with its jaguars and sharks in the night sky. She thought the boy was manipulating her somehow, but she couldn't see her way through him. She wrote down some titles.

Donalda Massie lived alone in a house by the lake. She'd been born there, in the black-framed iron bed upstairs.

She was the obedient one. Her older sister escaped at the beginning of the Second World War, joined the bomber-ferry service and flew Lancasters from the Canadian factories over the North Atlantic to bases in western England. She sent postcards to Donalda from wonderful blacked out bombed London. She died in the last days of the Blitz, blown apart in a pub at midnight. Donalda bundled up the postcards and put them in the attic in the trunk with her father's olive uniform from the war before. Her younger sister married and moved to the north of the city.

After the war there was a surge of babies. Donalda went to Normal School, learned to be a teacher, specializing in science, content in the big laboratory with the dissection tables and the rubber tubes that fed the Bunsen burners. She taught botany, biology, chemistry and physics, standing against the big chart of the periodic elements, and substituted for history and English teachers from time to time. Her father died soon after his elder daughter. Her mother died in the big black bed in 1960. Every year Donalda's routine became more hardened. The streetcar back and forth along the two miles to school. Church every other Sunday. Two weeks in the late summer at a lodge in the north; two weeks in Europe in midwinter, focusing every year on a particular new country or region. Once or twice a year a visit from her sister and brother-in-law with their bumptious, running young boy.

She had two passions.

The first was astronomy, and it arrived like a thunderbolt, on a Normal School visit to the university planetarium. The students bent over one by one to peer into the little shielded tube that thrust out at a right angle from the great shaft of the telescope. When she fitted her eye to the opening, she saw the faint red smudge of Mars, and it struck her like an axe, opening simultaneously an immense distance and an immeasurable intimacy, a huge mystery that ran on a known set of rules, precise, calculable movements that accumulated in overwhelming grandeur. Her legs buckled. Mars disappeared and she reached out to the wide, rising shape of the telescope to keep herself from falling. That weekend she bought a telescope of her own and set it up beside the south window in the attic.

Her second passion was cats, and it infiltrated her life later, without much fuss. One autumn morning the year before she retired from teaching, the same year she met Ivan, she woke up to a sound in her kitchen downstairs. A grey tomcat had squeezed under a window sash and was pacing the room. She opened the door to let it out. It pressed itself against her leg and purred. It had no collar. She poured a little milk into a flowered china dish and put it on the floor.

He was the first, and an abiding pleasure, an intelligent animal, she thought, a coper-with-life, who knew the richness of a settled routine. And perhaps like the tramps she'd heard her mother talk about, he'd put some kind of secret mark on her fence that meant Shelter Here, because two weeks later the grey tom brought home a little battered white cat with one ear gone and the other slashed in half.

The two cats took up an increasing amount of space in her thoughts. At school the hours rolled by like boxcars on a slow train, dropping their cargoes of botany and chemistry, but between periods against the trudge and bang of students outside her classroom door she'd think about her cats and smile. At night she delighted in them. They had a look and smell of wildness, and they brought her old place alive. They stretched in the oblong patch of sunlight on her faded rug, chased each other down the hallways and found little resting places in crannies and odd corners.

In the spring two more arrived. She gave them names, reconsidered and gave them new ones, then began simply calling them whatever names came to mind. The grey tom was Jupiter, then Pharisee, then Richard, then Longshanks. She scooped out their litterboxes and spread chemicals over them, but there was always a sharp smell of urine in the house. Then the big orange tom arrived, pushed the grey aside and took command. There was never any doubt about his name. From the beginning he was Mars.

She couldn't wait to leave her springtime retirement party, almost bolted the staff lounge in the middle of the principal's speech. "Her career has featured dedication and reliability. She is a pedagogue, in the highest sense. I need not remind you of the derivation of that term . . ." She waited while the staff raised their plastic cups of wine to her, said a few words and left for home and her cats.

That summer three more arrived. She seldom went out of the house now. She ordered what she needed over the phone, leaving cheques in the mailbox, and dropped her tidy little bags of trash onto the porch to be retrieved, as a special favour, by the garbageman. She read astronomy journals, watched the stars and sat in the front parlour with the white plaster circle on the ceiling, closing her eyes and waiting for the feeling of her cats sliding against her.

She usually wore a nightgown and a red bathrobe. She kept a pair of light blue slippers by the front door, since she disliked the feeling of the dusty wood of the porch under her feet. One August morning she opened the door to fetch the mail and saw one of her former students riding a bicycle down her street.

Donalda Massie's house was on Ivan's drugstore route. He brought medicated soap to the neighbour on her left and laxatives to the Ukrainian who lived on the other side. He had never made a delivery to her and didn't know where she lived. Now, strangely, here she was, in her bathrobe at her front door. It was as though she'd been cut out of one picture and pasted into another.

"Miss Massie?"

It had been three months since she'd left the school. She'd forgotten his name. "You're the Mexican boy. The Mayan boy."

"Is this your house, Miss Massie? It's a wonderful house." He was standing astride his bicycle, looking up at her. He hadn't spent much time in houses. He knew his family's apartment and the big public buildings, the churches and the schools, but the idea of a private house as big as two or three apartments put together was unsettling.

The big orange tom was peering at him from behind her robe.

"That's quite a cat there. What's his name?"

"This is Mars. Do you like cats?"

"Love cats. I'm a cat guy." He felt a strong desire to get

past her into the house. He had no idea what he'd find. A library, a sunroom, sculptures, a big iron safe in the wall with a heavy dial? He felt small and temporary, unmoored, looking at the house. It made him angry.

"You have cats?"

"No, I—" He pulled a story out of his head. It came as easily as silk. "We used to have one but my mother got allergies, and we had to give it—her—away. Her name was Minnie."

"For Minerva. A deity. Like Mars here."

He sensed there was a kind of chance in this setup for him. The old woman had something he needed, perhaps knowledge or some sort of hidden strength he could take from her if he was careful and smart. He wheeled the bicycle up the sidewalk. The orange cat turned and went back into the house.

"Mars!" The cat ignored her. From below the steps Ivan could see gliding forms and glowing eyes.

"How many cats do you have?"

"Well, six, seven—it's temporary." She seemed a little embarrassed. "They come in, I keep them for a while, then they move away or somebody takes them. It's really just something that needs doing. They are so hungry, some-times, when they come to the door."

"I think it's wonderful."

She scrutinized him for seriousness. She remembered his eyes from her class: the pupils two emphatic small black circles, the irises very pale blue, bleached, almost transparent, fading into the white.

"Then you must visit someday and I will show them to you."

He turned the bicycle around and heaved the delivery pack up onto his shoulders. "I'd like to do that very much. I'll just come around sometime, if you like."

For the next week he took care to ride past her house once or twice a day, not stopping but looking at the door as he went by. He thought even if the old woman wasn't watching she might sense him nearby. At night he lay in the dark and imagined what he might find in the old house—gold, pearls, perfumes, old books and maps, treasures like the ones in Sinbad's sudden bright cave. And he'd fly away on the back of an enormous bird with his pockets full of money.

Ivan was sixteen, smart enough now to know he had to be patient, wait for some opening. So he took the campaign slowly, one visit every few days.

First he came with a present, a herbal tea he took from the pharmacy right under Mrs. Godwin's nose. Miss Massie came to the front door, accepted the package and allowed him to pick up and caress a ragged white cat that crouched on the floor near her slippers.

A week later he knocked on the door, with an expression of concern. It was past dusk, and there was no light on: was she away, or perhaps ill? He just wanted to check. "I was sleeping," she said, and waved away his apology with an invitation to come in and try some of the tea he'd brought her.

It was a little like the beginning of his daydream about Sinbad's treasure. Through the entrance and down a long, dark, wooden corridor, then doors to his left and his right—monsters behind one, maybe, and riches behind another. They sat in the living room. He breathed through his mouth to try to keep the cat stink out. There were more than six or seven animals here. Ten, maybe, or a dozen. Three of them stayed in the living room watching him as she poured the thin bitter tea.

"And are you planning to go into one of the professions?"

"Oh, business, I suppose. My dad has a drugstore."

"In the neighbourhood?"

"Just up around the corner."

"Oh, that place. I used to go in for school supplies when I was working, years ago, lined paper and such. For my medicines I shop at the Independent in the mall. They deliver."

"Well, I deliver too."

"So you do. But of course they have all my paperwork."

She was sitting with her knees drawn together, he noticed, and smiling, her eyes attentively moving across his face. She drank with little sips, making her mouth a rosebud at the rim of the cup.

"Well," he said, "you just call the store if you need me for anything."

"Now, young man," she said, flirting creakily, "you're going to get me in trouble with the neighbours."

When he left she shook his hand, pressing her dry fingers into his palm; he didn't really focus on her last words until a few minutes later, and then he slid to a stop while he thought about them. "Get me in trouble with the neighbours. . . ." It was teasing, a joke about a man and a woman alone, but below that some real feeling he couldn't quite pin down. Two feelings, yes, half-contradictory but equal. One minute she thought they were friends, an old woman and a young man—that was one movie, with a rueful unspoken reference to what might have been. And the next minute she was running or rerunning some other script in her head: she was young and he was her young suitor. The daintiness over tea, the polite talk about his prospects—it was an eldest daughter at home to a caller making cultivated conversation with her parents on patrol in the hallway. And a dozen cats peeing on the rug. She was crazy, clearly crazy, and of course that changed everything. Probably changed everything.

Donalda Massie had been losing keys, fumbling names, forgetting what to call things. Out on the street she'd lose track of herself, caught in a sudden parenthesis as the world rushed past her. The matter in her head turned like tiles in a kaleidoscope and tumbled into some other arrangement and she lost her place. She had a wasting, hardening condition of the brain. Her doctor had confirmed it after a test at a table in his office, a child's exam—she remembered something like it from Normal School, fitting bright cut-out shapes through holes in a hollow plastic sphere, a triangle, a square, stars. She couldn't manage it. The doctor explained what she could expect and how she might prepare.

"You have family that can take care of some of these things for you?"

"Not really." The boy, the policeman. No.

"Well, there are a number of agencies, you know. And I would advise, uh, I would advise some attention to your estate sometime soon. Not to say you won't be bright as a button for years yet."

Her big old house stood by a wide boardwalk that ran for miles beside the lake. The earth-packed stone in the basement was original, and the front windows still had redwood shutters that slid into recesses below the sill. When she got the news about her illness, she thought about rearranging the place so that someone in a state of confusion could find her way from one room to another. But then she realized she didn't know where to begin. It all seemed perfect to her. She stood in the living room under the ornate plaster circle on the ceiling and felt the place settle in around her. There were hidden strata of wallpaper, dull brass plates on the doors, electric switches with round cylindrical ivory buttons and a long dusty shaft that ran behind the wall from the back bedroom to the kitchen. She settled for little notes that she pasted to the refrigerator, stove and toilet. She'd read somewhere that identifying notes could reassure people when they'd forgotten what the things in the kitchen and bathroom were.

She thought she could feel her mind pulling apart into sections like an old orange drying inside its rind, past in one place, present in another, with no section at all set aside for the future. Strangely, although the present was more distinctly separated from the past now, it took no effort at all to move between them. When she was in the present she felt dull and shabby, but in an instant she could turn to the memories that suffused the house, mild memories of conversations or shared music. She wanted to escape but couldn't, wanted to surrender and sink into the dusty wood and marble but couldn't do that either. She lived in the place lightly, trying not to touch anything more than she had to, visiting the attic on clear nights to stare at the sky through her telescope, turning her attention as far away as possible, following the tracks of the moons of Jupiter. She gazed at them as the astronomers of the Yucatán had a thousand years before.

The other houses along the lake changed, grew wings and skylights. There was a ten-year movement toward Mediterranean concrete-and-iron porches and then a movement away again. Lawns were covered with concrete for parking, the concrete pulled up again and replaced with wood chips and crushed stone, and then the lawns came back. Donalda's house stayed as it was, with its thin wires, brittle pipes and roof shingles sliding into the yard.

Her sister had married a machinist named Judd. When they visited years ago they'd let their son, Stephen, run wild; he scampered up and down the hallways and burrowed through the attic trunks. He found sabres and a rusted pistol from an overseas war and strode downstairs shouting orders in a harsh treble voice. He made Donalda uncomfortable with his rummaging through resting things, his changing of real weapons into toys, but he loved finding treasures in the big brass-locked containers. When she couldn't find the keys, he'd use a screwdriver to pry the locks apart, leaving the line of trunks looking like squat panting old men with their brass tongues hanging out.

When the boy grew up, he went to police college. His high voice deepened but remained harsh. The sister and the husband were dead now, but the policeman still came to visit once a month or so, spending an hour or less in her parlour. He'd become a big man, but she still thought he

looked as foolish and false as the little boy in his grand-
father's khaki uniform. The cats disliked him and stayed
upstairs when he came to the house.

He tried to impress her with his official policeman's
voice. He'd stop at the front door on the way out and peer
at the chain. "When's the last time you had the locks
changed on this place?"

"I don't know. Quite a few years, I guess. But I'm the
only one with a key."

"Guys on the street have stuff now could whip through
this chain of yours in half a minute. And then where would
you be?"

"I don't know. Right here, I guess." And she looked stu-
pidly at him, knowing it annoyed him. He reminded her of
her old students, the unfocused, bullying ones who hated
her and the schoolwork and tried to make sure nobody
else liked it either.

"And that back shed. Just rotten and falling down and so
close to the house that a firebug could put one can of gas
down back there and have the whole place going in a
minute. And don't think it don't happen. I know guys they
get sexual satisfaction from watching a fire like that."

He was trying to shock her. It was stupid and intrusive,
a grown-up version of his noisy parades on the stairs. She
watched him change on his monthly visits, with his belly
pushing out more every year. He wanted the house. He'd
sell it straightaway, she knew that, and throw all her cats
out on the street. She was always relieved when he left.

The cat population grew to fifteen, shrank to eight,
settled at about ten. Some were visitors, never really

attached to her or her house, and some were so much at home that they seemed to fit the house better than she did, as if she was living in their house, passed down to them from generations of successful business cats who had ridden out the Depression and the wars.

Three or four became close friends and sat in her lap as she dreamed. Primrose, Sweetie, Tuffy. Their cool, smooth fur under her fingers helped her think. In the weeks after her diagnosis she spent more and more time in reverie in her old scarlet chair, trying to force her brain to clear itself.

The words in her head marched in orderly sentences and paragraphs, just like the texts she used to teach in class. She could see them rising on their own from the wet decaying corrugations of her brain. They seemed to echo a series of notes for a book on astronomy she'd thought of writing years ago, but they curved into the personal, and sometimes they were pained or insulting. She marked them down on scraps of paper, taped them to the refrigerator door, the cupboards, hid them under piles of sheets in the linen closet and rolled them up in balls to throw for the cats.

The moon is at the beginning of its cycle tonight. It's a bright new curve that will grow in the Arabic way right to left. The moon's weight is constant, but some feel that it is heavier at this point in its revolution, as though its mass actually pressed down on them from a distance.

A scurry from the floor above, dust from the heavy curtains spinning in the sunlight, irregular hollow sounds from the tennis club across the street.

The newspaper says spaceships have mapped the other side of the moon but not closely. There could be a million things hidden in the shadows there.

Can you strengthen your brain by breaking it out of its ordinary circuits? How big would you have to think, how bright, how far?

Fixed to doors with masking tape, the other more practi cal notes to herself: Bathroom. Kitchen. Clear out the milk.

Barney the botanist back there years ago rubbing his head shyly, coming to bed and trying to stir me up, then off to his wife every time. Dead now. That fellow I met once. Two others, but really only Barney. Ten years of every so often.

Cat food. Table.

Barney had died three years before. She'd got the news in the teachers' lounge—great big growth inside him. The geography teacher's brother had done the operation, a peek and eek, as the doctors said—take a quick look and sew him up again, nothing to be done. She stayed away from the funeral. She did think a little about the death of the only images anyone really had of her naked on her high bed. She wondered if those pictures rushed past him in his final moments when you're supposed to see the whole march of your life. Likely it was all wife and children.

Fur sliding against her calf, Tuffy pressing against her, hungry boy.

I'd look at Callisto again tonight, but I feel like resting and the moon is restful, so well known. I won't climb the stairs. I'll watch the moon from my big red chair.

Ivan kept at it. He wasn't quite sure what he was doing—trying out stances and approaches or angling for some unknown payoff. He was eighteen now, had graduated from high school and was on his way to business college. Miss Massie was the first adult he could have a conversation with. He couldn't talk with his mother, his father wouldn't talk with him, and his aunts and uncles were pale and thick, like potatoes just dug up from the ground.

The only conversation he knew came from movies. In Miss Massie's presence, he became characters and told lies. Little ones at first, then outlandish ones: "I won the mathematics prize last year, after you left, you know. Solid geometry and a little calculus. It seems to come easy to me." In fact he'd just scraped into college, but she seemed to believe it, sitting in her fraying overstuffed chair with a grey cat on her lap.

"You enjoy mathematics, then?" she said. "It must be fascinating. A lot of astronomy has to do with mathematics, of course."

"Sure," he said. He could have told her he was a brain surgeon or a test pilot. It was like throwing a ball against a building—whatever you put into it came back to you.

"Would you care for some tea?"

He'd excuse himself sometimes to go to the bathroom, a dank upstairs cabinet with ragged towels on a tilting rack and a stinking box of cat litter beside the toilet. There was an overflowing supply of pills in the medicine cabinet behind the hinged mirror but nothing that was worth stealing. He'd take a moment or two for reconnaissance, stepping softly into her bedroom, taking note of the ragged bedspread and the thicket of empty perfume and cologne bottles on the beside stand. There was a telescope in the attic that might fetch a few dollars at a pawnshop, but that was about it.

Downstairs she'd have some tea ready, and a plate of stale arrowroot cookies. When he thought about Donalda years later the wooden taste of the arrowroots would seep back into his mouth.

It wasn't worth his while, but he kept going back. She had something he needed. It was exasperating; sometimes he thought she was drifting away, didn't give a shit about him one way or another, and he thought of the ways he could end it. He rolled out the sequences in his mind as he lay in bed at night. He could kiss her, or shout at her, or turn as he left and call back to her, "You really have gone gaga, haven't you? You've really lost it." But he couldn't do it. Throw a stone in the water and it splashes, ripples and closes again. There wouldn't even be much point in hitting her. Five minutes later she'd wonder why her face hurt.

Then there was a scary visit late in September. He was at business college already. The house smelled even more than usual, and her robe was askew—he could see a slight rise of flesh through the V of the collar. Usually she called him Ivan, but this time she didn't use his name or look at him directly.

"Is there something wrong?" he asked. "Are you not feeling well?"

"I don't know," she said. Then she smiled, looked at him directly and said very clearly, with a sudden hardness in her voice, "I can see you."

He felt like a thief caught in a sudden light. He'd wanted her to look at him, and now she was doing it. He felt she could see through his skin, into his heart, lungs and nerves, that she could follow every thought in his head; he was like the flayed man in his father's store, opened up and folded out.

Ivan jumped up, walked quickly to the door and looked back at her. She was still staring at the chair next to her, as though he'd left an afterimage of himself for her to examine. He opened his mouth to try to tell her she was crazy but found his throat jammed with fear. A cat called at his feet and swirled against him.

"What the fuck?" A big man with a pot-belly was standing on the front porch. "Hey! Who the fuck are you?"

"Sir?"

"What the fuck are you doing in this house?"

"Drugstore guy. I'm the drugstore guy." And he ran. Grabbed his bike at the front of the yard and rolled off down the street. His face was burning, torrid, and his throat was clogged; he was next to tears, for Christ's sake. The pot-bellied guy knew he didn't belong in a house like that.

Currents of ionized particles on their way from one galaxy to the next one. Birthing stars. Veils in space. Cat litter. Tissue.

Eight

THERE WERE SIX lions in the enclosure, the old male, two adolescent males and three new arrivals, a lioness and her two cubs. They had come from different parts of the world, some from captivity, some from the open, and the keepers had to be careful—the group was asymmetrical, there wasn't much to restrain the younger males, the lioness was confused and easily irritated and sometimes there would be flare-ups and even serious battles without warning.

The lioness, who had been captured pregnant, gave birth at the zoo and almost destroyed her first litter. She refused to nurse and snarled at the two kits—the keepers had to take them away, feed them by hand and then carefully bring them back to the enclosure.

The lioness just ignored them now. She had other things to worry about. She had to learn to eat killed food. She was used to taking her own. She'd dance around the big plain of the lion enclosure snapping at flies and birds, stalking squirrels. The cubs liked to watch her but were careful not to get close. The old male ignored her. He still ate first when the meat truck came.

They fed in the early morning and dozed through the day. The old male would wake up and prowl at four o'clock, staring at the crowds on the other side of the fence, his tawny black-centred eyes picking out animals that seemed weak or sick. She'd run hard to the crest of the hill and back, turning, leaping, roaring.

The little cat came up the far side of the hill in the late

afternoon, the smells becoming more intense and confusing. He was moving very carefully, stepping around leaves and sticks, scanning the ground and the air. He was thinking about birds. When he got to the top of the hill, the wind was coming from below and he caught the full scent of the lions: bitter, strong, threatening, muscular, clinging. Every tuft and clump that rose above the ground was marked. He looked over the lip of the hill.

The male was patrolling the fence. The lioness was on her back, rolling in the hot sand near the water.

The male turned and stalked away, the muscles sliding under the skin. He was about twenty feet from the top of the hill when the wind shifted for a moment and he caught the faint scent of the little cat.

The lioness caught it too. She froze, arched, leapt to her feet and came running.

The male moved closer to the brow of the hill. The cat was crouched on the grass behind an unavailing shred of bush. He saw the big bulk moving up toward him, the golden black-slitted gaze, caught the huge cat smell rolling ahead and felt the movement of the earth as the lioness ran closer.

The lion looked down, rumbled in his throat. The cat's ears went back. He flattened himself to the earth.

The lioness was gathering herself for a leap over the lion. He turned and hit her hard as she jumped, his right front paw clubbing her on the muzzle, turning her body so she flew over the cat and hit the ground hard to one side of him. She screamed. The cat jumped up and started to run down the hill. The lion bellowed. The cat froze. The lioness stayed where she was on the ground, staring at the other two animals, her teeth showing.

The two men in the security room had forty-six screens to monitor, signals from the elephant paddock, the monkey house and all the rest. They started to focus on the middle screen from the cameras at the lion enclosure when the lioness charged.

"Something's up with that," said the first man, and manipulated the controls on his console. The camera moved in on the two big animals.

"No, come back a bit," said the second man. The lioness was still on the ground. The lion was walking slowly, with a cub beside him. Not a cub.

"A fucking ocelot?"

"What is that?"

"Have we got tape rolling on this?"

"It's a fucking house cat, some kind of stray house cat. The old bastard is walking it around like they're having a date, for fucksake. And look at Her Highness back there on her ass. Pissed or what?"

The image was black and white but clear, the little cat moving gravely beside the big one, under his protection, past the crowd, the children laughing and shrieking. When the pair got to the far side of the wire, the two men cut to the south camera. It gave them a clear picture of the lion leaning against the wire, pressing against it with all his weight. The fence bulged outward, and the metal at the bottom raised slightly, making just enough space for the little cat to squeeze through. The cat ran away past the children and the parents toward the park gates, his paws padding lightly in the dust.

That night the television station played the images from the security camera at the end of the news. Black-and-white pictures of the little cat walking through the lion enclosure, escorted by the great-maned male, with the lioness staring at them. The newscaster made a little joke or two.

Julia Will looked at the image and felt the skin of her face and the back of her neck go cold. She felt dizzy and sat down heavily in the leather chair by the television set. Even in the fuzzy footage she recognized the irregular flash of white on the cat's left front leg and his jaunty saunter, his air of intelligence and independence. Jones was leading the lion around. She let out her breath, her mouth making a little wailing sound, and she was suddenly full of an intense sadness. The textures and shapes around her faded, and she concentrated on this sharp new pain, marvelling at it, wondering what it meant.

The picture of the little cat and the space he'd left behind, the bowl his body had made in the cushioned back of the sofa all seemed clear and real, and the rest of the well-ordered world around her seemed poor, old and abstract.

She went to her bedroom and changed into her running clothes, a light shirt and loose pants, jogging shoes. The stone front steps felt greasy under her feet. She ran across the big front lawn and along the inside of the fence, moving clockwise past the steel pipes sunk into the earth. The surface underneath her changed from grass to gravel to dirt. She usually ran on summer mornings when the sun was still low. She felt weightless in the air when its temperature was neutral, neither hot nor cold. Now it was early evening and the ground felt hard, tamped down by the heat.

She'd been married for two and a half years. She'd spent a year exploring the life of the well-to-do, the buttery leathers, sweet scents and doors that opened before she reached them. But the pleasures receded. Coddling and swaddling, she said to herself, life with François was coddling and swaddling. She ran to keep her body hard, to break out of the cradle and to focus on what she'd been before the luxury wrapped itself around her and fuzzed her out entirely.

She liked herself, her own body and mind, although she had to work to maintain them both. She liked her mother, who lived in the big house with them: she was rude and self-indulgent, a plump, demanding presence but in her own way loving. And she liked her little pet store cat. The breath came hard from her mouth, the bones of her chest ached and she was weeping. She reached the front of the big house again and stood panting at the foot of the steps. François and her mother were waiting for her.

"You shouldn't run like that," said her mother. "That constant pounding and pounding is not good for the internal organs."

"Lillian, that's stupid," said François.

It irritated Julia's mother that he called her by her first name. It seemed familiar and almost disrespectful, considering her years. She would have preferred Mother. François's own mother had been dead for years, and not much loss to the world the way she heard it, so where was the harm. "This is the *female* organs I am speaking about," she said.

"My female organs are fine," said Julia.

Julia sat down on the steps and looked out along the driveway, past the long shining cars to the steel gate. Six acres of enclosed land on this side, and the world beyond it. He was out there, she thought, maybe looking for real life again. Maybe he likes all this about as much as I do.

"Now, he wouldn't have gone to the highway," said Julia's mother, sitting down beside her. "All that noise would have scared him away. A cat wouldn't like the smell of it."

"Then why do you see all those cats smushed up on the road?"

"Those are dogs," said François. "She's right, you know. You really only see cats smushed on the city streets."

"Shit," said Julia. "Shit shit."

"We should organize a search party," said Julia's mother, who read English mystery novels. "Quarter the grounds, get the staff in order, sweep the property."

"Lillian, that's stupid," said François. "You can't find a cat that way."

"I'm tired of talking about this," said Julia. "I am *tired* of talking about this." She rose and started up the steps. François saw the pressed line of her mouth.

"What do you know about finding a cat?" said Julia's mother.

Julia was almost through the door.

"Hey!" said François. A plan had come into his head, as a plan always did when he needed one. When a storm broke he could think up an umbrella before the first drop reached his naked head. He was lucky that way.

"Look," he said. "Look, it's easy. He was around the zoo, probably in the woods around there—maybe he's still there. We have people looking. Or maybe he got onto somebody's property—maybe somebody took him, or somebody found him. That's okay. We have a picture, we can identify him. And we'll offer a reward. A thousand dollars. A thousand-dollar reward. Five thousand."

She was staring down at him from the steps. The umbrella in his mind snapped open and turned to gold: a brilliant thought, bold, a perfect stroke. "A million. A million dollars."

"A million dollars?"

"Why not?" he said. "A million dollars. If it takes a million dollars to get—"

"—Jones—"

"—back, I will pay a million dollars."

"A million dollars?" said Julia's mother. "That's the most foolish thing I ever heard."

"It is strange," said Julia. "It wouldn't be sensible. It would look very . . ."

"Who cares?"

"A million dollars?" said Julia's mother. "Who would pay a million dollars for a cat? For a stupid *cat?*"

"It's my money," said François. "And I won't miss it. Why not?"

"It's just enormous," said Julia. "It's such a big thing."

"You want your cat back?"

"Oh, yes. Yes."

"Well, then, Christ, leave it to me." A million dollars, yes, big enough to catch the eye but not a crippling expenditure, in line with his promotional cash flow. Tax deductible, if the accountants could do it—a business expense. He'd build a commercial campaign around it. He'd be the sausage maker who cared deeply for animals.

And in any case he'd pay a million to calm his wife down.

"A million dollars?" said Julia's mother, waving her plump arms in the evening air. "For a cat? For a stray cat? Do you know what you could *buy* with a million dollars?"

"Yes, I do," said François.

Sergeant Judd sometimes stopped in at the Tropicana, a strip club on Sylvan Street, to screen for changes in the flesh-hound scene and have a drink. Each dancer usually did one song clothed, one song topless, one song naked, but his favourite, Gracie, liked to strip down right at the beginning and spend her three songs whirling around the vertical brass bar, grasping it with her hands and one bent knee, sometimes climbing up the pole and turning upside down, sometimes spinning around it so that her vulva gaped at the men in the front row. Between sets she'd sit at his table and take sips from his Stolichnaya, bending over to hide from the manager, who liked the girls on fifty-dollar champagne.

"Going to get your tits done, Gracie?"

"Going to help me?" She was trying to save five thousand dollars to pump up her breasts to match the sumptuous globes attached to the other girls on the circuit, but she was always spending her money on shoes and purses. She had sixty purses in her little apartment and nothing much in any of them. She was tiny and sprightly as a monkey.

"You help me and I'll help you." Sometimes Gracie did pass on vague news about the subterranean life of 17. She'd hear about some power-powder coming to rest in a backroom somewhere or a squad of bank robbers chilling from the last job in the suburbs. He'd slip a twenty in her bag. The division had a snitch fund, a box of cash the plain-clothesmen dipped into for little gratuities for their informants. Tips for tips.

One morning about four o'clock, when her shift was over and his was winding down, they had bumped into each other in a burger joint near the Tropicana. The place was full of nodding junkies and sharp-nailed whores adding up their nights. He'd usually get his food to go because his police instincts told him if the low-life saw him eating like a common person they'd lose respect. But this time when he saw Gracie he stopped and bought her a hot chicken sandwich.

He knew every plane and fold of her body, but seeing it enclosed in her shirt and jeans excited him. She had a hard-luck story, no better or worse than most. She was from a mining town up north, a bad marriage and a string of two-week jobs working for pigs or hags for peanuts. She liked the night, the music, she looked good and was witty with her body; flashing and hiding, she made the drinkers laugh. She liked their lust.

They watched her with their mouths open and glisten-ing in the lights, their eyes shining. She could prance down the runway and stop every drink in mid-air. Sometimes a mixed bunch would come in late after an office party and sit down front. Some of the women would look away, some would stare at her and nothing more, a few would grin and whoop like the men, and she'd squat in front of them and slyly open her legs, then jump up and shimmy on down toward the glowing bar.

Gracie loved dancing, loved the life, almost all of it. She remembered a cartoon she used to watch when she was young, a lady cat who walked with a grinning tomcat, his eyes shut, floating in the air behind her, levitated by her scent, steered by a single slender finger under the point of his chin. She wanted that power, and now that she was a dancer sometimes she thought she'd almost found it. Some nights she felt she could levitate the whole bunch of them, make every drinker in the place float right up out of their chairs and follow her out of the bar in a wavy chain pulled along by her merry bent finger hooked into their trouser fronts.

"Some old stoner around the place last night was talking about PCP. I never heard of that."

"Horse tranquilizer, Gracie. Bad news. Blow up your head."

"Well, he was just talking, I guess." She looked around at the greasy faces, fake fur, salty boots, the wiped-out Chinese counterman pouring vinegary coffee. Faces yellow in the light coming in from the night street.

"Keep in mind I got a little more money if you hear stuff."

"Well, I heard of peace pills come in." Little white ones that would keep you up on a plateau for a day and a night with wind in your head and then drop you down into the canyon with steel bands around your brain. Then another peace pill and unity with everything. The bikers made them in farmhouse bathrooms, jugs linked with plastic hose and flames from portable burners driving the chemicals down the tubes. Wholesale nine dollars a hundred, retail a dollar a pill.

"I just heard they were bringing it in sometime later this week, early next week. One of the girls was talking about it in the dressing room."

"Which girl?"

Her little mouth turned down. "I forget."

Judd felt a surge of warm feeling. She was loyal. She was in his power. He could take her down to the beach the way the other cops did and threaten what he wanted out of her, but she was a real human being. What's more, she liked him—he could see it—and she was afraid of him but not too much. It was like his daughters a little.

There was a rumble from the front of the restaurant. The Chinese counterman was arguing with a customer, a high whine from one and a roar from the other, a huge man complaining about the oil used to fry his pastry, animal fat in it, he was sure. He was pointing to the counterman's leather belt and yelling about murder. "What died so you could hold up your fucking pants?"

"Crazy! You're crazy!" The counterman was just about crazy himself, going to university in the daytime, studying for his anthropology finals in the evening, then holding up the derelict shift in a grease joint beside a titty bar. He was so far out of patience that he was reaching under the counter for something when Judd walked into the argument.

"Let's just move it along, please," he said. The giant looked him up and down. Judd's wristwatch strap was metal and his jacket was wool, stripped roughly from sheep but still acceptable. The giant smiled at Judd and threw five dollars on the counter.

"Crazy fool," said the counterman under his breath.

Judd put a hand on the giant's shoulder and began to think how he might handle him if he turned, a shoe to the side of the knee, an elbow to the belly, then catch him by the waist and run him forward, opening the door with the top of the giant's head, out onto the street and down. Quickly, because the counterman had hot grease close by in the fryer. But the big bearded man moved off like a boat setting out from the dock, weighty, graceful, grand.

"Jeez," said Gracie when the sergeant came back, "you just talked to them and it all cleared up like that, you know?"

She cocked her head, as though she was trying to get a better sense of him by seeing him slightly sideways.

"Those peace pills," he said. "You got anything more you can tell me about them?"

"Just end of this week, next week," she said. "I heard maybe from the States, New York state somewhere."

He paid the silent counterman and slipped two twenties into her coat pocket as they left. She touched the money in her pocket and smiled at him. "Hey," she said. "I'll buy you a drink next time. Stoli and one ice cube."

"Breakfast of champions."

Sometimes he dreamed of following up on the thing with Gracie, but the idea of waking up with her, realizing he'd broken a promise to his wife and family, turned his stomach. And anyway Gracie seemed to be a good girl, still clean somehow, sunny and drug-free, a little peep of light on the dark street.

Her goodness and his forbearance made him happy, and his light mood lasted until he got home in the morning. Then he looked at the mailbox. He couldn't avoid it; he always tried to command his gaze the other way, but the mailbox called his eyes, summoned his mind and filled it with threats and insults. The bank wanted this, the credit card company wanted that, the world was losing patience with him and a resolution was imperative. He kissed his daughters, feeling the smoothness of their faces on his lips, kissed his wife and went upstairs to bed.

The cat was weary. His leg dragged a little, so that at every step his back foot rubbed against the ground. He ran across a wide street, a motorcycle shrieking past him, the rider wobbling and yelling, into a park. He found a harbour under a big wooden platform, a pretend pirate ship with steering wheels and rigging.

Car doors slammed. Calling voices, ringing phones, thin, forced sounds from television sets. An old man watered his garden, staring narrowly at passing dogs. The sun hammered the ground.

The pain gave him direction. It was as though something had taken a needle, threaded his body with it and was using the line to pull him toward the lake. He licked his back paw. The musk from the lions was still on his fur.

A sudden sharp prodding pain. He whirled. A boy with a sharp stick, poking him. A little flash of teeth. He backed farther under the platform. The stick came closer. Freshly pulled off the tree, the bark at the end torn and wet. Going for his eyes. He growled, then wailed. The stick prodded, caught him in the leg. He wailed again and limped out from underneath the platform. The boy came after him, and he ran.

It hurt to move, but he reached cover behind a group of metal garbage cans and the boy moved away. The pattern of the houses changed. The crammed-together boxes and chain link of the outer suburbs gave way to old, wider buildings. There were bigger trees with thick trunks that could take him up and away from dogs, if he could climb. There were food smells from the doors.

He was afraid of his own hunger, of not finding another safe place to sleep, especially afraid of everything that was chasing him, the lioness, the fox and the boy with the stick. He could smell dogs' breath from a block away, foul and tangy, and he knew if one of them caught him, that would be the last thing he'd know, the loathsome dog-mouth stink. And he was afraid of the pain, which was growing, moving up and along his flank.

The moon rose in the south, drawing him toward the good plant. He'd been wandering for two days, eating bits and scraps and drinking from dirty puddles shrunk by the heat.

He caught a smell from a laneway, rancid, rich, faint at first but growing stronger as he got closer, a food smell mixed with oil and dirt. It was in a laneway by a wooden garage with a half-open door. It was a hamburger, one big ragged-moon bite out of it but smelling like a serenade, like minced-meat cat food but with more blood to it. He was crouched over the hamburger when the bucket came down.

Sudden black, smell of dirt, oil and metal, a clang, a lurch upward, crazily rocking light, a wire grid clapped over the top of the steel container that had come down on the cat. He jumped for the wire mesh, got a claw through it, sank it into skin. There was a yowl from the pet shop man, the bucket spun sideways, the mesh slid away and the cat fell and jumped at the same time, the pet shop man sucking his torn finger and swearing. The cat crouched when he hit the ground and then spun left toward a welcoming smell coming from the shadows. He ran for cover, to the smell, under a gap in a wooden plank fence, to a concrete porch. The odour was coming from inside the house. It smelled like him, but magnified, the acid smell of a hundred cats on the city wind.

He moved carefully up onto the porch. Buckets of earth with dead plants, sweet hollow sounds from an old wind chime that hung from the porch roof. He sat, opened his mouth, yowled a huge hurt sound, all the pain and fear of the day's journey coming out of his core, yowled for relief. The door opened and he went inside.

Nine

LONG BEFORE HE met his wife, long before he owned his own business, François Will was conscious of his appearance and his manner. He often skipped lunch to save money for clothes so that when he worked on the trading floor entering numbers into the electronic display, his shirtsleeves would be clean and white and there would be some suggestion placed in the minds of the men who held his career in their hands that he might be half a grade finer than the others his age.

He was the descendant of a veteran of Wolfe's army who'd married a habitant's daughter and submerged himself in the Quebec tide. After six generations, all that was left of him was his surname and a vague family joke, but something about the dead man called out to François. He practised his English, talking back to the radio and reading English magazines about matters he knew already, hockey, singers and gangsters, putting the familiar images together with the clumsy, chunky English words.

He improved his short, weak body by doing exercises set out in a pamphlet published by the Canadian Forces. He jogged, jumped and pressed until his shoulders bulked out and his waist pinched in. He applied himself to his schoolwork, memorizing mathematical proofs and actuarial formulae. He scrambled hand over hand up from the dairy farm on the south bank of the St. Lawrence, stepping on the heads and fingers of his competitors, seizing scholarships and bursaries, because he saw himself as his British ancestor, but disciplined and wealthy.

When François got a job as a clerk at the national exchange, he listened for scraps and hints on the floor, pushed together a tiny clutch of savings and doubled it on a quick long shot on a gold mine. But then he pissed his profits away on shares in a weapons manufacturer that was supposed to win a government contract and lost it. He watched the numbers spin and stall and shoot straight down the drain. At home in his little apartment, he pounded his head with the heels of his hands, trying to beat good sense into himself.

One morning he stared at his image in the mirror, wondering how he could add strength and solidity to his image. He noticed that his left sideburn was almost a half an inch longer than the right one. He had no idea how long they had been that way. It looked lazy, even rebellious. He was angry. He rubbed shaving cream into the left sideburn and scraped down hard with the safety razor. He wiped off the cream and looked again. Now the right sideburn was longer. He shouted with rage. He rubbed the cream on both sides, right up to the level of his eyebrows, turning his head back and forth, tracing lines with the side of the razor in the cream, finally, gritting his teeth, cutting down sharply through the hair above the level of his cheekbones.

Still crooked. Now he looked ludicrous, infantile. He couldn't go to work like this, like a comedy stooge with a crooked bowl of hair. Shit! Shit! In a rage he raised the metal again and cut a swath through the hair on his right temple, then hacked on the other side. And then he saw a curl of red reaching out from the edge of his hairline.

He wiped it with a washcloth, but it wasn't blood. It

was a scarlet stain on his scalp, shaped like a crooked thumb. It disappeared into the hair below the curve of his skull. He moved away from the mirror, out of the bathroom, walked around his little apartment, shocked. He'd been carrying a stain on his head, above his brain, for twenty-three years. Or had he? He must have been bald when he was a baby. He tried to remember his baby pictures. He thought they showed him unmarked. Did these things grow later, creep onto somebody's head under cover of the hair?

He walked back into the bathroom and stared again at the stain. Maybe it ended just beyond the new edge of his hairline. Maybe it swooped and stretched all over his head like a tonsure. His hair looked idiotic now anyway, with white wings of skin on the sides of his head. He swallowed once, reached for the shaving cream and began to rub a mound of lather into the hair at the top of his skull.

It was more difficult than he'd expected. The hair came away in clots, exposing skin that hadn't seen light for two decades. The red stain curved toward the back of his head and then tapered off; its shape, when revealed entirely, was a crescent with its leading edge smooth and its trailing edge scalloped. It was strange and almost sinister. The hair and shaving cream filled the sink.

He stared at himself. He had chosen to be bald. His eyes suddenly took on a special intensity, and the scarlet crescent on his head was aristocratic and intimidating. He was an entirely new man, dangerous, full of possibility.

At work that morning the other clerks stared but said nothing. He no longer seemed one of them. There was something new not only about his scalp but also in the way he walked and the light that beamed from his eyes. The traders, who had never noticed him before, wondered who the new, tough, smart-looking clerk was.

Outside at lunchtime the moist sun-heated air clung to his scalp, and he felt a prickling, a warning. He bought a beret, the only possible covering, it seemed, for an entirely and voluntarily naked scalp. It added a note of cultivation to his new presence. He was unforgettable. He walked the streets of the city, looking for opportunity.

It took months before the right thing came along. He didn't want to be an investor, a little-fish shareholder in some business run by someone else. He wanted his own enterprise. He wanted to grab something away from a rival, seize it and hold it and wave it over his head like a newly taken scalp.

One winter evening at sunset, long after the exchange was closed, the cold wind scouring the city with grains of ice, François was walking along the tracks near the dock-yard, thinking about the dentists and accountants who bought boxcars and leased them back to the railway. In the morning it had looked like a smart opportunity, but now it seemed a plodding, stupid way to make money, no possible big killing, just an annuity. He was always having bright thoughts and then shooting them down. Nothing seemed to fit his dream.

He heard a roaring squeal from the building before him. It was a great concrete block with loading docks at the side. No signs, no windows, a blanked-out world. A truck was parked at the bottom of a ramp and two men were banging clubs on its slatted metal sides, sending its cargo of hogs up the frozen ramp and into the slaughterhouse.

François saw a raised corridor that connected the slaughterhouse with the building next to it, and walked on through the piercing wind till he came to the front. It was a glassed-in, friendly sight, a big butcher shop with cheerful servers in white aprons and boxy white hats. The sign read, "Frost: Fine Meats and Sausages."

And there they were, wrapped in little plastic-foam cartons. Loins of pork, spareribs and trotters, sitting on absorbent pads, and clusters of sausages, minced meat and spices wrapped in intestine, a constellation of sausages, Polish, mild and spicy Italian, Czech, Slovak, Chinese, flavoured with oregano, star anise, chili, sea salt, bursting with fat, and beside them shelves of mild and hot mustard from France, hot sauce from the West Indies, soy seasoning from Taiwan and racks of shining forks, spatulas and tongs.

A fat man in a heavy parka was standing in front of the sausage counter. Melting slush was sliding off his boots onto the dark green linoleum floor. His big face was sandwiched between a thick Russian fur hat and an odd thick pink scarf that matched the colour of his lips. His nose was pressed against the glass on the front of the display case. His gloved right hand was directing the girl behind the counter to the sausages he wanted.

"That one, the chori——" Something choked him, and he waved his hand impatiently. "The next tray. The orange, with the flecks . . . yes. The second one from the front, the fourth, the fifth—the two at the back. And now some of the bratwurst, from the lighter batch, at the side." A little drop of saliva fell from his mouth and landed on his scarf. There were two other customers, one casual but the other, a thin woman in a flimsy coat, equally intense, scrutinizing a square pile of smoked hamhocks.

François felt the powerful emanation of their appetites. He was almost shocked by the intensity. You could make something big of this. You could construct a vertical organization, from farmyard to feeding pen to abattoir, packing, sales, advertising, transport: an empire with outlying principalities for the leather, the lard, the prime meats, the bones, innards and offal but founded on this focused taste for spiced fatty salted meat forced into tubes and grilled over an open fire or fried in its own grease.

A corollary, a secondary inspiration burst inside François' head: kindness. The animals would die, indeed, but in comfort and ease. The advertising cameras would show them going calmly to a set of kindly knives. There would be music, loving care and respect as the pigs, horses, goats, sheep and cattle came to their final release. Friendly Franks.

It took him a year to put together a commanding position in the Frost Company. The Frost brothers were absentees, travelling the world on their dividends, old twin bachelors who monitored their empire from a resort in the Florida Keys and a beach in Hawaii, between slithery sessions with bulky boys on the sand. Their sister stayed behind in the city and did the books. He picked up a block of stock from the estate of the company's first lawyer and then went to work on the rest.

François Will in his best suit sympathized and soothed under the great flabby leaves of the rubber plants in the sister's greenhouse, listened to her complaints as she weeded and fertilized, repotted and grafted. Her brothers, he suggested, had a duty to choose between their pursuits abroad and their true roles at home. It was her place as a sister to tell them so, or have him do it for her.

"My father built this company from nothing," she said, thrusting her trowel into the spongy earth. "He lived for this company, and in the end he worked himself to death. Right on the floor with a bone saw in his hand. His heart." Twenty years of grievance throbbed in her voice.

The brothers returned for the company's brief annual general meeting with tans and boxes of chocolate-covered macadamia nuts under their arms. François Will announced that their sister had tendered him her proxy and that this position along with his accumulated holdings gave him the power to reorganize the board. The brothers were quickly dispatched, thanked for their services and shown out, reduced to non-voting shareholders, still carrying their chocolates, too surprised to complain.

François Will set out to redesign his slaughterhouse. He made it pig friendly, horse happy, a place in which he thought his four-legged creatures, given a choice, would choose to die. The air was warm and full of calming music. The stunmen stood around a sharp bend from the loading dock ramp and placed their boltguns gently on the pigs' brows as they turned the corner one by one. The bodies fell onto padded belts and were borne away to the blades.

By the time the major meat packers woke up he'd grabbed ten per cent of the dressed steak, loin and side market, thirteen per cent of the ribs and twenty-one per cent of the fancy sausages and was getting ready to go national.

Ten

DONALDA PUT THE black cat down on the kitchen floor and watched him begin to take stock of the place. There were three other cats in the room.

She wondered how they radiated information to each other, signals about their strength and mood and expectations. It might be a little like magnetism, received through the whiskers.

There was a thump as a heavy animal jumped off the arm of the red chair in the living room. The big orange cat came into the kitchen.

The black cat froze. His green eyes widened. The big orange had white stripes that ran the length of his body and came to a concentrated point between his eyes. He looked as though he was thrusting himself forward like a spear. The big orange sniffed at the black cat for a moment or two.

She'd seen the orange attack new cats. She was indifferent—the animals would live or die no matter what she did—but fighting was noisy. She'd considered throwing the orange out the door and back onto the street he'd come from, but she still remembered and loved the way he'd shouldered his way into her life, Mars, the god of war.

The orange sniffed the black cat's flank. The black knew he was being placed in some local arrangement of power and status with the orange at the top, and that the pain and weakness in his leg put him farther down the scale than he liked. He flattened his ears against the top of his head and murmured. The orange looked him squarely in the face and then turned and walked to the food bowl. The black could eat when he was finished.

Donalda picked up the new cat and put him in her lap while she looked at the sky. He was content to sit there. He was obviously a house cat, not wild, perhaps badly missed in the place he'd left. He was welcome to stay here.

Judd never liked his aunt's cats; they'd never liked him. He thought cats were annoying, pompous, stupid, whether they lived with his aunt or not. His wife used to keep an old tom with a yellow eye that shredded the furniture and spat at him. His daughters dressed it in shirts and hats; it complained without scratching, as though it knew if it touched the girls with a claw he'd drown it in the tub. When it disappeared, his daughters wept for days. On the street he saw stray cats scrounging in the trash, pulling old chicken bones out of cardboard boxes. Their eyes glowed in his headlights as he drove by.

He thought about tracking down Lukey, taking that snake of his and throwing it in through his aunt's front door. It would slide from room to room, fastening the cats in their tracks with its shining gaze, wrapping itself around them in a smooth hug, opening its mouth, dislocating its lower jaw, squeezing them so hard their bones melted and then sliding them into its tubular throat. It would suck down the cats one by one, then shed its skin, emerging bigger and meaner, and then finally it would slither on down to Donalda Massie, smothering her squawks and flutters, catch her by the head and start inching her down into its long shaft. When he came back there would be only her slack shod feet sticking out of its mouth, wide as a wastebasket, and the snake's wise gaze on him.

He could see himself living in that house with his girls. They'd play in the attic the way he had, even play soldiers in the same old uniform and wear the same medals. It was a good neighbourhood. As he walked them to school in the morning, they'd pass polite children and respectful, warmly nodding parents on their way to responsible jobs. It would do for a year or two; he'd clean it up, repair it, paint it— then sell it for enough money that perhaps he could afford their ultimate dream house, in the country beside a smoothly flowing stream and stands of cedar, with a big fireplace in a high rough-timbered living room, far away from the city. The girls would go to a private school with spacious grounds not so far away and come home at night to their wooden house overlooking a field of wildflowers. They would walk in the pine woods, down old settlers' tracks half hidden with new growth, looking at the over-grown squares of old stones where there had been cabins.

His aunt sat on a pile of her parents' money in her par-ents' house, and when he visited he could see the money disappearing into a flock of sharp-voiced, whining pests. When he brought his girls to call, she ignored them, and they hated the dirty-litter smell of the house and the old furniture with the aroma of dead people's sweat. When the bills had started to pile up on his kitchen table, he had started a serious campaign to win her over. One winter afternoon about three months before the black cat arrived, he brought her a gift, an electric footbath; she filled it with water and switched it on, then sat with it in the living room under the great plaster circle. Her feet were yellow, seamed and thick with calluses, although she never seemed to walk anywhere.

"I was thinking," he told her as she soaked her feet, "that I would send the girls to private school."

"Yes?" She was fussing with one of the animals, dangling a piece of paper, folded and tied up with string, in front of its nose. The cat batted and pounced.

"The public schools are getting very rough, very, like, slummy now, downtown. Lots of kids you don't know what kinds of families."

"William Strachan Public School," she said, looking at the cat. "I was by there just the other day. Just walking by the playground. School I went to sixty years ago, just as neat as it was then. Little children on the swings."

"It's very hard raising the children in the Division. Some of the parents—they know what I do. I've even put the arm on some of them once or twice, and the girls, they pay for that in the schoolyard, you see."

"They must be very proud to be a policeman's children."

Was she stupid, losing it, entirely soft, or was she just playing with him? He could barely hear her dry voice in the sweltering room. In the fireplace dead black logs from God knows when. Dust on the dark tables.

"When they come home from school, they seem a little rougher somehow than they were in the morning, you know? The world just gets to them."

"Sweet girls," she said. "They'll be all right."

He remembered boxing once at police college with another recruit, a Turk with a supple back who would lean just a little whenever Judd threw a punch, sway like a sapling out of the way of Judd's glove, avoiding, deflecting, until Judd's shoulders were aching and the man was still standing there in front of him, his tooth protector showing purple in a big grin. The Turk was back home now, living fat, he guessed. And here he was with his begging bowl.

A plane descended over the house, heading for the downtown airport, and when she said something, looking at him directly at last, he lost it in the sound of its engine. It was something about money. He saw the shape of the words on her old lips. Now she was smiling, clicking her damn false teeth together. He knew she was irrational, given to rages. The board had been relieved to get rid of her since she'd started to shout at her classes and fall into reverie by the blackboard; she'd spent the last three months of her career in the library, sorting and endlessly reshelving books on astronomy.

He couldn't press her. If she'd said she'd give him money, she'd take it back if he annoyed her. The cat in her lap looked at him, purring, smiling like the Turk. He jumped to his feet, grinning desperately, holding his clenched hands behind his back, leaned over and touched her on the side of the face with his lips.

"Remember what I said," she whispered, her breath on his cheek. But what he remembered suddenly was the grey steel safe he'd seen years ago when he was a kid, snooping in his aunt's bedroom. Two feet long, a foot wide, six inches high, a tough combination lock and strong enough to survive a flood or a fire. He'd picked one or two out of the ashes in his time.

Outside he found someone had run a key along the length of his car, both sides, scratches from behind the headlight to the back of the rear fender.

That night under the pink light Gracie showed the front row a new trick. She had a snake, a big constrictor; Lukey sat in the front row and grinned as it bent and swayed around her naked body. The snake liked the heat of the lights and maybe the feel of the bass and the drums and held its little blunt face up in the brightness. Judd came in halfway through the routine and saw the two of them together and felt as though someone had taken his club and given him a shot in the gut. The snake pressed against her breasts so they squeezed out under its body. It covered her between her legs. The guys in the front row didn't care. Lukey clapped to the beat. She came over to Judd later, when she saw the way he was looking at her, depressed or mad. "Got to have some show business," she said. For the first time he found himself looking through the opening of the thin robe, copping a peek. "The guys get tired of the straight stuff, you know?"

"You got anything for me?"

"Nothing new. Jesus. You was just here day before yesterday."

It was true. His routine took him to the bar maybe once a week; he was well before schedule and feeling not much in command, just ground down with all the voices in his life. His new captain, a fat woman who spoke through her nose and looked down at him along it at the same time. His aunt and his letter box. Tricky, superior, snotty. One of his daughters, dropping a plate in the kitchen, had said "Hell, shit" when it hit the floor. Eight years old, language like that. He was very strict about swearing, but you couldn't do anything about it—they picked it up. And this deal with Lukey's constrictor, a surprise. He hated the thing.

The men along the edge of the runway were shouting for more. The emcee was calling her back. The other dancers were looking mean, but Gracie was enchanting, running to the stage, shucking her robe, taking the weight of the snake as Lukey hoisted it up onto her shoulders.

Judd watched her coldly. She looked as if she was having a good time in the middle of this hard boozy shuck, but he missed her nakedness. The constrictor concealed her and slowed her up and made the dance look crude. She strode down the runway, turned and strode back, her shoulders square and the snake letting its back half fall behind her like a tail. Maybe she was screwing Lukey. Wriggling away in the back of the bar, the two of them covered with that big brown booster's coat. He finished his vodka and left.

François Will first saw Julia in the outer lobby of the stock-brokers' office; he'd left two years before to take over the meat business, but his investments remained conservative placements in banking and insurance shares. Julia was collecting a package from the receptionist.

She seemed so perfectly elegant that he lost strength in his legs and had to sit down beside a stack of magazines, the shocked blood racing in his body. He had never seen anything or anyone so beautiful. She turned and walked back into the inner office, leaving him sweating on his chair.

Obviously she had seen him gawking at her like a rube. Anyone who looked like that would be used to it, wouldn't make anything of it, although obviously she would never think of him now as anything but a stupid goof, if she ever thought of him at all.

His embarrassment began to turn to irritation. He had made mistakes in the past but had always caught and corrected them before anyone could laugh at him. Now this woman had seen him in a state of complete confusion, seen through him and dismissed him. He would not accept it. He was a man of action, the top of his head smooth as a torpedo and crested like a warplane, and he made his own way through all opposition toward any target he chose.

He went to the library and consulted the catalogue. He was embarrassed to ask for help from the librarian to find material on his particular challenge, the pursuit of a beautiful girl, but after an hour he came across a poem on the subject by a disappointed and long-dead German and a cynical little pamphlet sold by mail order thirty years ago from an office in Chicago. The poem was no help at all, but the pamphlet, "How to Make Love to a Beauty," was clear and ruthless. Be unapproachable, it said. Pretend she doesn't affect you. Tempt her with your unavailability. The novelty will bring her to you. If he could place himself in her path somehow and then clearly but tastefully indicate she didn't attract him, she would have no choice but to launch herself into his arms. The most beautiful women, the pamphlet said, attached themselves to cold, unsuitable men. He could manage that. And in any case he was on his way to being rich.

He asked around about her. She was single. Men in the company had marched on her in ranks and had been rebuffed. He took his broker out to lunch and brought the subject around to quail, as the broker called women, and then to Julia. The broker said that she was an extremely expensive call girl. He saw her in the airport one day, being helped into a small private jet with Saudi Arabian markings.

"You're sure it was her?"

"Oh, yeah. Legs right up to her shoulders. What a quail." François, whose business killed and packaged stuffed quails for the gourmet market, imagined Julia running and peeping in a suburban barnyard, then shrink-wrapped and still on a white foam tray. He hated his broker.

He began to visit his money more often, and sometimes contrived to pass the big human resources pen on the seventh floor. He'd walk by and watch her at a keyboard or, once, watering a shabby little plant by the window. His heart jumped. The broker, it developed, was even more full of it than usual. She was a solitary girl, the office gossips conceded, nothing more, an ice princess, immune to men. Or maybe looking for a man with money.

He had money. But the money came from making sausages. He despaired. She was like white-hot platinum, precious, classy and beyond him. She would laugh at him, tell her friends about the little butcher who'd presumed to adore her. The thought of her threw him back into his old life with his diffidence, his hesitations and doubts, before he found the stain on his scalp and his sense of direction. He had terrifying fantasies. She would take him as a friend and tell him over lunch of her heartbreaking affairs with others. She would make love to him once and never answer his calls again. She'd become a lesbian and sail away to Greece in a great yacht with a squat lady novelist while he yearned for her at home.

Once a year around the time of Julia's birthday, the accountant who administered the proceeds of her father's insurance policy sent a little extra cheque, a payment from the new dentist downstairs toward the purchase of the chair, the sinks and the glass-fronted cabinets. Lillian McCoy spent this little wad with abandon, lifting the two of them out of their small flat and off for a whirling week in Florida at an amusement park or Cuba at a cheap beach.

In time the trips dwindled to an expensive birthday lunch, but there was still an annual sense of celebration and freedom. For Julia's twenty-fourth birthday, Lillian chose the Café Cologne on the fringes of the financial district. The Cologne served thick raw steaks to brokers and vice-presidents, blood sitting in the seams and grooves of their mashed potatoes, and slim fillets of whitefish and garden salads to their wives. Newspaper columnists ate at the Cologne. Visiting movie stars sat on the banquettes at the back of the room.

In the kitchen there was the steamy hiss, bubble and spatter of cooking meat, the quick rapping of knives on wood and the bang of dishes pulled from hot water. The chef swabbed plates with his thumb; the saucier nicked his forefinger and bled into the Wellington; the salad master dropped romaine on the floor, picked it up, waved it in the air and smacked it down on the plates. At night the mice came to pick over the scraps of food on the floor, leaving their droppings under the counters.

The restaurant floor had fresh-cut flowers in glass bowls, crisp folded linen, soft alcoves in a dark purple that absorbed and hid the stains from food and wine and seemed as clean as new. At the entrance there were six wide, curving stairs. When Julia walked in looking for her mother, she felt like a nineteenth-century debutante entering a grand ballroom with swains, masked coquettes, glaring duennas and straight-backed dandies swirling toward her to fill up her card. The waiters twittered, cooed and swooped.

"It is time to get married," said her mother, digging into her appetizer, warm foie gras on a bed of baby greens. "High time."

"There's nobody on the horizon at all," said Julia. She'd had a few affairs, found the whole business unsatisfying and intrusive. She'd read manuals on sexuality and had tried to follow the instructions, but in bed every fellow seemed to lose focus and begin to thrash and stammer. There were unexpected greasy clefts and tufts of hair on the male body, and the erect penis seemed foreign, like an alien being that emerged suddenly from the torso and took over the whole operation. It filled her physical cavity, which felt pleasant, but nothing about the experience touched the small vacant space inside her.

"A woman can open herself to possibilities," said her

mother. Julia looked at the prawn on her plate, the tiny dead eyes and whiskery antennae. "You are, let's be honest, a very pretty girl, but these things pass, believe me. You'll be looking at yourself in the mirror and having regrets, you know, sooner than you'd think."

"I don't really feel it's very much of a priority," said Julia.

"It's just a question of attitude," said her mother, "and of course it is so much easier to find a superior person if you are still young and fresh." She bit into her white asparagus. She'd started to put on weight after Julia left home. She'd stand at the open refrigerator door and claw handfuls of pie out of a tin plate. She felt it was a sacrifice. She'd removed herself from the field of sex and left it clear for her daughter, although it seemed her daughter didn't appreciate it. The girl was cold sometimes. "I would never have met your father," she said, "if I had not made up my mind that I was tired of being alone. He would just have been the man who filled my teeth if I had kept on being selfish, but since I was thinking of family and children, well . . ."

The waiter, who was serving the entrees, moved sideways to look down Julia's blouse and poured hot béchamel sauce on his left hand.

"Now you see," said Julia's mother after the waiter left, "that used to happen to me all the time. It's only natural. Anyway, you need to put yourself in a receptive frame of mind. Nobody likes to be alone."

François Will came into the restaurant just then. He was making his rounds, trying to persuade the city's chefs to create new dishes with his sausages, using kiwi fruit or onion marmalade or caramelized leeks or strawberries.

When he saw Julia across the restaurant floor he blushed. It was a full, lustrous, beety flush that rose from his collar line and swept up past his cheeks through his forehead to the top of his head, a scarlet display like a baboon's ass, a flush that surrounded and overwhelmed the crimson stain on his scalp. He hustled across the room, bumped into a serving station, knocking three forks to the floor, and disappeared through the flapping door into the kitchen. Julia's mother watched the hook go in.

"I know that fellow," said Lillian. "That's the sausage man. He's got his face on the carts you see beside the ballpark. Does he know you?"

"We've seen each other," said Julia, remembering him from the broker's office. He was a big man, not bald but with a shaved head that suggested vanity. Not her type—but what was her type? Men couldn't reach her and women didn't like her.

"*Gnädige Frau, Fräulein*," said the head waiter, in a half crouch of deep respect, offering more wine.

"The man who came through here just now, the sausage man, is he something to do with the restaurant?" asked Lillian.

"A supplier, *signora*," said the head waiter.

"I believe I must know him from our church," Lillian lied, touching her lips with her napkin. "You might ask him to stop by our table if he has a moment. Just to say hello."

A week after the birthday lunch, Julia and François went out to a bowling alley. His company sponsored a team in a workers' league, and François often threw the ceremonial first ball. He was entirely constricted, stopped up with fear, his smooth battering-ram head pulled down toward his shoulders. He felt completely absurd. The printed advice about how to make love to a beautiful woman sneered in his head.

It was night and the bowling alley had set out balls and pins that glowed in ultraviolet light. He could see her teeth and the flash of her eye. She was an excellent bowler, propelling her balls perfectly down the long wooden alley. Her head pitched forward and her leg swung back in harmony. His throws flew into the gutter and rushed down the half tube, banging and swooping and thudding into the cushion. His feet felt grimy in the rented shoes.

Afterwards they walked back to her apartment, and he talked about sausages. She was a good listener, paying attention, asking smart questions. He knew the market was growing and open for exploitation. People were busier, eating away from home more, they wanted diversion, different flavours, more fat and fun, but they were worried about cruelty and death. His advertising campaign reassured them. He wanted to be very rich.

Outside the front door of her building, he stopped and turned. "Do I sound stupid?"

She looked at him. "No."

"Greedy?"

"No, not at all."

His nose was slightly pushed in, and his eyes were generously spaced, nobly set. He wasn't ugly. She was beginning to like the crested stain on his head.

"Look, I am . . . I'm going to be somebody," he said.

"Oh, you are somebody." Was she needling him? "Your face is all over the city."

"On packages."

"Well, what's wrong with that?"

In fact, she did like him. He was flustered around her, but she could tell he wasn't easily distracted in the rest of his life. She could see him driving through whole crowds of people, bashing through walls and kicking in doors to get what he wanted. And she thought he had the strength to take care of something he loved. He wasn't handsome in a magazine way, he wouldn't always be looking at himself in a mirror, but he was all right, presentable.

They agreed to meet again. When she turned and went into the apartment lobby, she found she had the image of his face set well in her mind, the shifting glow of lights on his bare scalp, his slightly indented nose and thin lips.

Jones was yowling, complaining about his late dinner. She opened a can of cat food and stared at the sticky disc of meat inside: eyes, no doubt, ears, elbows, bones, sinew. She felt clued in. The conversation with François about meat-packing had made her a kind of semi-expert. Jones bunted her calf, rubbed against her. She spooned out some of the meat and he leapt up onto the counter, unwilling to wait for her to put it on the floor. He tore into the meal as though he hadn't eaten for days, crouching over the bowl, protecting it with his chin.

She remembered François blushing in the restaurant. She recalled that colour perfectly, the wonderful advance of crimson up his cheeks and forehead and over the smooth marked crown of his head. That had interested her more than the rooster strutting about his business plans. Men liked to stamp and boast around her but didn't usually show that kind of helplessness. He could be embarrassed. He had some kind of inside. She was getting tired of constantly fending people off, deflecting her mother and squirming past the men in the office.

Julia visited François' meat-packing plant to watch him work. She was thrilled. He moved through the facility with confidence, showing complete understanding of every factor and facet. He was consulted respectfully by his employees, who obviously had a great opinion of his capacities, even a certain amount of affection for him. He was considerate of her feelings, suggesting that she bypass the killing operation at the head of the production line, but she refused.

The place had a pungent smell of blood, sweat and shit. They were doing hogs. There was a frenzy of shout, squeal, the bang of trotters on steel, but just before the hogs turned the corner to the slaughtering zone they felt a sudden silence, then the sound of music and a rush of sweet cool air. Most became very still. One by one the belt carried them into the zone. Then each heard the beginning of a crackling bang from a power gun wielded by a small strong man straddling the channel above the belt, a dart and a thump and nothing. Another man in a plastic suit drove spikes into their heads. The bodies twitched as they swayed up the line for the gutting crew with the masks, swords and sucking tubes. The intestines flowed into a slurp trough and down into barrels for fodder and tripe. The carcasses moved onward, heads down, throats gushing, to the cutters, grinders and renderers. A hog who entered the chute at nine and died five minutes later would be packaged and bound in various directions by eleven.

François shouted something to her, but she pressed her hand over his mouth, staring at the wonderfully logical, considerate and musical order of the killing. There was a beautiful flow of mass, fluid, muscle and steel. Very little was wasted: the bone went to button makers, the hide to the tanneries, the trotters to the glue makers. As they moved into the quieter spaces of the packing and sausage-stuffing works, she found herself listening to François with respectful attention. He was a man who had organized a complete world, made it safe, kept it clear and comprehensible and lived on its profits as cleanly and honourably as her ancestors had lived on the rabbits and potatoes of western Ireland.

In his office they drank brandy and ate little cut-up pieces of sausage on toothpicks. Two hours before, the meat had gone from the killing floor to the mixing bowls and then into the ovens. It was possible she had seen the death of the animal she was now putting into her mouth. She felt complete, the consumer, the destination that gave the entire chain meaning.

Eleven

IVAN TEUTI STUDIED marketing after high school. He liked the idea of hidden methods of persuasion, of catching and binding people with invisible ropes, using their own needs to control them.

The college was a collection of warehouses with underground tunnels to protect the students from the winter winds. The tunnels smelled of young bodies and steel and the walls were grainy painted concrete. Ivan walked between classes looking at the other students with his white-blue eyes and trying to decide how he might move some of them to his advantage.

One night when he came home, his father's chair was empty and his mother was rocking back and forth in prayer, coughing and communing. Between her God and her illness she heard nothing, and in her sadness she said very little. She never told Ivan what had happened, but he gathered after a couple of days that his father wasn't coming home; when he walked past the drugstore there was the old man still, with his hairy arms encased in shining white, pouring tablets into brown bottles. Mrs. Godwin was enthroned behind the cash register on a high stool cushioned with an embroidered pillow. Ivan didn't go in.

His mother went completely mute. Nothing in the new language, nothing in the old. She'd point and gesture but she would not speak. For the first time Ivan wished he had a friend, someone who could give him a place to sleep away from home, but since he didn't know how to go about making a friend, he continued to come back to the apartment, spending his nights in his father's chair watching his father's television set and listening to his mother's bubbling cough in the kitchen.

One evening after school he stopped at the old Swede's store to look at the magazines. The Swede was a gnome, right out of the Grimms' fairy tales Ivan had read years ago. He had thick tufts of hair growing out of his ears and nose and black brows that matched his eyes. He sat at his counter every day from eight in the morning to eleven at night. His prices were high and his products were shabby: the can openers splayed and broke on the first twist, the milk was old, the soda bottles covered in thick dust. He grew so used to complaints that every sale became the preliminary round of an argument. He'd slap his dried-out candy down on the counter and glare at the customer, putting him on notice that the transaction was complete and final.

The Swede knew he was being robbed. Every day he could feel the stock leaking out of the place, tucked inside school bags and stuffed into pockets. He'd prowl up and down his aisles of boxes and bags, shifting the older stuff to the front of the shelves, seeing holes where packets of candy, pasta and margarine had vaporized and blown right past his money drawer. People were thieves, and even if he kept his bags of milk past their due dates and stocked cans with dents turned to the back, it was impossible to get even.

Every child and adolescent in the neighbourhood had been barred from the Swede's at one time or another. He'd take them by the collar and hold their faces close to his, staring with his snapping black eyes. "Robber! Killer!"

They'd come back in a week or so when he'd lost track of their faces and steal a water pistol or a tube of toothpaste in the name of justice.

Ivan felt the old man's stare as soon as he walked in. He hadn't been inside the place for months, and it seemed during the interval that the Swede had passed over into some unknown zone of craziness. He leaned out from his counter as Ivan walked down the aisle, watching for a sideways movement as Ivan slipped something into his coat.

Ivan saw a new neatness on the old Swede's shelves. The boxes of cereal were lined up exactly, and the plastic envelopes of frozen vegetables were laid out precisely on the steel racks in the freezer. The Swede had scraped away years of frost from inside the machine so he could look in and take stock instantly.

Ivan was irritated by the old man's birdy peering. He shoved an old bag of potatoes from a bottom shelf with his foot and called out, "Mr. Olaffson!"

"What? What? The Swede was on his feet, rushing down the aisle as though the place were on fire.

"This place is a mess. You want to be careful—people could trip on something like that and kill themselves."

The old man started talking loudly about murderers and cheats who would fall down on his property and claim on his insurance. Ivan knelt down and shoved the bag back into line. The old man picked up speed: the world was shit, this country was shit, full of shitters. Ivan walked back to the front of the store, the old Swede following him. Ivan turned around and spread his arms wide, showing the old man all the pockets he had, all the places he could have stashed a bag of peanuts or a pack of cigarettes, and then, smiling, he turned again and walked out the door, the Swede's cracked voice rising behind him.

He almost skipped down the sidewalk. The Swede had started a fight, taken offence when none was meant, made accusations that were undeserved and at the same time shown Ivan how nutty and vulnerable he was. He had invited punishment and shown Ivan exactly how to deliver it.

He let a week or two go by and then he went back. The old Swede glared at him. Ivan smiled, strolled to the back of the store and quickly exchanged an old, yellowed plastic package of spaghetti for a tub of ice cream. He left the pasta to freeze in the white glass-topped box and the ice cream to melt on the shelf. He took three scrub brushes and hid them behind the new milk. He swapped six cans of cheap cat food for six cans of beef stew. Then he bought some chewing gum and left.

Every other day that spring he returned, entering the store when it was busy and mixing up the old man's stock. He could see the Swede staring at him and then swivelling to put a purchase into a bag and make change, counting out the coins slowly, then poking his head out again to look down the aisle. The old man was getting skinnier, his body contracting inside his dirty dungaree jacket. The hair from his nose and ears was jutting out farther, making him look as though he'd been electrified.

Ivan borrowed a Swedish-English dictionary from the library and memorized a couple of phrases, which he whispered when the old man was distracted, hoping the words would infiltrate his mind and take root there:

"Where's your money? The milk is bad. Who is the thief?" The Swede's hands began to tremble, and the spots on them turned a deeper shade of brown.

The campaign lasted four months. Ivan was getting ready to write his final examinations at the college, his marks were high, he was gifted at manipulation, his model scripts for television commercials were witty and direct, and his private target, the Swede, was fraying and fading.

Early one morning before the Swede came downstairs from his apartment over the store, Ivan took some newspapers out of the tied-up stack left for the Swede by the overnight driver and slipped exactly half the money owing under the brown wrapping. That afternoon he drank a third of the cream in a wax container in the refrigerator and closed the carton again. He smeared a packet of nylon stockings with mustard from the shelf above. That night he telephoned the ward alderman to make an anonymous complaint about rats in the Swede's basement. The inspectors arrived, looked, shrugged, warned the old man and moved on.

What pushed the Swede over the edge finally was the swastika he found scraped on the inside of the store's front window. Ivan had to time his move precisely when the old man was distracted at the back of the store. He used his apartment key to cut the swastika into the glass just above the collection of dirty dolls and cologne placed there years ago. He left before the old man saw it, but a minute later he could hear him wailing from down the street.

The next day the old man was gone from the cash register, and the day after as well. The door was open and the customers strolled in and out, picking up what they wanted and leaving a little money or not. Then a beat cop noticed something out of whack and came in to look around. He found the old Swede dressed in a parka and crouched in the big freezer, solid and blue with a shotgun gripped in his hands. He'd apparently planned to wait for his tormentor and then spring out and shoot him. It must have taken him hours to lose consciousness, die and congeal. Ivan spent some of these hours writing his final marketing exam.

The cat was finding it more and more difficult to move around. The trip across the city had kept his hip loose, but the slow life inside the woman's house meant the sickness had a chance to take hold of his body. It had begun to reach out along his lower back and even as far as the root of his tail, and that affected his balance. Once he tried to spring from the floor to the table, felt his leg buckle as he launched himself, hit the solid wood with his shoulder and fell back. The big eyes of the other cats noted this, and he slipped farther down the social ladder.

It wasn't always clear from day to day what the social order was. There was a puffy white longhair with a hollow cry; he seemed to take command when the orange was on another floor but backed off when he returned. A one-eyed tabby was pregnant and defended her space in the cupboard with great fierceness. The rest of the structure was unstable except for the orange tom's place at the top. He was huge, with a wide nose and great meaty haunches.

The orange seemed bothered by the black and liked to

find him and face him down. There were customary
stances for this: the orange would stalk toward the black,
his ears flat against his head, and the black would crouch
and fall on his side, ready to submit or, if the challenge
grew harsher, to try to use his back claws on the orange's
belly. The orange would push the confrontation almost to
the breaking point, leaning against the black with his full
weight and hissing through his teeth. The old woman
watched these encounters calmly.

She sensed the vulnerability in the black cat. She took
him again on her lap one night and stroked him gently,
rhythmically, waking soft memories of the other woman
from his former life. He stretched and splayed his claws
and closed his eyes.

Donalda dreamed of her few nights with Barney the
botanist, in the summers when his wife was out of town
with the children. He'd come to her house carrying a bottle of wine, with another half bottle already in him. They'd
sit in her living room, she'd sip quietly, he'd charge into the
bottle like a soldier, tossing back whole glasses and wiping
his chin. There would be silences and incomplete sentences.
Having a man in her house made her uncomfortable.

"Old place, eh? Built when, 1850s? Look at the plaster
angels." Dancing cherubs in still revels above their heads.
Outlines of maidens' faces, tailed with braids, repeating
on the faded wallpaper.

"Like the wine? This is Bulgarian wine." The second-
cheapest bottle on the import shelves. The alcohol gave
her a quick headache.

There was always an awkwardness when it came time to go to the bedroom. Neither knew how to suggest it. She usually just left silently and went upstairs as if to make some adjustment to her clothes and then waited for him to come up after her. Once she heard him at the door, she could turn and hold out her arms.

This happened for three-week periods three summers running. She saw him occasionally in the school hallway in the wintertime and heard his high, bubbling laugh in neighbouring schoolrooms. Sometimes she could feel him looking at her. They spoke briefly once or twice at the front entrance after school, little exchanges about the weather or the athletic teams. Then he'd call in early July as though nothing had changed: "It's Barney Oliver. Care for a drink?"

Her body was wide and her small breasts had brown swollen-looking nipples that were sensitive to his mouth. She'd sometimes wonder if it wouldn't be better to send him off, and then he'd start sucking away at her, and her stomach would curl and she could feel herself beginning to yield. Afterwards she could never remember much about the pleasure, and she'd feel annoyed, watching him climb into his underwear, the sticky cluster of penis and balls sagging toward the oak floor.

He'd turn in the moonlight and say, "I'll give you a call."

"You'll call," she'd say into the pillow as he left. She knew she ought to feel humiliated; he was using her, obviously, as a receptacle, a spittoon, as her mother would say. But there was so little in her life besides him, her pets and her telescope and her garden and nothing more that she couldn't bear the idea of reducing it further.

Sometimes she thought of the three sides of her life together, the man, the planets and the animals. She made up a picture of herself dancing with Barney on a carpet of stars, with heavenly globes wheeling around them, comets in her hair and two cats at their feet circling and grazing their legs. They danced the foxtrot. They would become constellations. She'd quickly realize this was foolish.

One summer Barney stayed away. She expected him to show up after the end of school; she spent some time tidying and cleaning, even put entirely new sheets beside her bed so she could change it at the last minute and their bodies could lie in cleanliness and luxury. The summer turned hot. The city proclaimed a water shortage, and the lawns began to turn brown; the police scolded people who used their hoses. She was afraid to leave the house and miss his call. She ordered groceries by phone and went no farther than her front porch, listening for the ring through the open door. That fall she heard he'd moved north to the small town where his wife was born to take over some kind of family business. She thought she might hear from him if it was the kind of business that sent the owner to the city from time to time, but she never did. That fall the third of the cats came to stay, howling on the porch until she let him in, and then she realized she was becoming the kind of woman who opened her door to animals and not to people.

The last struggle between the orange and the black began in the hallway. The orange was sniffing at the black's flank again, and then began to grin and pant, the sense organ in his throat grasping for the scent of the black as though the black were a female in heat. The black backed away and the orange came after him. The black's ears went back and he crouched, his back against the wooden panelling. The orange began to growl, a warning sound, even though he was the aggressor. It didn't make sense. The orange was insane, or at least prepared to violate custom and throw the place into chaos. The black took a swipe at the orange and one of the claws on his right front paw grazed the other cat's left eye.

The black jumped over the orange and ran into the living room. Most of the other cats were under the shuttered windows, arranged in ragged rows. The orange was coming after him, and his hip was hurting, a new needling pain radiating from the centre of the weakness. He scanned the room for a way out.

It was late at night. There were oblong boxes of moonlight on the threadbare carpet. There were hiding places behind or under the furniture, but he knew the orange would never let him get away. He felt a thump at his back and leapt for the windowsill. The orange leapt just behind him, miscalculated, hit the wall and fell backward, turning.

The black was gasping for breath. His hip was burning. He heard a rattle and a splash behind him. The orange cat's head had hit the hard plastic frame of the footbath. When the black looked down, he could just make out the shape of the orange standing in the water, shaking his head. The black could smell the blood that leaked from the orange's left eye.

The black jumped down into the water, wincing as the

liquid rose up the sides of his body, grasped the orange by the neck with his teeth and pushed his head down into the footbath. The orange writhed. His muzzle broke the surface once, and he got a half mouthful of air before the black plunged him back into the rolling water again. His back bulged and twisted in the water, but his claws couldn't catch hold on the hard smooth plastic. The black pressed down. Finally the orange lost strength, gave up, went limp and died. The black was still holding his head under the water when the old woman came into the room.

The black cat climbed out of the footbath, jumped back up onto the windowsill and began to lick his fur.

"Brave boy," said the old woman. The body of the orange cat rolled in the bubbles.

Donalda didn't watch television, but the rest of the city did. The image of the cat, caught on the security cameras, strolling across the brown prairie of the zoo, accompanied and protected by the lion, struck a deep chord. He was so cute, so brave. Then the news of the reward sent a wave of energy through the city.

Captain Liz and Sergeant Judd were summoned to headquarters with the senior members of the other divisions.

The central atrium of the headquarters building was designed to concentrate light so that when you walked through the entranceway onto the white stone floor the light burst at you from the ceiling, made you feel translucent, your insides visible. There were police cars from a hundred years ago on display and pictures of police officers who had died in the line of duty, all bleached by the light.

Headquarters liked life to work like a fugue, all parts synchronized, the city advancing and receding in harmony. Headquarters stood plumply in the briefing theatre with a hundred police officers in ranks before him and laid down the law about the snitch fund. There had been questions in the papers. There would be answers or it would be somebody's ass.

"Not my ass," said the captain to herself, and Judd looked at her mouth moving. They called her Liz because she seemed like a lizard. She'd be still and cold and look at you with flat unreadable eyes, and suddenly you'd be snapped into the air and dead.

Captain Liz and Judd walked out through the shining atrium, their boots banging on the tile floor.

"It's yours," said Liz.

"Mine?"

"The snitch box. You bring it up to the line. If we're short, you fix it."

"Well, shit, how do I do that?"

"Listen, Judd," said Liz, "you are my Operations guy and this is definitely Operations. If I do it then it's Admin and we get the HQ bean-counters involved." Her thin lips pressed together at the thought.

"But where do I get the numbers?"

"Well, Sergeant," said his boss, "why don't you take twenty bucks from the snitch box and go buy some?"

Early the next morning Judd was waiting outside the bar, his big body tense behind the wheel, off his schedule, out of control, watching the bartenders, waiters and dancers come out into the night. Jesus. There had never been paper to cover the snitch box. It was filled with money that drifted in from drug busts and out of the pockets of housebreakers, and it went to informants across the city, twenty here, fifty there, informal grease to smooth the big police machine. Accounting? Sometimes there was ten thousand bucks in there. Sometimes it was down to fifty. Sometimes he took a hundred or so to cover some bill or other, but everybody did that. It was informal overtime. An accounting. How was he going to square that?

He was waiting for Gracie in his big police Plymouth. He'd pulled some of the fast-food wrappers out from under his front seat and thrown them into the street.

She was dressed in a little plaid skirt and a white blouse. She looked like a girl from private school.

He pushed the passenger door open. She got in. They were silent.

The Plymouth moved out into the smoke and grime.

She smelled the alcohol on his breath, sweet and stinging in the dark. She thought she knew him, but he was in a strange mood now. Cops were usually very direct. When they wanted a quick suck or hand job they just grabbed you and told you, and she had been through some of those scenes but she'd never given in; she had never whored for anyone. If he wanted something like that, he could lean his big body on her, even pull his gun the way she'd heard cops did sometimes, but he'd have to force her. She looked at his face, but he seemed distracted—not focused on her. Maybe he was taking her somewhere to identify someone she'd told him about, one of the Dominican dealers who had landed two kilos of coke six weeks ago. If they knew it was her, she could find herself in a ditch a day later with her neck cut right through to her backbone.

West on Lake Drive. Maybe he was taking her to the beach. Sometimes cops took people to the beach where nobody lived and whaled them for information. She never thought Judd was like that, but something had changed.

Left off Lake, north on Dennison and right again on Hepburn. Rooming houses opposite the park, whoops from underneath the black shapes of the trees and a blue-white light from the greenhouse. He was driving her home. She hadn't known he knew where she lived.

"How'd the dancing go tonight, Gracie?"

"Okay."

"You do your thing with the snake?"

His voice wasn't contemptuous or brutal. He sounded like a husband trying to make conversation with a wife who had a mildly interesting job.

"We had a few laughs."

He smiled. A cat flashed across the wide road in front of the car. He jerked the steering wheel. The car missed the cat by a few inches, and it disappeared into the blackness under a panel truck.

One boyfriend of hers, a messenger driver, used to try to hit cats on the road, gunning the car toward them or swerving into them as they reached the sidewalk. He hit maybe one a day. She couldn't tell whether the sergeant had been trying to hit the cat or avoid it.

The stoplights at this time of night were flashing red and orange to let the light traffic through easily. Their faces behind the windshields pulsed in the dark.

He turned into the parking lot of her building. She wondered if he wanted to come up. She half wanted him to, but she still wondered why he was trying to crowd into her life like this.

She picked up her purse, held it on her lap. The whole scene was completely, dangerously alien and unknown.

"Does your wife dance?" What a stupid thing to say. Would he think she was calling his wife a stripper?

"My children dance."

He parked the car. His big, meaty face turned to her.

"Your children?"

"My two girls."

He gave her a sharp, concentrated look, his huge body twisting on the seat, and she reached out to him and patted his big face. It was almost romance. But once that same boyfriend who liked to hit cats had given her a look like this and then driven away forever. She didn't know what to do with this cop. She didn't want to get physical, but she didn't want him to go away angry.

"Aw, Gracie," he said.

An hour later they were lying on her living room floor, still dressed, and she was mostly relieved, if a little let down. It seemed all he wanted was a consoling body against his, for his hands stayed at his sides and he stared at the ceiling. He was a gentleman.

But in the darkness he was already clenching his big fists, angry with himself and angry with her for her stale little living place. He was thinking of his daughters in a few years in a ratty room like this with skinny sticks of incense burning in a glass pot and half-finished drinks on the rug.

His girls roughened, smiling like hookers, pumping away at big fat slobs like him. He groaned a little. Gracie thought it was the sound of love for her breaking out of the big guy.

At the beginning of the next shift he found a note from Captain Liz in his mail slot: *Snitch box is fifteen thousand short. I need this in two weeks.*

Twelve

Ivan Teuti knew he wanted to work in television. He loved the flatness of the images and how if you came close to the machine you could see the way the people were composed of constantly shifting lines. When he graduated, he took his résumé to six television stations.

They all had impermeable surfaces, like television sets. He seemed to bounce off them without leaving an impression. At his final stop, at the local independent station, he had a short interview with a fat blond woman with a keyhole mouth and a metallic voice. He focused all his charming intense attention on her and elaborated on his improved résumé with phony cable television experience, counterfeit athletic achievements and made-up periods of volunteer service in an imaginary downtown soup kitchen. She dropped the résumé on a pile of papers and said that if anything came open that seemed to suit his talents she would certainly get in touch with him. He left smiling, saying her name three times under his breath to make sure he remembered it.

That night he woke up furious and ashamed, writhing at the memory of her offhand rejection and the condescending reception at the other places. They were even worse. He replayed every moment of every approach. The humble walk through the glass-plated revolving doors, the dismissive glance of the security guard and the outstretched hand of the receptionist as she took his envelope without looking at him—an automatic gesture, as though she was taking a transfer from a subway machine or change from a token vendor, looking away, continuing her telephone chat. It was as if there was nothing at all about him that would catch the fancy of any successful person. He felt like an ugly child peering at the back of the television set, looking for a way into that little world. The entrances were blocked and would open only for people who were more clever, more good-looking or better spoken.

It was unfair and insulting. He deserved to be where he wanted to be, and he deserved to be treated with respect. He turned on the light and looked around the shabby room. The brown wallpaper had been untouched for as long as he could remember, repeating patterns of cowboys, horses, cactus and crouching Indians, and it was starting to come away where the wall joined the ceiling so that the endlessly multiplied Western universe he'd known forever was developing a dingy yellow sky. He walked through the apartment, looking around with a new hatred. His mother's sour old-country food in the refrigerator, all hard grains and salt-bitter pickles. His father's empty television chair and the television set itself, with its excluding world inside.

Since his father had left, his mother kept busy constructing sacrifices in her bedroom out of materials from the bathroom: little sticks with tufts of cotton on either end wound in toilet paper, drenched in nail polish remover. She'd carry these totems into the bathroom and carefully place them on plastic film she'd stretched over the oval hole of the toilet seat. She was aiming at two targets: Jesus and her husband. Both had left and she wanted them back. Exactly at midnight she'd touch a lighted match to her construction. The flames would balloon in a flash of fierce light and burn the plastic film, and the ball of fire would fall into the toilet and congeal into black strips and coils that she studied for messages. The apartment smelled like a campsite.

He'd yelled and threatened and tried hiding the stuff she used for the sacrifices. Nothing stopped her. He shoved open the unlocked bathroom door and there she was, dressed in her green printed robe, the rolls of fat accordioning down from her waist and her flat empty breasts pressed against the porcelain toilet, peering into the bowl. She looked at him, put her finger to her lips and smiled.

So he was twenty years old, his mother was insane, he lived in a shithole and he couldn't force his way out. The burning stink wriggled into his nose and bloomed inside his head. He shouted something. His mother shushed him again, cocking her smiling face to the toilet bowl to listen for Jesus and the druggist.

He had no real idea how to break the barrier between where he was and where he ought to be. He floated free, walked the streets outside the television stations, looking at the people who entered and left, trying to memorize their expressions and stances. One evening he waited outside the station where he'd had the interview with the fat lady, trying to figure out how to push his way in. Then he saw her coming out of the building in the dusk, a sudden sweat breaking out on her forehead at the heat of the evening. She wore stockings with seams. He followed her.

They got on a streetcar that took them rolling west past

small shops that sold incense, charms, fast food and used furniture. The car was crowded, and he found himself standing in the aisle next to the fat woman. He looked at her plump nape and sent a mental beam toward her, Jeannette, assistant personnel manager, television division. But Jeannette merely swatted her neck and rode on, chewing something, staring blankly at the street. He was so close that his flank was pressed against the length of her leg and backside, and still she was completely unaware of him. He felt a strange calm rage.

There was a tangle of rails at an junction where six streets came together; she reached up for the signal cord, the razor burn pink in the flesh of her armpits. She sighed and edged through the crowd to the door and jounced down onto the step of the streetcar. Ivan followed. She stopped on the corner, looking at the little stores in front of her as if she was making a selection for the night: the laundromat, the fast-food joint, the antique store, the bar.

She blew a strand of hair off her face and went into the bar.

He followed after a moment. She was just settling onto a stool opposite the rows of liquor bottles. She was big but not huge, not repulsive, just exaggerated, the humps of her breasts visible through the armholes of her sleeveless purple dress. She carried a big wicker bag with a matching wicker wallet inside. There was a big-screen television set playing tapes of old football games and a skeletal bald man wiping the bar. Clashing steel guitars and bass coming out of speakers in the ceiling. She ordered a rye and ginger ale.

He sat three stools away. They were the only customers.

He could see her image in the mirror, in a gap between the tequila and the fruit liqueurs. He sent her another flashing mental message, thunderbolts of thought, calling her attention. Her eyes drifted over to him, paused and moved away.

She didn't recognize him. In the five minutes he had spent in her office he had made no impression at all. She had taken his careful résumé and tossed it onto a stack of useless paper, where it would sit until a hurricane blew it away or a nuclear explosion set it on fire. The rage came up in him again, as he was faced once more with this impenetrable shell, the wall of not noticing that kept him from the real world. He wanted to throw her fat ass off the bar stool onto the floor.

He ordered a rye and ginger, and she looked up again. She watched the skinny man pour it and deliver it. Her mouth trembled. She wanted both drinks for herself. He raised his glass in a little toast, sipped his drink and made a slight face at the bittersweet sting. Her eyes clouded for a second, as though some memory was troubling her.

"Chin-chin," she said flatly, and the flesh below her jaw moved a little.

"Cheers," said Ivan Teuti.

"Still hot out there?" asked the bartender, recalling his duty. He had eight strands of black hair wound and plastered over his scalp, and his shirt glowed blue in the artificial light.

"Hot as a bastard," she said, and smiled.

"Hot as a two-dollar pistol," said Ivan, remembering the phrase from a detective story he'd read years ago. That was his role, of course: young but tough, hard-boiled, seen the world, been hurt, not much time for dames. Broads. That would pull her in; she'd have spent hundreds of brain-dead hours watching old movies in her living room and yearning for some wounded stud.

"Some summer," she said. Her behind made a lush horseshoe around the plastic stool.

He sucked on her breasts an hour later in her musty bed above the antique store next door. First the left, then the right. They were firmer than he'd expected, and mounded upward, not falling to either side of her rib cage, but her thighs swelled out in bags. His hand was busy between them. Her heat and scent came up to his nose. "Aw, jeez," she said, arching her back and reaching down.

He'd been a little worried about this, on the walk up the narrow stairs to her flat. Pictures of naked women didn't do much for him, and once when he'd tried making out with a girl from class his dick had failed him. He kept a photograph in his bedroom, a portrait of a tall dark woman in expensive clothes, the line of her breast hidden under an expensive shawl, only the shape of her thigh tight against the white cloth. She always got him going. She was pure, rich and cold. With the picture in his left hand, the magazine folded over, he could bring himself up to a good-time level and stay there for half an hour. Jeannette's hams in her purple dress ground in front of his eyes, and he couldn't feel a thing down there; he had no tightening in his stomach and no inner press against his pants, but as things turned out it was all right. Somehow as they'd kissed, kissed hard, stood, struggled together past the couch into the girlish bedroom, the family pictures on the bedside table, fallen onto the white bedspread, stripped the clothes from each other, fumbling and pulling, raising their bodies as the garments slid underneath, somehow during all that his cock had joined the party.

"Ah, God, jeez," she said again, and pulled on it. He moved over her. Her parents looked on fondly from a foot away. She shoved him in, grunting. Her face was sweaty and there were blond hairs lying flat and wet on her forehead.

He put his hands on her forearms and stopped moving. He stared down at her. She looked up at him, saw his pale milk-white eyes. "What's wrong?" she said.

"Nothing," said Ivan Teuti. "Nothing. But remember me."

"Oh, Christ," she said, "oh, baby, baby, I will remember you."

She fell asleep in the descending darkness with her plump hand on him. His fluid grew cold on the sheets. He rolled away, found his clothes and spent a little time in the living room, prowling around her territory, touching her magazines, her ashtray, her cheap glass-and-iron table. He looked in the refrigerator: some fruit, some yogourt, diet ice cream in the freezer, almost finished. The ice was melted in their drinks on the glass table. He thought about leaving some kind of mark, the kind of thing a burglar did when he finished the job, but decided against it. As he let himself out the door, he could hear a bubbling sigh, a little call from the bedroom. He walked down the stairs carefully, stepping near the wall, trying to make sure the risers didn't creak.

At home he heard his mother rustling in her bedroom, assembling another contrivance for a midnight bonfire. He lay down on his bed and reached for his magazine. The dark woman looked even more scornful than usual. The leashed dog at her side stared out at Ivan with good humour; the set of his muzzle, his pink lascivious tongue, showed he know what the score was. He could smell Jeannette on himself. He went to sleep.

That afternoon he went again to the independent television station, told the receptionist he had an interview with the assistant personnel manager and after an hour was shown again to Jeannette's office. She had her back to the door as he came in, another copy of his résumé in his hand. He placed it gently on her desk. She turned, looked down and then looked up at him. Her eyes widened and she smiled. He sat down and crossed his legs.

"Jeez," she said.

"I think I'm well qualified for an entry-level position in your company," he said. He'd rehearsed this. He had to switch from the hard-boiled detective to the bright and dapper young up-and-comer. He wanted her gasping from a change in air pressure.

Her smile faded.

"I'm a self-starter, highly motivated, a people person. I can take responsibility and work well as a member of a team," he said.

"But you——" She stopped. She looked at the name on the resume. "Ivan?"

"Teuti, pronounced Tooty, Eastern European family, originally Finnish, born here but I have the language, which is quite a considerable asset in a multicultural city, I'd say." He was enjoying it. He could almost hear her thoughts: it's the same guy, the same voice she'd heard from between her legs twelve hours before, but here he was sitting brightly on the other side of her desk, smiling as though nothing had happened—he loved it, loved the luxury of controlling both tracks of a conversation.

"Surely we've met?" she said.

"Oh, sure, maybe, but I think you'd . . . remember," he said, punching out the word, leaning forward a little. He saw the word jolt into her head. "Technical training, excellent academic record, volunteer service. I think you'd really be very well advised to put that résumé in your active file. Your active file. You don't know what could happen if you missed an opportunity like this one." He was still smiling, but now there was a sense of threat in the room. She'd been stone drunk the night before. She could probably still taste the rye. She had to be wondering if she remembered everything they'd done.

"The active file," he said again.

She didn't move.

He took the paper from her hand, placed it carefully on the desk. "I really think you will like what happens if you put my résumé in your active file."

"What would . . . what would your initial salary expectation be?" Not the way she usually said it. She was jittery.

"Oh, I know you'll be fair," he said. "I just know that by looking at you."

She picked up the phone and punched in the extension of the technical director and told him she had someone to fill the trainee spot in the camera room.

The station was all steel and vinyl, flat shiny surfaces, with monitors along the walls, the station's signal multiplied a hundred times. There were photographs in the corridors of people who once worked at the station or still did: confident, smiling people with high cheekbones and the large frank eyes of children. Ivan loved it, felt part of it right from the beginning, walking down the hall behind Jeannette's fat butt to the office of the technical director. Busy people passed him on important missions. Little white-bloused girls with clipboards covering their chests, wide belts, pulled-back hair, clicking heels. Makeup ladies with crimson lips. Thin men with hair caught back with rubber bands. Exotic coffees in waxed cardboard cups and glass doors with banks of computers, fat sloppy attendants and bespectacled engineers moving between them.

When Jeannette reached the technical director's office, she looked up at Ivan for a long minute, trying to read the inside of his head. The technical director looked at the two of them and smiled.

"Ivan Teuti, Bob. Marketing graduate, young." She put his résumé on the technical director's desk. "Hungry."

"Great. We like them hungry."

She left. Ivan sat down on the steel-and-leather chair.

"I always ask this. Do you want to be in television or do you want to be on television?" said the technical director. He was expecting the usual blather from a beginner— don't care where I start as long as I can work hard and do well. They all wanted to be anchormen, and they all lied, which was maybe a fair qualification.

He almost jumped at the intensity of the little man with

the blue-white eyes. "I don't care. I just love television. It's the most incredible thing in the world. It reaches everywhere. It's amazing. I want to get right inside it." Well, that was a cut above the usual self-serving babble. The technical director knew a few people who felt that way, who tuned themselves in to the frequency and power of the screen, and they were the best workers in the station. They never went home, couldn't leave the buzz. They wanted to straddle television and hold its reins.

The technical director looked at Ivan Teuti's pale eyes. He didn't seem to be crazy, although maybe there was a little vicious streak in there. That would serve him nicely in the television world. He was smart, from the look of his exam results, well-spoken, and he seemed to have the consuming, yearning need for control that pushed people up the scale.

"I like you," he said to Ivan Teuti, who did not react. "This production assistant thing. It's really more or less an intern position. You'd be pulling cables and running the teleprompter and going for coffee and helping out on the remote shoots. Not a whole lot of money but that's the way we like to begin our people here."

"I'll take it," said Ivan.

"You don't want to know the salary?"

"In a year it won't matter," Ivan said, and the technical producer felt a sudden coolness in the room. This guy was something, even for television.

Ivan thought he was going to like it, but he loved it. Loved it. Showed up early for his shift, stayed late to hang lights and sweep studio floors, made friends with his modest smile and pleasant manner. He studied the framed pictures in the hallway, looking for common qualities in the eyes, the smiles and nicely arranged hair. He could feel his walk and his posture change. When he looked in the mirror he saw his smile had changed. He bought new clothes, designer sweatshirts and close-fitting jeans. He smiled at Jeannette when they met in the lobby beside the smoothly rolling steel-and-rubber escalator. He fitted in beautifully.

In his second month of training he was assigned to carry lighting cases for a field cameraman. Their first assignment was at François Will's estate, to record his appeal for his wife's lost pet. François Will was an advertiser, and the news department had extended him a small courtesy. The lineup editor thought it might make a little kicker at the end of the newscast—even business hotshot not immune to grief for lost pet kind of thing. And there was that strange black-and-white footage from the zoo, with the big heavy prowling lion and the tiny cat strolling beside it. Images to talk over.

The cameraman usually worked by himself, recording interviews as he ran the equipment. The interviews were a pain in the ass because all he really cared about was the luxurious feeling of the lights. He gloried in the exact placement of the spots and fills, and he loved to paint faces with luscious gels. Ivan was along to learn the ropes, and so for once the cameraman had someone to ask the questions while he stared through the lens, and this time there was something to stare at for sure. The guy's wife was a knockout, a big slim blonde with a face he wanted to glaze with beige and steel filters. Ivan thought he knew what she was: a trophy, a status blonde, the kind of hurdle he expected he'd hop over in a year or two.

He attached a microphone to François' shirt and asked Julia to run the other one up under her blouse. He could almost feel the little metal cylinder and the string of plastic cord trailing against her skin.

They were arranged on the big couch in front of the bar with the lights bouncing off the expensive decanters behind them.

"We are rolling," said the cameraman.

"We would like to make a little—" said François.

"Excuse me," said Ivan, "but this will go a little more quickly if you let me ask the questions. And it would be more natural."

"Oh, fine, sorry," said François. The cameraman was blocking Julia's view of Ivan, but suddenly she wanted to see him. She had a faint memory of strange eyes.

"What can you tell me about your cat?"

"Oh, he's . . . he's a member of the family, really. My wife had him before we met, that's five, six years ago now, and he's really a very nice cat." François was jumpy, annoyed with himself. He didn't know what he expected, but this seemed out of his control, undignified.

"His name is Jones," said Julia, and the camera moved to her. "He is a domestic breed, a black cat with a white mark on his left front paw, and this is a picture of him." The camera moved in for a closeup of the snapshot of Jones lying in Julia's arms, the two of them staring at the lens. "We miss him a great deal. We think he may have gotten away a couple of days ago when someone here left a window open. That little cat in the picture from the zoo—I think that's him."

"We are offering a reward," said François, feeling a loss of command. The camera stayed on the snapshot for another moment and then moved upward to Julia's face.

"We really, really want our lovely Jones back," said Julia, and her warm smile glowed in the lens.

"We are very fond of animals. We adore animals," said François, thinking about the marketing, "and we are offering a substantial reward." The camera didn't move.

"We are offering a reward of two million dollars," said François. There was a slight pause, and the camera frame panned back to his face.

"Two million dollars?" said Julia.

"Two million dollars," said François. He was in close-up. He had regained control of the situation. He could tell his wife was moved, and even the kid asking the questions from behind the camera seemed to be impressed. And it wasn't bad publicity, after all. It could translate the smiling face on the packages of sausages into the image of a real man with real feeling, a warmth toward animals and a great love for his wife. Suddenly he felt that he had come into focus as a loving husband and a showman, a great businessman and one of the luckiest guys in the world.

Thirteen

IVAN TEUTI'S MOTHER started sending notes to Jesus and the police and people she saw on television, complaining that her son was putting things in her food to interfere with her prayers and preventing her husband's return to her. Not even Jesus, it seemed, was stronger than her son. Finally she lit one of her pyres in front of Ivan's bedroom door, and when the police showed up she was happy enough to go along with them to wait for her husband in a secure nursing home. Ivan pushed a note through the mail slot of the drugstore one night to tell his father that the old apartment was vacant and bundled the stuff he wanted into a rented truck.

His father took over the place, along with Mrs. Godwin and her children. Ivan had kept a key and came back once, letting himself in during the afternoon, looking the place over, moving from room to room, seeing the changes the new woman was making. Curtains. Cutlery. On the big bed a new comforter and sheets and beside it magazines and a box of condoms. His old room held her children's clothes and toys. The place left him cold. They were welcome to it.

His new apartment was in Chinatown, above a store that sold vases and little wooden Buddhas to tourists. At night he could hear the owner downstairs praying and, it seemed to Ivan, apologizing to his inventory of cement, wood and stone statues. Or maybe the owner was counting or singing or something. During the day he moved the statues out at a brisk enough clip. Ivan couldn't understand the vague sounds he heard from the floor below and that suited him. He liked his disconnection with Chinatown. His neighbours walked past him without looking at him, speaking in a language nobody expected him to understand. The hallways smelled of ginger, garlic, five-spice powder, anise and sesame oil. On the street he walked past stores selling medicines made from parts of bears, tigers and monkeys.

His landlord's tall young son was the intermediary and acted as though he owned his father's six shabby properties himself. His shiny black hair was coated with oil, and he carried a finely tooled leather briefcase. He was refining his techniques as a businessman before he moved on to larger and more upscale properties. He handed out a printed list of rules: no holes in the walls for pictures, no music after 11:00 p.m., garbage to be put in the backyard bin at certain hours only. None of it made the least difference to Ivan, who looked at the landlord's son indifferently with his blue-white eyes.

The son was curious. "What's a guy like you want to live here for? This is for Chinese people."

"Close to work."

"What kind of work do you do?"

"Television."

"No drugs!" The son leaned down to put his face close to Ivan's. "If you think this is some kind of place for an opium den you better think again, you know. If I see anything like that I call the cops right away. I don't need that."

"No drugs." But the guy was starting to piss Ivan off.

That night Ivan sat on the bench below the front window and looked out into the street, watching the white-aproned grocery clerks stacking onions and cabbage, the idlers reading their papers right to left, the cops' foot patrol past the produce bins and the ironic tourists laughing on their way to dinner. There were competing sounds from the street. The gift store loudspeaker played Chinese music, the grocery store old American pop songs, and both were cranked up to top volume. They jammed together in the air. He reached over to open the window a little wider and caught the web of his right hand, between the thumb and the forefinger, on a sharp metal edge.

The blood welled up quickly. He felt a slight shock, like a quick rap to the top of his head. He raised his hand and watched blood flow down past the meat of the thumb, down the wrist, past the slight bulges at the end of the forearm and down the skin to his elbow.

The blood slowed. He could sense his body moving against the rupture. He imagined the squads of cells forming around the edges of the cut, producing healing chemicals to cauterize and seal off the opening. His body was returning itself to the way it ought to be. It had a constant desire to maintain its perfect form.

He turned his arm in the purple-pink flashing light from the street. His blood was congealing. He had the feeling he was greeting an old friend, a never-failing friend, moving in a calm river in and out of his heart, washing impurities away.

Ivan remembered the mouse and the Swede and Bill's grey face after his ribs broke. It seemed to him that there should be some feeling about that and that it should flow as evenly and automatically as his blood and then pass on, but he didn't seem to feel anything in particular about any of it. There was a high whinny of argument from the grocery store, and a scent of burning sesame oil from the barbecue joint. He tried to use the sound and smell as guides into his own head, riding them in as they penetrated his brain. He beat his palms against his face, trying to jostle an entryway into himself.

What did he feel? What did he remember? There were flickers. A Sunday school cartoon drawing of a happy lamb with Cyrillic letters beneath it. The arch of a house next to a bus stop beside the library. His father's face intent, his lips pursed as he poured capsules down a paper funnel into a little brown bottle.

The blood was crusting on his forehead where he had slapped himself. He could see his dim reflection in the window. Streaks of red that looked like war paint. He could be an Iroquois fresh from a raid, and that would be an enemy warrior's blood, sprayed out from the cleft his hatchet had cut. Or a Mayan king with red hands under the sun.

He washed and slept, and in the morning he felt strong and solid, as though the loss of blood had freshened his body. A little of the fantasy stayed with him as he walked to work. He saw himself running amok down the street, swiping and jabbing with a sharp curling kris.

"Hey!" It was the gift shop owner, an olive-skinned stooped man with a bad limp. Ivan had watched him from the window, moving cases of souvenirs and cheap art from his truck into his store, bamboo screens, tea sets, mahogany letter openers, mah-jongg sets with plastic tiles.

"You the guy upstairs!"

"Yeah."

"You on TV!" The man was smiling like a friend.

"No. I just work at a TV station."

"My son tell me you on TV!" The man dug into his pocket, fished around and brought out a little dark red carved Buddha. It was smiling and big bellied like thousands sold in Chinatown every day to dangle from the city's key chains. It was cheap and crudely made. You rubbed its belly for luck. It meant nothing to Ivan. He put it in his pocket.

He had never wanted his face and voice on the screen. They'd shot a student commercial at the business school, and he'd had to face the camera; he was a little repulsed by the sight of his white stare and the sound of his high tenor. But the day he'd gone out to the Will estate, the lineup editor got into a big fight with the anchor when Ivan brought the tape with the cat stuff back to the newsroom.

"It's rolling over for an advertiser," said the anchor, who had been at a conference on journalistic ethics the weekend before.

"Horseshit," said the lineup editor. "A two-million-dollar reward for a cat? I'd lead with that if it was *your* damn cat."

"Well, fuck you, I'm not voicing it," said the anchor. He pouted.

"Well, fuck you, I'll get the kid to voice it," said the lineup editor, and Ivan did his best, which was not bad, and even recorded a piece of script directly to a camera outside the studio, his pale-eyed stare giving the story extra mystery. It became the lead item, and the anchor read the intro with a little added edge to his voice after a conversation with the executive producer. Julia watched at home. The snapshot of Jones brought on a rush of love that took in the cat, and François, and even Ivan Teuti, who delivered the report, she thought, with respect and clarity.

That night the worm hunters who picked their way over the lawns of north 17 found themselves in the company of squads of cat hunters, many half-drunk, with bags and nooses and little plastic satchels of cat food. The worm hunters had lamps strapped to their heads. The cat hunters had flashlights in their hands and big floodlights swivelling from the roofs of their vans and trucks. There were arguments and then fights and a worm picker wound up in hospital with a broken leg and a bruised face after a cat hunter drove over him.

One of the newspapers did a front-page feature story on what two million dollars would buy you, and the next night, with pictures of endless vacations and long yachts in their heads, a thousand people were out on the streets flashing lights in trees and roaming through parking lots. There were more arguments, more fights, even gunshots in a schoolyard when a group of cat-hunting teenagers intruded on a drug deal.

Judd had a bad night chasing squabbles and rhubarbs around 17, and the morning was worse. When he got home his wife and daughters were in the living room. The mistress of the dancing school, a spiteful Hungarian, had called the girls out onto the floor in front of the entire class and waved a cheque at them. It had been, she said, "dishonoured by the bank and that brings dishonour on the class and on your family." And she had made them wait for their mother on the sidewalk outside the school. He could imagine their pale, shamed faces and their pure little bodies in the open air as they waited for the car. Anyone could have done anything with them.

The two girls had been crying all night. His wife sat on the rust-coloured couch with the cheque in her hand.

"Well, why the fuck did you write it if you knew there wasn't enough money in the fucking bank to cover it?" he said.

"Daddy . . ." said his older girl.

He flushed. "I'm sorry. But why?"

"Am I supposed to be your bookkeeper, too?" asked his wife. "Who made me the manager here?"

He was bursting with humiliation. His stomach went rigid and then seemed strangely to start falling. He had the sense he was diving off a steep cliff and would keep falling forever, alone.

"What else are you doing with your time?"

He might have been able to stop this, but his shame made him vindictive, and now he had brought up a forbidden subject, her unemployment and depressed solitude. He braced himself.

"You're drunk," she said.

"I am not drunk."

"You're shit-faced. I know how much you drink. You spend all the money out there. . . . You expose us this way?

We're not protected! You don't protect us!" Her words rasped at him, opening him up, and the girls' looks heated the wound.

"Look at this place!" she said. "Provider!"

He felt the heaviness of the pistol in its holster under his arm. He could reach for it now, press it to his head, wait for a second to seize the final image of his life, there would be intaken breath, then silence, then the beginnings of the final explosion, and then he'd feel heat and the start of the pressure on the side of his head. Or he could turn the gun outward, immobilize her with it, extend his arm and hold her rigid with the threat of it, get up, go over to her, force it into her mouth—or even, for mercy, he could turn the gun on the girls first. He imagined his dead heavy body falling on top of the dead girls with the gun dropping from his hand.

He walked out of the room, her voice coming after him—"Drunk. You can't even walk straight. Look at you. And look at us."

He took off his clothes and lay on the bed, listening to the noises from the floor below. He could hear anger and shame in every click and bang. He glowed with rage. Suicide among policemen was called eating your gun, and it was common. There were funerals with honour guards for men who ate their guns and pensions for the widows.

Even his crazy aunt would come out for that. She'd be dressed in old fur, and her cat stink would carry before her as she came down the aisle in the church.

If he divided his life between those who deserved better and those who deserved worse, then obviously he and his family were on one side and his aunt was on the other. The girls were vulnerable. His wife was sick, shamed, desperate about money. He felt her sometimes in the dark staring up at the ceiling. He could feel and see what she was thinking: she was imagining the bank's locksmith at the door and the bailiffs stacking their furniture on the lawn. He thought of Captain Liz and the fifteen thousand dollars. He looked sideways at the alarm clock and watched the glowing second hand moving in the dark. There were limits to this. Next time or the time after that he would reach into his jacket and end it one way or another. He didn't know whether it would be just him or all of them. It probably depended on what his wife said to him just before.

In any case it was absolutely clear that the medical cleanup company would be rolling up wet rugs in this house, and soon.

Which led to that idea again.

Gracie liked to walk through the university campus. It wasn't far from her apartment, and it made a change from the bar; she could blend into the flocks of students and think for a minute that she was a co-ed herself, appearing onstage in the university theatre. In the Engineers' Follies, maybe, in a red sequined bikini, as Miss VaVoom. An agent would see her perfect teeth and nice if small breasts and take her off to the movies.

She wasn't looking where she was going, and slipped on a crack in the concrete near the top of some stairs that led from the groomed university lawn down to the road. She fell forward. She was in mid-air, in a spinning arc. Her head stayed roughly motionless, it seemed, as her feet orbited around it.

Time slowed. She thought that this was bound to be a dramatic, life-changing moment one way or another. Maybe life ending, if the weight of her body drove her head down onto the pavement. It would tilt one way or the other and her body would keep going and her spine would snap. She would die as though hanged, but by compression. She could see this quite clearly, and could also see the next possibility, landing hard on her tailbone, cracking it, crunching the backbone, lying helpless, the passersby picking her up, the nerves inside the spinal column fraying, parting, the lower half of her going dead. Which would be about it for dancing. Or a pinpoint landing on an elbow. Same result. She reached the limit of her momentum, hung feet over head for an instant, her legs continuing their grave wheel, her head motionless, and then began to come down.

She had picked up some counterclockwise torque and when she was three feet off the ground saw that she was heading for a fire hydrant that had bolt heads projecting from its cap. She imagined her jaw, nose and teeth shattering. She extended her left arm and imagined the bones of the hand breaking, the stunned flesh of the palm pierced by the bolts, the nerves stretching and tangling. In the moment before she actually hit the hydrant she felt a strange peace, her soul settling, coming to rest.

Her left cheek banged the hydrant, her sweaty flesh adhered to the metal and then broke away, leaving a ragged blotch on her skin. Time jerked forward with the pain and accelerated as though trying to make up for its loss as the impact changed her trajectory and brought her slamming to the sidewalk on her back. She lay breathless, the back of her head aching, her cheek screaming.

Suddenly she was lifted into a kindly cradle. A huge man had picked her up and was holding her like a child. The enormous face with its black beard stared down at her.

"My poor dear girl," said the enormous mouth, with its small white teeth perfectly spaced inside the great black beard, "let me get you inside." It was the weird old giant that Sergeant Judd had chased from the greasy spoon.

He carried Gracie tenderly, sweetly, up the steps and into the grey building that housed the university's dental school.

She thought that inside these places would look a bit like her high school, with high windows and pictures of blowing pines and graduating students on the walls, but it was grander, much grander, with marble floors and great bronze chandeliers. It looked like a movie set: the castle at the top of the hill, fogged in and full of creaks. And she was being carried along in huge arms. The students blinked and whispered as they went by. Maybe he was like the monster in the movie about Dr. Frankenstein. Big and warm-hearted but quick to snap.

The wide corridors were full of young men and women in white coats, carrying books, chattering to each other and falling silent when they saw her. As Gracie was borne past the classrooms she could hear more scraps of sound from inside, high whines and low grinding. Her face was burning where the ragged edges of the wound from the hydrant met the air.

The huge man carried Gracie through a high wooden door with a clouded glass panel and a sign on it: "Restricted: Animal Quarters." He set her down gently on a wide table, took a handkerchief out of his pocket and patted the blood on her mouth.

There were cages along the walls on either side of her, one section for mice and rats, another for cats. Three plump chimpanzees sat in a special pen fastened to the wall above the table. At the other end of the room there were stacks of cages filled with dogs. Students stood beside the cages writing in notebooks. The dogs yelped and roared. The monkeys screamed. The sharp noise from the animals cut into her head.

"How are you feeling now?" asked the big man. He was fumbling in a drawer set underneath the table.

"A little banged up. And my head hurts."

"Well, yeah," he said. "Quite a thump you gave yourself there. Saw you go up in the air like a, well, not like a bird, exactly."

A chimpanzee on the wall above her jumped and clung to the front bars of his cage, jerked and swayed, shrieked, his big yellow teeth showing inside an oval grin. A hamster ran in a ticking wheel. The footsteps of the students in the hallway overhead made little distant bumping sliding sounds.

The big man found a clear glass jar with a grainy brown salve inside it. He unscrewed the top, reached in with his right forefinger, drew out some salve and pressed it gently to the cut on her cheek. She thought of bugs and germs swarming into her body from the dirty paste and she tried to jerk away, but he held her head still with his left hand. The salve stung, then prickled; then she could feel the wound tighten and begin to dry.

A kid in a lab coat at the far end of the big room was shovelling food into wide tubes that led to feeding bowls for the dogs. He put his left hand in its thick leather glove against the bars and let the dogs tear away at it while he measured their meals with his right hand. Gracie could hear the dogs' teeth clicking against the wire, their deep roars and high yaps.

"That'll do you," said the big bearded man. "You'll be just as pretty as you ever were, in the morning."

The chimpanzee above her grinned again. She could see metal in his mouth: steel bands straddling the upper row of teeth. When the chimp opened his mouth to shriek, the back teeth were grey with fillings.

"Practice for the kids," said the big man. "The second-year students take turns putting him to sleep, yanking out the fillings and putting them back in again. Braces on the tops—he's going to look like a star by the time he's through." Dogs paced and grinned. Most of the cats were asleep. There was a gaggle of white coats at the end of the room. One of the male students had a limp cat in his hands. He was making its mouth move as he talked in a high sweet little voice: "Give me suction! Give me a number six!" The other students laughed.

Gracie sat up slowly. Her face was still burning. The big bearded man put out his hand and steadied her.

"Open, please," said the big man.

"What?"

"Open, please," he repeated. "My dear, this is a dental school. This is a place where we study teeth. I would like to see your teeth."

She opened her mouth. He peered inside, hooked one cheek wide with a forefinger. He stared some more, then tapped her jaw upward and closed with a forefinger.

"They could be perfect," he said. "They could be perfect."

She thought about dazzling movie teeth, set between crimson lips. If she had perfect teeth she would sing and dance and not take her clothes off until late in the movie, maybe. The big man smiled at her. She closed her eyes.

Fourteen

THE CITY LIVED on television, breathed it. Everywhere there were moving images beaming out to fill the spaces between real objects, submerging the city in smiles, requests and commands. There were little screens tucked under the cabinets in kitchens, medium screens beside oak desks, screens in elevators, in bus shelters, in libraries, in schools, in hospitals, screens that displayed daily dramas that moved from murder to rape to love to massive swindles, screens with news that shifted from fire to burglary to pear-shaped police captains talking into microphones, screens that listened to you while you talked to them on the telephone, screens with animated pictures of jelly, baseball, old men with white beards who represented God, the germs that cause halitosis, cars, underwear. François Will's company had the Friendly Dancing Pig that tapped across the city's screens from breakfast to bedtime celebrating its own flesh. At the end of every message François' face popped up in the corner of the image and said in a voice of surprised discovery, "They're good!"

And now François had a double hit, an advertiser's dream: heavy rotation in the commercial slots and featured play in the news: each signal radiated positive feedback and resonated with the other. He was becoming a big item.

Every night there were new pictures of Julia winding her damp handkerchief around her fingers. The newspapers added interviews with psychologists and sociologists, and commentators pointed out the irony of a two-million-dollar reward for an animal when so many people were homeless and hungry. The homeless and hungry carried pictures of Jones in their empty wallets and spent nights turning over garbage cans and peering under porches. A designer created a scandal by dressing his models in cat skin. The models threw coins into the audience, calling out for Jones.

All this time Jones stayed in the old woman's house. He ranged from the attic to the basement, nosing behind the furnace, jumping up to the window over the oil tank and patting the glass, but there was no way out he could find. His hip was stiff in the mornings, it was taking longer and longer to stretch and lick the feeling out, and his sense of the healing plant was starting to fade.

One night he was at the basement window peering through the cobwebs at the bushes outside when he heard the crunch of boots.

Sergeant Judd was looking through the back shed for the third time. He had left his car three blocks away. He had a green plastic bag over his shoulder. He knew the layout; he could find his way easily down the narrow walk at the side of the house, unlatch the gate and find the back porch with the tips of his fingers, even on a moonless night.

There was a light at the front of the top floor and a glint from the back room. She was at her telescope again, studying the moons of Jupiter or something. He had heard so much about the moons of Jupiter that he thought he could say them off by heart. The shed was dry and rotting and tilted so that it touched the back porch of the house.

He had spent weeks looking for the cat, pummelling his informants, cruising the back alleys. He was a public searcher and a private one; if he found the cat alive he'd send in a bum to collect the reward and take it from him afterwards. The cat would answer everything and change his life absolutely, square the snitch box and pull his daughters out of the garbage. But he'd given up the dream now. He was absolutely sure the cat was dead, bug food somewhere. He'd have to make his own luck.

He had done nothing, absolutely nothing, that could be used against him in any court. He had bought fuel, but that was because he was planning to fill the camp stove he took on trips with his daughters. He had walked around the old woman's backyard, but as a relative he had a duty to observe and supervise her property.

There was a sudden moving shaft of light from the alley, and he flinched and sidestepped into the shadow by the side of the road. He had always been the man behind the light. Now he was in front of it, avoiding it, looking for darkness. He was behaving like one of the street operators down at the bottom of 17, the housebreakers and bad boys who spent their time hiding from his spotlight.

Many of the bad boys had families. There were hard-working burglars who kept their children in good schools and broke into tears when they were arrested. He was hard-working, too, but no amount of work would keep his children safe. He could shovel the city's shit until the end of his life and he'd still watch them roughening, becoming coarse. And the old woman who could save them was fixed on the night sky while her house stank up the neighbourhood.

He took the three canisters of camp fuel out of the green plastic bag and put them in the shed. It was still completely legitimate. He intended to go camping with his daughters but was storing the fuel here to be picked up after a visit to their aunt on the way north, or something. Perhaps he would offer to take the old woman on the trip. If he stopped now, the cans could lie there until doomsday. Nobody would ever ask what he had really been thinking about. He could move back to his own side of the line.

The cat heard the soft sounds as the plastic canisters thumped together. The moon was old, left-handed, crooking toward the centre of the sky.

At four o'clock the next morning Judd was back at the bar, waiting to give Gracie a lift.

The bar door swung open. He leaned over to the passenger's seat, pushed the handle, nudged the car door. There was a rumbling in the dark sky, a white line flickering and suddenly hard rain whipped by wind. Gracie got into the car. There were braces on her teeth, glinting in the fluorescent glow from the street light.

He drove silently out along the harbour highway, the sound of the police radio bristling in the still air, pops and hisses from the headquarters microphone. The car's wipers thumped on the glass.

She looked at him in the dark, his profile shining and fading as cars passed. He had a cradle of flesh under his jaw, pouches under his eyes; when he turned his face to her she could see two diagonal seams in his forehead that made the shape of a rooftop in his skin. When he frowned they made his face look tight and fierce.

"Fucking cat, Gracie," he said. "You heard anything about the cat?"

Rain pooling above the wipers making a face, a sharp nose that dissolved and guttered away.

"Some guys in the bar went out looking," she said. "Took some flashlights. They killed a skunk with a shovel. Stank up Sylvan Street."

"No cat," he said.

"They didn't find him," she said. What was the deal here? They'd drunk, lain down together, embraced. Now what?

She had her hair pulled back and caught behind her head with a rubber band. He turned onto the beach road. Her small full mouth made an oval. Her stomach rose.

There was an old freighter tied up to the splintering wharf, seized by creditors. Its Polish crew was forbidden to set foot on the land. The Poles were broke, searching the ship for old cans and mouldy bread. The women in the crew stayed below, but there were always a few men on the deck, even at night, even when it rained. They whistled at girls and begged men to throw coins or food. Two of them watched the police car pull up and park. The moon sank.

"A hundred years ago," Judd said, "there was all kinds of stuff here. Freighters up from the Atlantic, from Europe, taking stuff off the trains, wood from the North, iron, copper. Two hundred years ago they were cutting masts up there, shipping them through here all over the world. I read about it. Now look at it. Users and crooks and these guys jumping ship, bad guys coming in, the Chinese smuggling people in, hookers, you know."

What was he talking about? He didn't know. She didn't know.

"You get bad elements wherever you go."

"The shit piles up here," he said. A pause. "So what do you think, this cat, this cat's dead?"

She was shocked. "Oh, God, no. No, no. No, I feel him out there. I really believe he's out there." She surprised herself. She didn't know she felt this way, didn't even know she'd thought about it, but Jones on the run out there seemed important to her somehow.

"What are you, psychic?"

Was she? She'd had faint wisps of sorrow or happiness sometimes, moods she hardly noticed but seemed to predict the kind of day she was going to have. Sometimes she could look at a phone and know it was going to ring, even know what kind of call it was going to be, good or bad.

"Are you?" He'd raised his voice. She could feel its force against her face, pushing her away.

"I don't know."

"Well, shit." He wondered himself what he wanted. Directions? "Indians, you know, used to come in their boats along the shoreline here, meet down the beach where the river ends, big strong guys, and now look at them, drunk Indians all over the street. It's just all crap, you know."

"There's good in everybody."

The big face turned. "You think so?"

"That's right."

His hand was inside his jacket, moving on his holstered gun, feeling the leather and steel. His mouth was dry.

"Not much difference for those Indians. Like the good ones and the bad ones. Just life will push you one way or the other way. One day you're good and the next day . . ."

He'd forgotten she was there. He had a sudden sharp desire to look at his pistol. He pulled it out of the holster and into the light. She pushed open the door, jumped out of the car and ran. He sat still. The Poles on deck howled and hooted at her. He flicked off the safety catch and fired one shot into the ground outside the car. The Poles knew the sound. They were silent. The sound of her shoes thumping on the old wharf.

He felt suspended, weightless, powerless. There was a siren down the highway, but it faded.

When François Will married Julia, at her suggestion he carried her back to the factory in his limousine and lifted her over the threshold of the packing plant to the cheers of the workers. At first they had lived in a waterfront condominium while the builders prepared their estate on the edge of the northern suburbs. Jones had dozed in her lap on the balcony as she looked out over the lake.

She had felt a relaxation of pressure and thought she might be happy. In the evenings the two of them drank wine and looked out over the harbour where vendors cooked and sold sausages from packages bearing his face.

"Do you mind being the wife of a sausage-maker?"

"No, no. I think it's sexy." She wasn't really sure what she meant by that, but it always aroused him. She'd call his socks sexy, or his business plans, and François would leap up and move toward her.

François had a determination to please that brought her to a state of contentment. Sex was pleasant and even something more than that. She found that her body was sometimes capable of climax; the change seemed to be related to a quality in his lovemaking that was safe, reassuring and even amusing, a friendliness and competence. It was much like his comportment on the factory floor—assured and considerate.

"Do you dream?" he asked one night.

"Oh, yes," she said, and told him a story about a woman running through a transparent tube, a shaft that narrowed at the end and injected her into a pool of flowers in which she swam until she reached a pile of sand, salt and money. She made it up as she went along. She never remembered her dreams.

"Do you dream?" she asked him.

"No," he said. "Never." His stray toenail clippings were sharp under her feet on the cold tile floor of the bathroom, and she was shy about her toiletries, hiding her packages of menstrual goods behind a box of bath salts. But all in all life was pretty good.

Fifteen

THE RAINSTORM THAT began before dawn continued all day. It was the product of the latest in a series of large, slow-circling masses of wet air that followed a line of lakes toward the city. The rain was hot and left dirty spots on clothing. *Mugged,* said the newspapers, and the television screens showed river levels rising and children fishing for tainted fish in sloppy, hurrying water. The heat clung. In the dark tunnels the trains ran slowly, their wheels grinding and screaming over the swollen tracks, the cooling fans pushed beyond their limits, the cars forcing plugs of steamy air ahead of them into the stations.

The cow manure the farmer had dumped washed down the stream and into an open channel that followed a gouge left ten thousand years before by a melting glacier. The mass of bacteria in the water spilled and smashed as it hit the smooth rock. The water swept into a wide concrete half tube and down again through a long sluice that carried it to the city's big steel intake pipe. There was so much water that the intake was choked. The force of the flow smashed the main control valve. There was a sudden rush of dirty fluid down the inward channel. It broke through the primary filter that anchored the city's water system. Tons of water, speckled with dirt, oil and metal, boiling with bacteria, gushed out into the holding ponds and flooded into the channel that ran to the city's taps.

The technicians in the water control room were on summer shift, double duty to cover those who were away.

The student on quality monitoring was on the phone to his girlfriend, murmuring about the night before. He missed the upward yank of the needles on the console, and the music from his radio covered the crashing of the filters in the caverns below. When he finally looked up and said, "Oh, shit," the grimy water had been flowing into the city's pipes for eleven minutes.

The student spent another quarter of an hour poking, peering and sweating, his throat getting tight, before he gave up and called for help. The maintenance supervisor pulled some secondary switches, rechannelled the flow and told him to forget it. There were redundancies and backups.

The germs in the manure found the dark, warm pools friendly. Their rate of reproduction increased as they eased their way through the city lagoons. The stillness of the holding tanks suited them even better. When the health inspectors did a routine round of tests two days later the germ count in the city's water was over the red line; an hour later and then two hours later, it was still rising.

When Ivan Teuti's mother ran away from her nursing home, she wound up in a women's shelter, whispering to Jesus from her bunk and writing Him notes she'd burn in the garbage pail in the women's washroom.

I want a word with You. I served You all my life, and You know I'm good. Why am I floating by myself on the sea with the garbage all around looking for You? Are You sailing an ocean liner on Your way to get me? Or are You on some other world? Give me a sign. Did You break open Your Mother when You were born? I know my maiden membrane broke when he went into me and grew back and broke again when his son came out of me and grew back because God wants me to be a Virgin. Have You talked to Him? Am I getting this right? Send me an angel.

Ivan kept an eye out for her as his camera car drove around the city. He didn't have a clue where she could have gone. Once or twice he talked to the cops, but she was an adult, after all.

One night he went to a baseball game. He thought he remembered the section where his father used to sit, down near the right-field baseline, and picked out a seat behind it from the chart at the ticket window. The baseball park was a huge steel-and-concrete tank half filled with flesh and air, ringing with sound, flashing images, swooping birds, the calls of vendors and the crash of sound effects. It was the middle of the first inning, and the technicians in the control room were already cueing up the sounds of bells for foul balls and rifle shots for strikes. People glanced in his direction as he walked down the wide stairs. A beer seller stopped in front of him—"Aren't you the guy on TV?"—and poured him a plastic cup on the house.

He wasn't happy about this. He liked to go to the ballpark and slide around the sections, moving from one empty seat to another, looking around him, smelling the air, the scents of the women, checking the concrete floor for bags left behind. Once he'd lifted a camera in a brown leather case, just to see if he could do it. A little pantomime. He had sat down, put his cup of beer on the floor, watched a batter swing and strike out, got up to leave, snapped his fingers, reached down for the beer and the camera at the same time, lifted them and sidled off down the row of plump knees, waiting for a call from behind him, getting clear. He threw the camera into a trash can. Now he wouldn't be able to do anything like that. He had a label, the TV guy, the cat guy. It was his story.

"Ladies and gentlemen, a warm welcome, please, for our special guests this evening, the well-known business-man François Will and his wife, Julia. Give it up!" Their faces huge and golden on the screen. François smiling. Julia looking as if she was there against her better judgment.

Ivan felt a little burn in his stomach. He was in the stands, locked up, shut away, neutralized. He thought at least if he went on television he'd gain a real place in the world, but he was still on the outside. The main players were down on the field and up on the electronic billboard. He felt servile. He'd broken through one membrane but still faced another, stronger, barrier between the people who described and the people who acted.

A snapshot of the cat flashed on the giant screen. Jones lying on the back of the couch, a puddle of black with hot green eyes. A caption flashing: *Two million dollars.* François waving to the roaring crowd.

All the same, the television work was all right. He was the king of the cat reporters, had the story nailed even though he was figuring out how to do the job as he went along. Every evening the city tuned in to his station for news of the cat. It was amazing how surely the interest held, con-sidering that there hadn't really been much new for weeks. Ivan spun out sidebars on children who dressed up as cats and ministers who preached about social values, using the search for the cat as an example of irresponsible wealth and the cat himself as the ideal we treasure but can never reach. The other reporters gave him piercing looks. He was invited to have coffee with the president of the station and several important sponsors. François Will bought a concentrated new round of advertising slots during the evening news. Sausage sales were up.

Every morning when the animal shelter opened its doors, a crowd of people ran to the cages, thinking one of them could be the first to recognize the two-million-dollar cat lying languidly on a layer of shredded paper. But the animal workers had already checked every one that came in, and the garbage workers raked through every truckload that went into the dump, looking for a little stiffening black body. Psychics posted signs in their windows offering infallible help in finding the cat. Libraries ran out of books on hunting and feline behaviour.

The president of the television station called Ivan into the boardroom and confirmed him as a reporter, gave him a modest raise and sketched out the great things that might be in store for him in the television industry. The president spoke in a calm, confiding whisper. Ivan listened unmoved. His new career was alien. He was impervious. In the end his cool, colourless stare gave the president the creeps, but half the employees did that one way or the other.

François and Julia watched the tapes of their interviews at home. François spent extra time with the first one, spinning it back five times to the point at which he had increased the reward from one million dollars to two. The camera had been on Julia, and he picked up a flicker of surprised disapproval in her face.

"Why did you look like that when I announced the reward?"

"Like what?" This made her uneasy. She tried not to watch herself.

"Like this." He rolled the tape back and forward. "You look like a pickle, a sour dill pickle." Her eyes had narrowed very slightly when he said the number two million. If he could increase the magnification, he thought, he would see her pupils contracting in irritation. He tried to zoom right through them into her brain and read her thoughts, but the frame was pulling away. He thought he saw the beginning of an upward tilt to her face as though she were about to look at the ceiling in exasperation.

"I wasn't looking like anything. I was listening to you."

"Did you like it when I increased the money like that?"

"I was surprised. I guess I knew it meant you loved me."

"But did you like it?"

"I was surprised. You can't *buy* me on this."

"I'm not trying to *buy* you."

"Don't be exasperating." She used words like this when she was annoyed, words like provocative, incomprehensible, ungraceful. She'd whip him with syllables. Then she'd walk away and spend an hour doing God knows what in her bedroom and come back as though nothing had happened.

Her mouth *had* compressed when he said two million. A pickle mouth. He had gone too far, maybe. He did that.

In fact, Julia did feel two million was boastful. The whole thing was offensive. He had turned a gift for her into a public ad for himself. The sight of the little play of annoyance on her televised face made her annoyed all over again. And it had made her look older, shown her what she'd look like in ten years. She had never worried about that, and she was irritated with herself for thinking about it now. It was his fault. In her bedroom mirror she looked at the slight pulse at the base of her neck where the blood constantly beat at her from the inside. She could feel time working. Before long the unending slight push would make the skin coarse and slack.

The only answer was to develop some kind of strength to take up the space left behind by disappearing beauty, but she didn't know how to do that. Sometimes she felt she was interesting, and other times she fell into a frenzy of boredom with herself. Again it was François who had triggered this with his stupid, clumsy generosity. Thoughtlessness. To do something like that in public, while she sat beside him, as though she were a little high school date and he was showing off by giving her two orchids instead of one.

Or maybe she was only angry at herself. In ten years she'd be another pissed-off divorcée with wrinkled lips and ropy tendons. Webbing at the neck. She felt ashamed and alone. She put on her running shoes and left the house.

A story got around somehow that the Lithuanian family above the used furniture store on Hebber Street had the cat locked up in their kitchen, waiting for François Will to increase the reward. Word was that they were ready to chop off the cat's front paw and mail it to Will's wife. The first stone went through the front window of the furniture store at eleven o'clock, and by the time Judd got there twenty minutes later a crowd of men had battered their way through the door, charged up the stairs and started throwing chairs and tables around. A squad from 17 managed to get cuffs on some of them, but the place was a wreck: the refrigerator lay on its side with its door flung open, milk, beans and cabbage spilled across the linoleum.

"What did you think?" Judd asked one of the men. "They were keeping the cat in the freezer?"

"Fuck you," said the man, and got the point of a club in his stomach. He threw up his food and beer on the greasy floor. The Lithuanians wailed. When Judd came in his own front door in the morning, he looked at his clean floor and his wife's red eyes.

He slept for twelve hours straight and dreamed of the old woman, her telescope and her piano. When he was a child she had always insisted he play something for her when he visited. When he finished his clumsy one-handed tune, she'd push him along the bench and play a mazurka or a waltz or a tango, with corny left-handed bass thumps and high romantic right-hand trills. Back then she smelled of strong soap and lavender. In his dream he was playing the tango with both hands, rolling the deep notes, and she was dipping and swaying on her old carpet among her cats.

When he woke up, his wife and daughters had finished dinner. He came downstairs in his bathrobe and looked into the kitchen. They were laughing over the sinkful of dishes but stopped when they saw him. He yearned for his children to go to sleep so he could hear the light rhythm of their breathing, but he couldn't stand the idea of spending two hours waiting for their bedtime. He dressed and left the house.

He spent the next couple of hours just driving around 17, stopping at the university to look at the night-school girls stepping quickly across the street, thinking of Gracie. She had braces on her teeth now—where had she gotten the money for that? Why had he taken her to the beach? She'd run away, run from him in fright, and then he'd heard the hooting from the Polish ship and fired the shot into the ground. He didn't know why he'd done that, but he knew how to clean his pistol and replace the bullet. He'd erased any sign the gun had been fired. He'd neatened up the past.

He was a senior sergeant, detached for special assignment to direct the city's search for the cat. He had his own car and the freedom to roam around anywhere he liked. He had the keys to the city. If she wanted to make trouble, she'd be crazy to take him on.

He drove east toward his aunt's house, veered north into the moneyed neighbourhoods on the ravine and parked his car outside a small bar on a side street. It was almost empty. The beat of the music videos on the television set bounced off the walls.

He ordered vodka, looked at the screen and tried to set his mind free. He wanted some kind of direction, some decision to rise up into his head from some other place inside him.

The bartender switched to the news. A little man with very pale blue eyes held up the cat's photograph. A band of the city's sewer workers had come in on their day off to tramp through the entire network of tubes and pipes below the street. The water levels were so high the sewage sometimes reached their shoulders but they wanted to reassure the city that Jones, dead or alive, was not trapped down there. They didn't find him. They were disappointed and relieved at the same time.

The little reporter had a smile on his face, and Judd thought it might as well be directed at him. This was the first time he'd heard about the sewer workers. He felt the threads of the city slipping from between his fingers. Two million dollars sliding around out there somewhere. He was the cop who knew every hole and hill and house and hump in 17 and beyond, and still he'd be the last to find it.

It was quite dark now. He got back into his car and drove south to the water, to the old woman's street. The vodka was acting as a distorting lens between him and the rest of the world. His hands on the steering wheel sometimes seemed too large and sometimes too small.

He parked the car four or five houses down from hers and sat protected by the night. Even now he was on legal ground. He was the senior male relative checking up on her safety and comfort. He got out of the car and walked down the sidewalk, looking around as he normally did, checking the lit rooms through the windows: a woman's still shape, a flowering plant, a strange cheap jagged painting. As he turned into the walkway beside his aunt's house, he reached into his jacket and pulled out a pair of work gloves.

The cat was in his usual place at the basement window above the oil tank when the boots came by again. They frightened him. He needed to be close to some way out. He ran up the dark wooden stairs and into the kitchen.

Judd pulled the door of the shed open. He thought for a moment that someone had taken the fuel, but then he saw the three cans along the far wall sitting on the dirt. He pulled them out one by one, loosened the cap on the first and put it down beside the back porch. He twisted off the second cap, took a breath and poured the liquid over the wooden steps. Its shifting weight made the can sway in his hands. He took the third and ran a trail of fuel along the ragged lawn to the back of the lot. He'd be her lone survivor. The insurance would come to him, and whatever was in the steel box under her bed.

The light was on in her attic. A car rolled down the alley behind him, the sound of its radio thudding against the wooden fences and doors. He crouched and pulled a packet of paper matches from his shirt pocket. The gloves made it hard to open the cover. He swore, the vodka rose up in his head and he staggered sideways, tearing the cardboard, fumbling out a match from the red-capped row and breaking it off. He swiped the match on the abrasive striking line. It didn't catch. He struck again, overbalancing and almost falling into the line of fuel, and struck for a third time—the match caught, but before he could lean over to put it in the fuel it fell and went out. He struck another match blindly and felt a sudden press of air against his face as the flame hit the fuel and sprang along its trail.

The cats in the house smelled the fuel and the flames and started to race from room to room.

The fire caught under the porch, ballooned a little

when it reached the first canister, paused and then exploded with a roar. There was a hot smell of gas and then a sudden thump as the flame reached the outside rim of the porch and then burst upward, leaping onto an old stained sofa and the plank that wedged the door closed. The paint began to curl off the outside of the window frames. The cats were running faster now, moving up the stairs, rebounding off the closed doors of the bedrooms, rushing into the bathroom, climbing the shower curtain.

The old woman pulled her eye away from the telescope and sniffed the air. She got up, went down a flight of stairs and saw a glow through the open bathroom door. She looked out the window into the backyard and saw an arm of flame reaching up past the glass. It smelled like the liquid she used to kill slugs in the garden. One of the cats screamed. Another swiped at the flame with its claws. Donalda ran halfway down the stairs, slipped on a tread, caught the handrail, gasping at a sudden stretch and tear in her shoulder. The odour was growing stronger, and the smoke smelled like wood. She limped to the back door, her shoulder stabbing. She could feel the fire in the backyard starting to eat away at her father's house. She coughed and pulled at the door. It didn't move. She could hear the wood beyond it snapping and creaking. The curtains over the window burst into sudden orange flame and the stench grew stronger. There was a common growing wail from the cats. She moved back toward the hallway and the front door, tripping over furniture and debris, then over the body of the black cat who had flattened himself on the floor and rolled onto his back, yielding. The old woman's heel caught him on his bad hip. He screamed. A painting of a Dutch village in the living room burst into flame, then the calendar on the desk, furling crisps of black paper falling to the floor. The smoke was forcing itself down her throat. Her lungs felt hot and bright.

She was coughing, crying. Suddenly her housecoat was on fire, the orange stripes seething in the light. It hurt. She wrenched the front door handle, the black cat crouching on the floor beside her. Her hair caught fire, and she could feel the skin on her face cracking. The doorknob burnt her hand to the bone; she fried her skin fumbling with the locks. She could see a man running outside with a coiled hose on his shoulder. She screamed, pulled at the door, screamed again, opened the door and a great blast of flame moved past her, knocked her off her feet, threw her to the floor, curled around her as it sought the outside air again, blowing the black cat past her, tumbling him down the steps, his white-lightning foot gleaming in the fire, Judd running forward, then seeing the cat, the photograph from the screen flashing into his mind, unbelieving then believing, screaming at the cat, almost reaching the cat who scrambled away, eluding him by a foot or two, yowling, the ceiling of the hallway pulled down onto her still body, the cat running, the street cold and stinging under his scorched paws. His black fur smoked in the darkness.

Sixteen

THE FIRE HAD singed Judd's big face, and a spark had caught in his hair and burned a swath across his scalp. The cops on the scene thought he was stunned and grief-stricken. He watched them take the old woman's body away in a white ambulance. A divisional commander stood beside him with an arm around his shoulder and promised him that the force would get the sons of bitches—kids, probably. There had been stuff like this in the neighbour-hood before, but nobody had died. It was a damn shame. Although she was of an age, wasn't she?

Judd thought he could smell fuel on his clothes, although he knew he hadn't touched the fluid except with his gloves, and he had thrown those into the hottest part of the flames when the fire got going. He could still see the cat bounding past him, the little white streak on its leg clear in the moving light. Two million dollars the old woman didn't know she had and he had been too slow to catch. He kept the image to himself. He thought he'd heard at the height of the fire the sound of the little metal safe falling through the floor and landing in the basement. He'd get whatever was in that, some stocks, maybe, and the records of her savings account. The insurance would come to him. But it wouldn't be two million dollars. And it wouldn't be anything at all if they nailed him for this. They couldn't, but if they did.

He washed at a gas station, punching out pink gobs of soap from the dispenser, lathering up and rinsing off a dozen times. He had a sudden jolt when he thought of the little paper receipt for the fuel tanks but then remembered he'd shoved it far down in a garbage can twenty blocks away from his aunt's house.

He drove again, up and down the alleys around the old woman's neighbourhood, gunning the car to frighten the cat out of hiding behind the garbage cans, old mattresses, half-open garage doors. The soap hadn't done a thing. The smell still clung to his hands and the pockets he'd put his hands in and the pants around the pockets, the odour so strong in the car now that surely some would seep out through the door when he opened it to get out, so clear that everyone around had to smell it.

The cat ran along the alley for two blocks, stopping for traffic on a cross street and then loping into the darkness again, jumping onto a fence to escape a lunging dog and waiting, his back arched and tail bushed, for the dog to lose interest. The dog snuffled, whined and reared up to put its front paws on the fence but couldn't reach him and finally turned and trotted away. The cat's heart and breathing slowed.

He heard a low grumbling from the blackness of an open doorway and smelled something familiar. He jumped down from the fence and followed the scent.

The raccoon was chewing an old piece of meat half wrapped in plastic, her black paws holding it down while she tore it with her teeth. She looked at the cat, moved slightly and let the cat in to work on the flesh.

Judd's car rolled by in the laneway. The meat was calf's

liver, dropped on its way from car to kitchen. The cat had never tasted anything this good. It was tangy and slick on the tongue. The two gorged and slept.

Ivan saw the images of the fire on the morning news. There was a close-up of the stupid plastic gnome the old woman had put in her front yard. It was black and half melted. The reporter's voice said that the occupant had died, and many animals with her. It got under his skin. He'd invested a lot of time in the old woman and then the cop had frightened him away, and that was a weakness that had led to a loss. Now she was out of the game. He couldn't go back and correct his mistake. Time and luck had finished his unfinished business for him. That wouldn't happen again.

Kessler the driver prowled all around the zoo and explored the woodland paths around it, stopping to sniff for signs of cat. He didn't believe the cat had got far. He took tiny little steps the size a cat might take and a few times got down on his hands and knees to look at the scene from a cat's point of view. It was pretty tough. Fucking Hiawatha couldn't find a cat in bush like this, with all the dogs and squirrels and toads and shit like that. Could have gone anywhere.

Julia was running more, and her body was becoming leaner, more muscular and more angular. Sometimes she'd run the perimeter of the grounds from eight o'clock in the morning until noon, and then again from three till six. She thought the simple signal of her footsteps might bring the cat back from wherever he'd gone, but no such luck.

Lillian was worried about her. This constant jogging couldn't be good for the feminine places where her grand-child would find life sooner or later. As Julia's body got harder, hers got softer. She gnawed through rounds of cheese, tubs of ice cream and buckets of fried chicken delivered to the front door, to the annoyance of the cook, by a saucy driver from a chicken palace a mile away.

François was thinking about increasing the reward again. It was just play money anyway, ghost hopes. What difference would it make, two million or five? The cat was gone, long gone, dead for sure. He talked it over with his public relations people but didn't mention it to Julia and finally postponed the whole thing; she was jittery and irra-tional, always running or shut away in her room.

He concentrated on Friendly Pig market share.

Julia had been to the zoo once with her mother when she was small. She remembered the raucous howler mon-keys, the cut-stone stare of the alligators and the big white polar bear pacing in his cage, five steps forward and swing-ing to walk five steps back. She had no idea how to get to the place now. She called her driver one morning after she'd finished her run.

Kessler drove Julia to the perimeter of the lion enclo-sure, near the place where the lion had held open the fenc-ing for the cat. She stared at the spot, then along the line of the moat and the mesh fence that stood between the inner line and the road. She could feel Jones thinking, moving up and down the gap, finding a raised log to leap from; she could see him almost slip on the other side of the moat, cling and scramble, get one hind leg up and then the other, surge forward, stop, gather himself and look around for a final passage through the mesh. She walked the line of fence. A puff of scrub grew along one ten-foot stretch, and when she pushed it away from the metal she saw a slight dip in the ground. He had gotten out of the zoo grounds here.

She turned, searched the road, feeling him freeze and wait until the flow of cars stopped for a moment; then she felt him run, as she ran, across the street to a decline in the ground where a wet path led to the beginning of a ravine. It connected with the city's park system, an archipelago of partly tended wilderness that led gradually southward along the line of a buried river to the lake.

She was certain he had gone that way. She could see him bounding down the path past the bushes and the strange rusted metal sculpture the city put at the verges of its parks. Jones was cutting down toward the heart of the city: she knew it.

She looked up and saw Kessler against the sky, lighting a cigarette. His lighter closed with a sharp steely clap.

The smoke plumed from the driver's cigarette. Julia started back up the inclined path and then stopped. She could feel Jones somewhere below her, in the park or near it, somewhere on the long sweep of ground down to the water.

She ran her hand over her face as if trying to wipe away the mist of luxury that separated her from everything.

She turned, went down the path and disappeared into the woods.

Hec Morton had bought the used video camera in a pawn-shop to take pictures of a woman he sometimes saw across the alley in her bedroom at night. He saw her twice undressed down to her waist, once all the way naked. He was pretty sure the guy in the pawnshop could tell why he wanted the thing, but neither of them cared. He could still see her as she remembered the open curtains and turned to close them, her heavy breasts swaying and a hand held over her crotch. Hec had moved back from the window quickly and closed his eyes to try to fix the image in his mind. She wasn't young, forty, forty-five, but still built more like a girl than the damp-haired barrel-waisted women who worked alongside him at the laundry.

The camera was very complicated, with switches to set a superimposition of date and time, buttons to control the magnification and frame, and even a control to remove the automatic balance and focus. The booklet said this would allow the operator to experiment with photographic techniques. Hec left the automatic on.

He pointed the camera out the window at the alley, dropped it to a sudden movement on the ground and found himself looking at a raccoon rolling on its stomach in the dirt. He could see the animal's little-black-kitten mouth with its pink tongue and white teeth. The raccoon looked up, and the camera swayed upward as well, toward the woman's window, but stopped at the level of the garage roof. There was a cat lying on his back in the sun.

There was something about the perfect relaxation of the cat, its left back leg easily hooked in the air and its body open to the sky, that made Hec Morton smile. He'd had a cat like that once. It had loved the sun, hunting birds and catching girls for Hec. He used to take it to the park on a little leash, and they always came rushing over to pet it and whisper to it. That cat was pure black. This one, when it rolled over, showed him a lightning-shaped blaze on its left front leg.

The frame shook a little as the camera zoomed in.

Hec stayed with it for a moment, scanning the animal from front to back. It was sure as hell the cat everybody was looking for or God's own copy of it.

He put the camera down and stepped back from the window. Maybe the motion attracted the cat's attention, because when Hec got down to the alley with an open can of tuna in his hand the cat was gone and the raccoon as well. He walked around the neighbourhood for a couple of hours but didn't see either of them. Then he went back home and watched the images through the camera's viewfinder. Hec felt a glorious excitement and confidence that his life at last had turned. He'd get his due. He had something the world would be interested in.

Kessler the driver had just called and told François that Julia had taken off, disappeared—he'd waited two hours and thought he'd better report in. That was the moment Ivan Teuti chose to show up with his crew and new footage of his wife's cat lounging on somebody's roof.

The reporter had a strange face, ordinary and neat but with eyes that seemed to disappear as though there were some kind of vacuum up there on top of his nose. He played François Hec Morton's images. Is that your cat?

François didn't really know one way or the other, and drummed his fingers on his thighs.

"And Mrs. Will . . ."

"Out looking. Looking for him."

She'd become weepy and dull and then sharp and withdrawn. Now she was vanishing. Her moods were a shifting problem he couldn't figure out, a messy, fluid puzzle with no consistency or direction and probably no solution at all. And she was a little less precisely beautiful than before; her loss of weight made her jaw look heavy.

Ivan thought François was lying. He sniffed for Julia; her scent was gone. Something funny here.

The city was electrified when it saw Hec Morton's new pictures of the two-million-dollar cat. Network newsrooms sent mobile transmission trailers to Hec's street in south 17. The subway was jammed with crowds of cat hunters carrying net bags and knapsacks, electrical tape, bits of hamburger, packets of catnip, bacon, pet carriers and rope. Captain Liz ordered barricades to seal off a four-block area, but the cat hunters were already inside, crashing through gardens and over fences and kicking in shed doors.

The cat and the raccoon had moved a few garages down and were sleeping under a loose pile of old tires. They were wakened by the sound of a gang of cat hunters pounding at the garage shown in Hec Morton's videotape. Hec was in the front of the gang with a satchel in one hand and his video camera in the other. Network cameramen were positioned up and down the alley. There was barking, shouting, a clatter and splinter as the wooden garage began to give way.

It was the woman Hec had seen naked who found the two of them. She crept up on the pile of tires with a cardboard box under her arm and a frozen disc of ground beef in her hand. She caught the raccoon in the beam of her flashlight. The raccoon growled and stamped. She moved forward, leaned over and flashed the light down the well of torn rubber. Jones stared back at her.

He looked unhappy, the pupils of his eyes contracting in the rich yellow beam. She rubbed the cold greasy meat with her left hand and held it out to him. Two million dollars in a little black package that was two feet away and almost hers.

He was still full of half-rotten liver and disgusted by the smell, but the pain in his hip was strong and he didn't complain when she picked him up and began to stroke him. He struggled a little and then settled into her arms. The raccoon growled. She laid the cat gently in the open cardboard box and folded the top closed.

She had almost gotten to the street with her box when the landlady and her fat son blocked her way. The landlady disliked her anyway, since it seemed she thought she was better than anyone else in the house. "And what is it you have under your arm here?"

Her son, confident after a half year of law school, said, "Would it be something you found on this property, which by rights belongs to the owner?"

She felt a crash of panic and disappointment. Everything in her life seemed to go this way: a lift and a sudden letdown. She tried to shove past the landlady. At that moment the raccoon emerged from the open garage door, her teeth gleaming and muzzle wrinkled. The land-lady's son shouted and pointed. The landlady shoved the tenant with one hand and grabbed the box with the other. It fell and flew open. The wincing cat ran down the passageway beside the house and into the street.

Two cameras caught him in their lenses as he moved haltingly toward the police barricade. There was a clamour of dogs, a stamp of boots and whisper of track shoes. A light curtain of rain swept down the street; the cat felt its mist in his eyes and the concrete underneath his feet felt suddenly thick. Two squads of cat catchers collided at the barricade, one man only a foot behind Jones, his arms out-stretched, running hard when he was tripped by the leader of the other group, a burly full-bearded cab driver with a shopping bag and a butterfly net. The cab driver reached into his shopping bag and pulled out a tire iron. The first man pulled out a small glinting blade. A patrolman stand-ing six feet away at the barricade pulled out a can of pep-per spray and pressed the trigger. When all that was over, the patrolman looked around for the cat, but he had clam-bered through the barricade and turned the corner.

The network news programs that night followed the cat hunters as they ranged along the street beyond the barri-cade, tramping through restaurant kitchens and turning over tables, shoving their way into laundries and picking through the hanging plastic-wrapped suits, bursting through the doors of grimy toilets in the gas stations. Hotels in the city were suddenly out of rooms, and the airlines and bus companies were reporting a large increase in traffic as cat hunters began to converge on the city from around the continent. The mayor asked his assistants whether he should declare a state of emergency.

Judd was running on anger and alcohol. Captain Liz wanted the fifteen thousand. The other cops in 17 thought about filling up the snitch box for him, but what the hell, he was a bit of a prick. Let him figure it out.

When he saw the latest pictures of the cat at the barricade he parked his car a half block away and settled down to wait.

Julia stumbled once over an exposed root and fell onto the wet leaves on the path, smearing her face. She lay still. She could feel her panting breath and her chest pressing against the soil underneath her. It was getting dark. There were lights flickering in the apartment buildings that overlooked the park. She sat up.

The pain in her face began to ease. She had a sense of immense moving life in the trees above her, in the ground around and beneath her. Creatures running on smooth-worn paths along branches from an oak to a linden, leaping and clinging or flying, beginning the rounds of the night, reaching out by scent and hearing to find sheltering things that might be food, or crowding into narrow spaces for shelter and protection, or lumbering through deep-sunk tunnels below her, nudging and bumping when they met at the junctures of a network beneath the earth; above them the worms on their random courses; far below the trapped water of the old river.

She looked straight up the trunk of a maple. It was raining a little; she could sense the water falling onto the leaves, bending them, pooling, dropping farther, breaking into spray, congealing again in the lower air. She could almost trace the tracks of the rain from the uppermost clouds to the surface of her skin.

She folded her hands over her breast the way her cat sometimes did when he was lying in a bunch on the top of the sofa.

A rasp and rustle from the bush. She jumped away from the path, one foot in the air, the other shifting and slipping on the wet ground, and pitched forward into an alcove of ferns and branches under a group of pines. Human-made. Abandoned now, and cold, but a made place. With—her hand happened on it—a sleeping bag, slimy on the outside but dry inside.

Sudden laughter from the dark path, a man's laughter, harsh and half-drunk. She found the zipper to the sleeping bag, pulled it down until it caught, jammed her legs into the opening, forced herself down into the cloth tube, felt a comforting enclosure and the beginnings of warmth in the light rain. The laughing man had moved past her, and now she was alone in her protected space, thinking about her husband, the driver, the house, her mother, her cat, and then thinking of nothing, nothing at all.

The cat's leg got looser as he ran away from the roadblock. The pain and the fright receded, and he began to feel better than he had since he left the big estate. The imagined taste of the healing grass filled his mouth.

He began to lose his breath after half a block, and suddenly there was a huge form in front of him, an immense brown horse with a man on its back. The horse reared, and the cat swerved away from its hooves, bounded up a concrete staircase and onto a windowsill. The horse was still bucking and the man on it was shouting. The window was open. The cat squeezed underneath the sash and dropped onto the floor of a large shadowed room.

A man in a wheelchair sat at the end of the big space. He raised his head when the cat landed on the wooden floor. His face had a seared redness across the left cheek. One eye was grown over with flaming skin, and the other was filmed with white.

The walls of the room were hung with pictures of the man in his winning days, his encased head poking above the cockpit of his racing car and a checkered flag in his gloved hand, or wheeling past the grandstand or holding a big champagne bottle like a machine gun and spraying the crowd, being kissed on the cheek by a brightly smiling young woman in a cap or a headdress or a crown, his oily plastic suit covered with crests and advertisements. Then, where two walls came together, there were pictures of the crash, his car bucking sideways, a burst of fire, squibs of flame rushing back at the driver from the engine, the car on its side hitting the fence that rammed his body back against the seat and compressed it against the protective cage, bent and snapped his spine.

He spent hours looking at the pictures, retracing the movements that led to the crash and the movements that followed it. When he had tried to pass on the high side, he touched, a very slight touch, the fender of Car 29; 29's driver jerked the wheel in fright or anger and banged him back; he felt a loss of contact, a sense of smoothness and then heard screams from the rubber as the tires began to sideslip against the track surface, his body swinging against the direction of the motion, spinning the wheel toward the skid, hoping the tires would guide the nose back into line, seeing the wall, spinning the wheel again to try to guide the car into a glancing hit, the sudden jolt from behind as 36 hit his left side and drove him directly into the corner at full speed.

He went through it again and again. There was video-tape and sometimes he watched that, controlling the image with a puff of breath into a tube, but most of the time he preferred to look at the still pictures. It was easier to remember the smells and sounds, the feel of the helmet against the skin of his head, the heaviness of the wheel and banging of the road through his bones.

He raised his head, turned his chair with a touch of the joystick and saw the cat crouched in the corner of the room. It had been months since there had been a strange presence in the apartment, and that suited the racer. He was at the mercy of Gamester on weekends and Hans Monday through Friday, and that was entirely enough.

The cat, settling down after his encounter with the horse, looked at the room, measured its exits, took in its antiseptic smell. Then he walked slowly, his tail lifted and curling slightly back and forth at the tip, to the racer in his chair and jumped up on the racer's lap.

The racer felt the beginnings of a shake in his body, the random firing of orphaned nerves and disconnected muscles. He could barely see the cat with his one half-good eye, and he was afraid the quaking of his body would frighten it away, but the cat sat firmly through the tremors, lightly hooking his claws into the dead flesh of the racer's legs. As the twitching died down, the racer heard the low sultry sound of the cat's purr.

He suddenly thought he could feel the pressure of the cat's body against his lap. It was a startling sensation—a *sensation*—solid, unmistakable, even unpleasant, because it was impossible. The nerves were dead. Some quirk of memory was simulating the weight and texture of a cat's body and sending it through his brain. But the feeling was so consistent and convincing that he began to look at the cat as something miraculous. For the first time in months he tried to press against the restraints that held him securely in the chair. The cat smelled slightly of smoke.

"You're a fine, sweet boy," he said to the cat.

The cat was still a little jumpy from the fire and the chase through the barricades. There was a new pulling sensation in the middle of his flank as though a cord had been drawn down from the area of weakness. He needed some quiet, and the man in the chair was quiet.

The next morning the cat patrolled the apartment looking for signs of other animals. He remembered the crush of bodies at the old woman's place, and he didn't want any more of that. He found a high window overlooking a tree that had a noisy population of birds. He got used to the low grinding whirr of the racer's chair.

The racer and the cat began to develop a routine for the hours they spent together. The cat came in at night and lay in the racer's bed, brushing against him or kneading his slack flesh. Every morning he left to avoid the caretakers. He'd crouch under a pile of junk in the courtyard while the helper moved dully through the apartment, cleaning and tidying, emptying the racer's bags and lifting him into bed or out. The racer asked his weekday man, Hans, to leave a little sandwich out near the bed, and Hans agreed, although it made him grin to think of the cripple hunching his way over to the plate in the dark and nibbling the sandwich, his useless arms dragged behind him under the covers. It seemed impossible, but in the morning the meat would be gone.

"Did you hear about the big cat chase?" asked Hans. The racer didn't follow the news.

"No."

"Some rich lady put up two million bucks for anyone could find her cat that run away a month ago. Must be some kind of talented cat."

"White cat?"

"Black cat with a white leg. Two million bucks. I tell you, I find that cat and this town won't get one good look at my ass leaving."

It was a lie. Hans loved the intimate details of his service; he relished the job of cleaning the racer's body and propping him up in his bed with the reading rack in front of him. Hans was born to serve, and loved the little tyrannies the servant imposes on the master. He rolled the racer back and forth in bed to neutralize developing sores. He nagged and pestered. He wanted to spend every minute in the racer's apartment but went home every night because he didn't want his employer to know how much he liked his life.

Hans tended the racer's body and was perfectly in tune with his moods. He dusted and straightened the pictures on the racer's wall. If the racer was in a bad state of mind and snapped at him, he'd go home with tears in his eyes and then sink into irritation. The next day he'd be a little rougher than usual for a minute or two as he turned the racer's limp body, but then he'd settle down to his usual kind routine. Hans was a big man, running to flab, with heavy black eyebrows that grew together over deeply socketed brown eyes. He'd failed at every job he'd held, from short-order cook to garbageman. He was easily distracted and often confused. Now he was happy tending the universe of a famous helpless person.

Sometimes the racer kept secrets from him, but Hans could always tell. There would be a kind of sudden shadow lying across the still form on the bed. Hans would become sharp and snippy, heaving the helpless flesh without tenderness. Eventually the racer would get tired of this and casually let his secret fall into the open—a newspaper interview over the phone, a new gadget for the racer's computer. The two men would be friendly again. "You're an asshole, Hans," the racer would say, as Hans cleaned and neatened him, fussing over the fit of his pyjamas, and Hans would agree.

The cat was the biggest secret of all, and when the racer thought about telling Hans he held back. If it was the cat with the reward, Hans would take the money and leave him, not need him any more, and the racer liked the idea of having a big, raw, strong man dependent on him for money and even more than that. And there was a little pleasure to keeping the secret. He could look at Hans's broad moving back as he dusted and swept and remember what he knew and Hans did not.

In the daytime the cat prowled the courtyard. It was a six-foot drop from the street, protected by rusting iron railings, and it had become a trash can for whatever passersby might think to throw away. A stained mattress, and underneath it a family of rats, the babies pink squealing commas in the darkness. Blown newspaper, dampened and dried again and again, faded and crusty. A pigeon that had come to the courtyard sick with an infected lung and died and dried, a bundle of faded grey and violet feathers. The custodian had given up on it a long time ago. In this part of town you could scrub the place hospital clean and an hour later it would have crap all over it again.

One night the racer looked at the cat hunched over the sandwich, pulling the meat out from the slices of bread. The racer had always loved knowing things other people didn't. He'd had little superstitions about which glove to put on first as well as bigger secrets like simultaneous girlfriends and bank accounts registered in false names. Now he had one final fact to keep all to himself. He felt like a djinn bent over a pile of gold he couldn't spend and had to protect.

The strange sensations in his body continued. It seemed to him he could feel not only the cat's fur but the texture of the sheets in his bed and the cloth of his shirt and underwear. He tried to imagine the sheathed nerves that had frayed and snapped at location C-5 reaching out to bind themselves together, the broken bone suffused with new blood and bonding in a new strong tube that would firm the softened muscles. But the sensations came and went. Sometimes he felt nothing beyond the boundary at his neck. He could see his body extending five feet beyond his ring of consciousness, but he felt no attachment to it; the body was just scenery.

Finally Hans noticed little toothmarks in the bread left behind.

"You got some kind of animal here," he said. The racer shook his head.

"You got rats, then, or a cat. I never seen a cat," said Hans.

The racer swore as the tremors began in his inert body, jouncing across his flesh. The attendant looked on as the dead muscles twitched and clenched.

"Shit," said Hans. "I didn't mean to upset you." He looked carefully around the room. Something was going on. His eyebrow lifted. The racer looked at him blankly.

Hans rode home on the subway, turning the puzzle over in his mind, and as the doors hissed open at his stop he saw a poster of the cat on the station wall, the black cat lying on the back of the sofa, and the cat's eyes burned into him, and he realized the secret the racer was keeping from him. He reached back for the conversation about the cat and the reward; he'd told the racer himself, like a fool, and ever since the cripple had been lying in bed laughing at him, keeping it from him, betraying him. His big heavy body stumbled down the platform and out into the rain.

That night the cat slept at the foot of the racer's bed, and the racer dreamed he was driving the greatest car in the world, a car that could roll up mountains and keep going up into the clouds and find unmarked highways in the air. He dreamed he was shifting the gears, stamping on the clutch, tapping the brake to ease into the turns. Then he dreamed he was in bed having the dream and his body was moving with the images, his arms and legs following the motions.

When the racer woke up he found the cat had curled up on his pillow. The early morning light made a pale wash on the bedroom wall. The cat was purring again. The racer reconnoitered his body. There was nothing below the collar-bone, blankness, just a dead bank of flesh below the covers.

The cat moved closer. The racer could hear the low rumble of the purr and feel the smooth fur on his cheek. The sensation was strong, burning. The sound of the purr filled his head. The cat's yellow-green eye was almost against his own, huge and questioning, the long curved pupil staring at him.

It seemed to the racer that the cat's gaze reached deeply into him, moving easily throughout his torn body, finding and pitying the decaying muscle, the frayed bone and nerve. He found meaning in the animal's gaze. The cat was making an offer.

"Yes," he said to the cat.

The cat lay down, his light body blocking the racer's mouth and nose.

The racer strained, the live tag end of his body still struggling to survive, one part of his mind fighting with the other. He could feel the base of his brain protesting, and to counter it he tried to push his face more firmly into the cat. The cat yawned and stretched, his muscles tensing and loosening, increasing the pressure of his body against the racer's mouth. The racer felt a sensation of heat in his throat and then sensed a jangle of music in his head, words, half thoughts and memories. The arch of a naked foot. The barking and rumbling of his car. Then a rush of pleasure, almost sexual. Behind his closed eyelids he could see spots of fiery light. Then the outer edge of a growing cone of darkness reached them and absorbed them. He fell, his body rotating in space, head over heels.

The cat felt the face underneath him go slack. He lay where he was for another hour until there was a clattering at the front door of the apartment.

The cat jumped off the bed and headed for the open window.

Hans came into the apartment with a plastic cage. He looked through the bedroom door at the dead racer, saw the pallid stillness, the empty dry open mouth, and then saw the cat crouched on the windowsill.

"Cocksucker," said Hans, and lumbered across the room. The cat turned, jumped lightly down onto the front steps of the building and ran down the street.

Seventeen

JULIA WOKE UP gradually, moving from a heavy dream to a lighter one and then to a wisp of a thought about the outdoors and small stones on a long descending path. She opened her eyes and saw the path six feet away. The sleeping bag stank of mildew and wine. Her body was stiff and her mouth tasted like mud.

She sat up and looked around at the screen of trees and bush and the damp walkway that descended beside the buried river. She felt a sudden pulse of delight. She reached out and felt the fallen leaves. Intense slickness, smoothness, decay. Barking dogs. A piercing close jangle. The cellular phone in her purse. She pulled it out, stared at it, turned it off and put it back.

Images fell into her consciousness and then quickly dissolved. Jones was somewhere to the south, stretching and yawning. He was crystalline, every hair defined, his yellow-green glossy eyes wide. He took up the centre of her mind. The city forest surrounded that, and beyond the forest were vague images of François and their house.

She began to walk along the path. The woods were dark under furrowed banks of grey cloud. The air seemed supersaturated, like a solution of water overstuffed with sugar, waiting for a disturbance of the surface to solidify it into a mass.

Julia tried to figure out the new rules as she walked. Would she have to stay in the forest? How would she eat? She'd cut herself off like a poisoned leg; or was she the body and the rest of the world the part that was separated and abandoned? Clearly there were no rules. She'd have to make her own. She felt the air flowing past her skin. It seemed she could feel the air above and around her, all the way to the fringes of space, lying gently on her body, keeping her in place. She'd always been good, had always followed the rules laid down by her mother, her school and her work, as well as the customs and understandings of what it meant to be a lady and a wife. She had always fitted into these outlines like a cut-out doll fitting her place on the page perfectly, with dresses and accessories in exact accompaniment. Now she was travelling on a wet trail far from home, a tramp, living beyond the borders.

She found a crumpled paper bag that held a piece of sausage and a half-eaten apple. Maybe she'd be able to live on what she found in the trees. She ate as she walked, biting into the brown flesh where the other mouth had stopped. Why had the person thrown the apple away? The taste filled her head.

Squirrels, roving dogs, the smell of a skunk as she moved south. The rain dropped through the trees, gathered for a moment where leaves came together; the wind bucked the little cradles and the water fell again. In clearings sometimes there was the light, quick sweep of a shower. A big curved furry back clambering into the brush: a badger? There were other people in the woods, mostly still and solitary. On a rotten log a huge man with swollen legs, gasping, his back rigid, his brown eyes folded in flesh tracking her as she passed.

His voice came in a thick whisper. "Looking for a secret?"

She stopped.

"Got a secret for you here." He seemed to be on the point of death. He was holding himself rigidly, taking little sips of breath. His lungs had been stretched into thin bags half-full of clear fluid. He was drowning himself.

She came closer, took his hand; the gluey flesh bunched and sagged. There was fungus growing on the log; the ears bent under his thick puckered thighs. The brown eyes, red rimmed, rolled at her.

The big lips smiled over tan teeth. His hand held hers. "Get it?" She tried to pull away; he held her. "Say it."

"You didn't say anything."

He took a great shuddering breath, coughed wetly and let her go. She moved down the track, looking back at him once, hearing his tender little gasps.

A skinny woman eating popcorn on a bench. A black man trudging behind a shopping cart, forcing it through the mud of the forest track, digging deep furrows, the cart filled with dirty clothes and pages of codes and conspiracies. Two wily-looking kids and then two high school girls sharing a bottle of cheap red wine, smoking, giggling. A small goateed man with big teeth, leading a brown dog on a leash. The dog sniffed her as she passed, and the small man stopped, looked at her again, choked, and said, "Aren't you—hey!"

Julia ran and the little man ran after her. His dog strained ahead, then stopped suddenly at some smell on a bush, and the little man crashed into him, fell over, smearing his bristling chin with mud. "Hey! Aren't you—" She ran on.

She conjured up François, made him trot alongside her and beg her pardon for something. He'd be panting, his shaved head glistening, his bulky body heaving along the path. He'd be justifying himself as he ran. "I never knew you were unhappy, you never told me, I never saw a thing—"

"But that's exactly it." She made him run into a thorny bush; the spikes pierced his flesh.

"What's it?"

"That's it." It was all beyond explanation, but she felt full of joy and framed with meaning. She sent him back home and to hell, still gabbling his half explanations. He'd done her no harm; he'd done nothing to her at all.

Life was piling up on François.

On one hand he was grieving and confused, and on the other he was beginning to calculate the costs, procedures and explanations involved in a divorce. The memory of Julia was already being supplanted by the solid fact of her mother. Lillian was spending most of her time in the kitchen, standing like a colossus on the groaning tiles, scooping mashed potatoes, cake, spaghetti, bagels, General Tso's chicken into her face as fast as the spoon could reach it. It seemed she was so shaken by her lost daughter and the idea of a two-million-dollar reward for a cat that she was trying to engulf his entire fortune before it could be paid.

"Are you going to come out to help us look for Julia, Mother?" he'd ask, with Kessler looking on disgusted from the hallway. But she'd keep eating in silence, her small fat-enfolded eyes watching him over her plate.

He was also dealing with an unfriendly acquisition, looping the last choking strands of a takeover around the neck of his major competitor. Fesnos sausages, dear to the southern Europeans, shot through with beads of cold fat, hard with grease. It was the culmination of a long process. Over months he'd quietly located and acquired pockets of Fesnos debt. Then he'd begun to squeeze the company, demanding payment. His agents persuaded supermarkets to move the Fesnos sausages to the bottom shelves and replace them with Friendly Pig products. The whole campaign had unfolded like an equation and the end would come quickly when the numbers became irrefutable, jeering in the faces of the Fesnos executives.

He loved that payoff. It showed how far he had come. His first takeover, when he sent the little brothers back to their beach in Hawaii, had taken place in a shabby boardroom above a stained killing room. Now he strode into the granite lobby of a modern manufacturing operation, past the cubicles of the clerical staff and the comfortable offices of the administrators, some people peeping quickly at him, others openly staring, their gazes lifting him up, filling him with joy, down the corridor lined with framed public service awards, his board nominees in a phalanx behind him, marching in unison on the linoleum, wood and carpet, through bright spaces and dim, into the boardroom where the senior staff of the Fesnos operation were gathered.

The chairman was a smooth young Fesnos with a law degree and a briefcase made of shining hide from the slaughterhouse floor; the company was diversifying, testing new uses for bone, blood and tallow. Not fast enough. François had them by the gullet.

"We are prepared to negotiate," said young Fesnos, looking at his lawyers.

François took him by the hand, looked warmly into his eyes, and said, "Not much point. It's over." And it was.

At first, the takeover went as he planned. A rustle of paper, the click of brass fastenings and the murmuring of executive consultants discussing outplacement packages with the dislodged senior executives. The white-collar staff milled in the cafeteria, waiting to learn who would be retained and who would not. But then there was a growing grumbling sound from the killing hall.

The Fesnos workers had shut down the plant and refused to let François' men inside. The noise from the floor was getting louder and clearer. It was a mass chant: "Fuck you! Fuck you!"

There was a metallic ringing as the workers hit the steel framework of the line with their knives and airguns.

The law gave him clear possession and control. But the clanging and crashing and the chant grew louder. François and his executives marched away.

Goddamnit: he had to wrestle for every inch now. His luck was out. He stood at the gates and listened to his chief lawyer read aloud the relevant clauses in the labour law. The Fesnos workers shouted and threw steaks, ground meat and chops over the security barricades. It was all on the news that night, with Ivan asking François questions in a rain of raw sausage.

"Two million dollars!" yelled the Fesnos men. They wanted for themselves what François would pay for his cat. "Two million dollars! We're not animals!"

"It's a question of principle," said François into Ivan's microphone.

"What principle is that?"

"Of management's right to deploy resources as management deems fit."

"I don't understand."

"Two million dollars!"

"There are rules and procedures. All I am asking is respect for established rules and procedures."

"Can you tell me," asked Ivan, the lens poking over his right shoulder, "exactly where your wife is now?"

"Fuck you! Fuck you!" yelled the butchers through the fence.

How did Teuti know? The search was still private; her picture had just gone out to the police divisions. "She has gone out on some little independent project of her own. Something to do with the cat, I think."

"Fuck you!" shouted a slaughterer, thin and watery-eyed, baying like a basset through the steel mesh.

"Is it true you've reported her to the police as a missing person?"

"Purely in a precautionary way, yes."

"Her last known whereabouts?"

"On the edge of the park system just opposite the lion enclosure."

"Do you think she is trying to retrace your cat's steps?"

"She is upset, very upset."

He felt weak and foolish, and angry at Julia; she'd left their superb life for a walk in the woods?

"So what's the future for François Will and Friendly Pig, with this kind of labour disruption here?"

"There is nothing as satisfying as making good food at a good price for good people," said François. "The people will decide. Friendly Pig means value for money. Fesnos— well, look around you." On television screens around the city the watery-eyed slaughterer shrieked. And Friendly Pig sausages flew off the carts, each customer making a statement of emotional solidarity with François Will and order and fairness, chewing the hot cylinders of pressed meat as they walked in the rain.

Julia trotted on through the city forest, living on scraps, dozing under blankets of piled damp leaves, finding sheltered caves and niches for her toilet, the image of Jones gathering intensity within her. She wanted the touch of his fur under her fingers. He was so pure.

Kessler was going after the boss's wife.

He was going to track her. He had read all the books about survival in the forest, and he was pretty sure he could do it. He saw himself living on the land up north somewhere, setting homemade wooden traps for beaver and marten, fishing with spears and deer tendons made into twine. He could tell north from south from the way moss grew on an exposed tree trunk, and that was a start.

Kessler packed his bush gear: collapsible tent, ground sheet, hatchet, twine, compass, matches, flashlight, collapsible cooking stove with collapsible frying pan and coffee pot, desiccated food, maps and clothing. He drove to the edge of the zoo and lumbered down the path toward the city forest. He was ready to live on the land for weeks and follow every bent twig and crushed blade of grass until he tracked his quarry to her lair. Then a ravening Westmoreland terrier came out of nowhere and began to savage his knee. He fell on a tree limb lying on the path and broke his left leg in two places. The terrier tore into his packsack. Kessler lay sombrely on the ground and felt stunning waves of pain shoot up from his ankle through his knee and thigh. This kind of thing never happened in the books.

The germs woke up from their exhausted lassitude in the holding ponds; they spread through the city's pipes, changing as they went. Some mutations died at once, but others found harbour in the nooks and coves of the underground network and evolved into forms of life never seen before: hook-headed microscopic monsters that attached themselves to intestines and drilled through the walls into the bloodstream, bringing their hosts to a sudden dead stop with septic shock. Some of the new germs chanced into specialties, combining with waste pharmaceutical products in the water and mutating into selectively potent microbes, making some people ill, leaving other people alone, attacking the old and the very young but leaving the rest, or the reverse, fastening on strong people at the height of their strength and turning their insides into glue.

The process took weeks. There was unexplained illness and then lines of cadavers lying in wrapped lines in hospital corridors. Then one strain of the germs began to dominate, assimilating or devouring the others, taking command of the foaming, lively broth in the city's pipes.

It was a seven-headed germ with extended talons and a semi-circular cutting edge at its rear, and it found refuge in the stomach linings of dogs. The larger dogs managed to absorb and neutralize the attack, but smaller dogs could not. The bacteria wormed their way into the inner parts of miniature schnauzers, Scottish terriers, toy poodles, cocker spaniels and scored their stomach linings with tiny bleeding cuts. The dogs became ravenously, insatiably hungry. As the collies and German shepherds looked on in confusion and fear, the small dogs turned on their owners, snapping at their fingers, lunging for their knees, sounding high howls at the windows, scrabbling to get out. Suddenly the city had herds of feral dachshunds, corgis, Maltese and bichons, their legs twinkling as they ran along the alleys, killing and eating whatever they could catch; squirrels died, their blood staining tiny muzzles, and cats ran from the nimble red-eyed Mexican hairless that bounded up trees after them to the height of six feet, her little lips white with foam. Ivan Teuti, reporting live from City Hall, had to kick a foaming cockapoo that was going for his groin.

Ivan was getting used to his celebrity. The glimmer of the lights followed him wherever he went. In a restaurant there was a mumble of recognition. The chef peered over the half doors of the kitchen. There was a swirl at the busboy station, and extra baskets of bread and butter arrived at his table. The meal came covered with shredded petals arranged in a lovely circle. After he paid the cheque the manageress took his arm and escorted him formally to the door, and one of the waitresses joined him in bed when her shift ended at midnight.

It was like the old game of snakes and ladders. He had found a hidden ladder from the bottom of the board almost to the top, and it allowed him to climb through all the barriers of money, class and personality. He brought a friendly intensity to the screen, and that made him a friend and even more to millions of people. Women came to the studio, sat in the outer lobby and sent in notes proclaiming their passion. All this had nothing to do with him, really.

He still loved the texture of the television world, the smoothness of the monitors, the steel cameras, the swooping, certain movements of the lenses. Everything was metallic, even the eyeshadow and the nose rings on the floor director who counted him down to air with diminishing fingers. It was a hard bright place. Heel clicks and the snap of tape-cassette boxes into slots, the whine of rewind, cold lights, hard shadows, and in the centre of it white-smiling, white-eyed Ivan Teuti.

A drunken producer, a broken man with a rabbit-pink nose, taught Ivan a few little tricks to squeeze emotion from someone he was interviewing. Half finish a sentence, let the ending trail away—the guest would be terrified by the silence and hurry to complete the thought, often adding something he'd been guarding. A disapproving or disappointed look when the camera was pointed the other way might tell a subject that the interview was failing, and he'd spill a secret to regain Ivan's respect. "They'll do anything to make you like them," the producer said, swaying in the waiting room as the makeup artist touched Ivan's face with powder. "Here you're Mummy, you're Daddy, you're home. They'll do anything to make you happy."

There was some pocket of his personality that gave the impression of amiability and kindly intelligence, but at his core he was still ice and stone, whirling alone deep in space. When he tried to climb into his own mind he found a separation there as well: the two halves of his brain had divided his personality into dark and light. The successful, pleasant televised image was taking on its own life outside him, and before long he would be left with nothing but the sour, tight, ravenous child.

Ivan invited François to the studio, making the invitation sound like a compliment. His instincts sensed a secret in François that might just come out in sweating, stammering close-up.

François was patted with makeup. Ivan poured him a cup of mineral water with his own hands. They sat in two low black leather chairs, against a black background: limbo. The camera went hot.

"Tell me again where you think your wife might be tonight."

François blinked, jerked. "She's . . . taking her own approach. Making an independent effort on this." Ivan's eyes, suddenly warm and large, waiting for him, the silence growing in force. "She's . . . not part of the organized effort. . . ." Silence. François could feel the camera frame squeezing his face, looking into his mind.

Ivan nodded, waited. The producer's voice slurred at him: *Shut up now. Here it comes.*

"The fact is I don't know where she is. She just left day

before yesterday, just left, disappeared. I don't know. The police don't know."

Ivan looked intensely sympathetic. "You must be terribly worried."

"It's lonely, it's— I'm afraid for her."

"Strange, in a way, that you should be paying for a cat you've lost, when what you've really lost—"

"Oh, yes. Oh, yes, I'd pay—"

"For her?"

"Yes, a reward—"

"Double?"

"Oh, yes, double. She's my wife."

"Four million dollars, then. Plus the two for the cat."

"Yes, yes." François was beginning to weep, partly in humiliation, partly in anger, partly in relief.

"You're a generous, kind-hearted man, and—" Ivan turned to the camera "—I think I can say the city won't rest until we find your wife."

"Julia—"

"Julia. And the cat, of course." And as the camera pulled back, Ivan Teuti was giving François a tissue for his tears.

The line of grey limestone buildings guarded a great green square, the main campus of the university. Young men ran for whirling plastic discs. Dogs' heads made of concrete watched from the eaves of the buildings, their teeth and tongues exposed to the wind.

In the basement of the dental school, dogs, apes, rats and cats sat in their steel cages. In the huge room above them under the smeared skylights other animals lay strapped in rows of dental chairs. The first-year students had to practice, and there were things not even rotting drunks would put up with. Computers didn't give them a feel for the mouth, you couldn't get a good grip on a plastic model, and when they tried to examine each other they'd wince at the pick and jerk away from the drill. So animals it was. You learned a lot about the manipulation of fine strands of steel when you put a set of braces on a dog, a monkey or a rabbit.

Gracie sat in a dentist's chair on a raised stage at the end of the room. It was a little like being on stage at the club, since she could feel the intense stare of the students, but here she had all her clothes on and there was no music, just the rolling baritone of the big bearded man, Dr. Levering, as he leaned over her, pointing out the wonderful features of her teeth. A slight malocclusion had required a slight pressure correction, but after only a month the braces were ready to come off, and as you can see, the results— the results are classic, absolutely perfect! This is what we work for! This is the ideal! A little camera transmitted the image of her open mouth onto a large screen above Levering's head. Around the room the students looked at Gracie's mouth, then into the little gaping mouths of their sleeping animals.

Levering was talking about the romance of the mouth. He said you couldn't stand to be a dentist if you didn't appreciate the poetry and architecture of the mouth, in particular the teeth, which were evidence of evolutionary genius and possibly divine design. The second-year students had already warned the freshmen about this, but there was no way out: the madman was head of the department, a lunatic for teeth, and slept on a cot next to his lab animals. Gracie found his voice soothing.

"The mouth is a warm, wet tube very much like the lower intestine, a kind of echo, in fact, or satire—in any case, equivalent engineering, interesting in its own way with its special receptors for taste and touch but remarkably conventional when compared to the teeth, the jewels of the mammal. They are exposed, improved, hardened skeleton. They are the leading edge of survival. In their finest form, in the pure carnivore, they act as both weapon and processor. They are the first tool, pre-mammalian, our common inheritance. In the omnivore, as here—open a little wider, dear—they are adapted and a little deteriorated, but still exquisite, exquisite constructions of pulp, nerve, blood and lovely enamel, irrigated and cleaned with saliva, fed with blood, groomed by the tongue, the entire thing harmonious, lovely in design. But piteously vulnerable to social changes and alterations in food patterns. Betrayed, in the human species, by developments in crops, technology and taste."

Gracie's mouth was braced open with a shining clamp. She swallowed. Her throat convulsed enormously over her head.

"Look, ladies and gentlemen, at the tiny pink plush of the gum line, the sensational seal of the flesh against the tooth. This is the ground on which the purity of the dental design fights its battles with the subtle corruptions of the modern diet. Sugar. Refined sugar. Sweet colas. Infiltrating the dental apparatus, subverting the border, prying the flesh away from the tooth with beachheads of degeneration. Even in our Gracie, here, our perfectly toothed northern girl—all right, Gracie?—you must be vigilant for tiny striations, the beginnings of decay—a tiny roughened spot here on the bicuspid, the wonderfully formed bicuspid, which might well, in time, deepen, soften and in the end rot. And die."

The students poked at the little mouths and giggled.

Gracie thought back to the herd of cows in her father's barn up north. Their flat, large, slow-grinding teeth. Their breath was steamy and sweet in the morning air, nothing but hay, grass and water moving through them, and the warm musty smell of the cow shit that fell to the concrete floor. She had hated the dead weight of the slop buckets with the thin steel handles cutting ridges in her fingers, but maybe the barn had been a good place after all, nothing bad in it but the people. Years ago those cows took their long, rattling ride down the highway in the ventilated truck, the wind from the road whipping across their flanks. Their eyes would roll and their tails bang against the restraints, but they would be crowded in too tightly to do anything but stand and moan. Then the chute at the other end. Her father poking a slim envelope into the pocket of his overalls.

"This is a pure mouth, undefiled," said Levering, putting his big hand on her shoulder. "Think about the ordinary mouth, with wretched gaps, piteous and ugly stains, deep grey smears where the dentist has packed in the cement. If we were artists we could restore all mouths to Gracie's state. But we are warriors. We fight our battles and we leave our ugly scars."

The students, bored to hysteria, were passing notes and whispering behind their hands. Some were smooching in the dim light at the back of the hall.

"Prehistoric man, yes, yes! Had teeth like this. Prehistoric man had a perfect mouth! It was the mixture of the diet, the commingling of grain, fruit, plant and meat that set up a perturbation and a confusion in the dental array! Pure diet is the only answer! Grasses, bark for roughage, reeds and flowers! This is Gracie's diet! This is the food of the future!"

Gracie was mostly a cheeseburger-and-fries kind of person, but life was full of unexpected developments. Flowers sounded like the right kind of food for a star.

On the roof, in the rain, a man and a woman crouched beside the skylight. Their feet slipped and skidded in the wet dead leaves. The woman had a camera. They recorded the images of the lecture room through the smeared glass: the lines of animals, the dental picks and drills and the little engines that shook the amalgam for the filling, Levering treading the stage, Gracie's huge mouth, her glistening tongue, the animals' jaws clamped open, the white jackets of the students, the slack paws and drooping tails, the white glowing lights.

Eighteen

ALICIA REMBUS WAS an enormous pain to her family and friends. She was querulous and self-righteous, her femininity aged and set like bone. She was full of shallow emphatic opinions, fat, pious, given to faints and seizures that would bring her crashing to the floor, sparking brief hope in the others present. She would then start upward, fanning herself with an open palm, a pitiable widow, a miser, the victim of a thousand illnesses and plots.

She'd had a flicker of madness in the afternoon rain, passing the park. A faint recollection of a sudden treat with her long-dead husband, fireman Bob, with the open laugh that had blunted her spite before the Lord took him from her, a memory of ice cream: maple walnut. Eaten out of a waxed cardboard tub with a flat wooden paddle, preferable to the ice cream sold in the stores, since no lady would eat a cone, the movements of the mouth being vulgar. She'd fished in her purse for a dollar, grumbling at the price, but given it to the little Chink who ran the cart, picked up her dish, spooned a tiny morsel of maple walnut into her bitter mouth, then pitched forward flat on her face unconscious, the cup landing in the running gutter.

She languished, her fever coming and going, the nurses and technicians in the hospital monitoring the balance of her salts and the progression of her acids. She murmured from time to time: "Don't . . . don't . . . put it away. . . . Dry that." Her brain was disordered by the pressure of the blood supplied by her narrowed arteries; her mental pathways were jumbled, and she dreamed of black angels with needles in their arms, Bob as God pissing on the world's fires, his organ thrust out in her dreams just as bold as you please, and the cat they'd been looking for, constantly patrolling, stopping, sitting, licking himself, one long leg stretched out, rising, pacing, his pink paws pattering on the tissue inside her head, the white and grey tissues yellowing with age, she could see, like a newspaper, the nervelets and ganglia tangling, the cat pushing and licking them, trying to put the disorder right.

Seven days in, she sat bolt upright and asked for rice pudding.

Her breath was restored after a week of rattling and wheezing, and her appetite was whole, and moreover she'd undergone a change of personality. She was suddenly and very strangely mild, secure and fulfilled. The relatives who had been quarrelling about the size and expense of her casket were astonished; it was an unknown Alicia, no longer the bitch queen of the family but polite, considerate, amusing.

"I walked on the edge of death," Alicia said as she left the hospital, "and the cat pulled me back. The cat showed me where I went wrong. I am reborn."

When Ivan Teuti came to interview Alicia Rembus, he was happy to find a shrine in her living room with the cat's picture on it and sticks of incense propped up in empty water glasses smoking in the darkened room. Alicia sat before it with her eyes lifted up to Jones's black blank face.

"What happened to you exactly, Mrs. Rembus?"

"I was dying. I saw a great light like a door opening, and

I heard the lovely music of a thousand voices, and then I saw the cat smiling on me."

"Did it say anything—meow, or what?"

"It said, 'Alicia, this is not your time. Your family needs you. I will protect you and keep you strong.' And then I woke up." She ate rice pudding for the camera to prove it.

Ivan looked at her calm, kindly face and thought of his own lost mother, on the run, raving at her God, sending Him letters, copies to her husband, copies to her son: *Jesus, protect him, put Your hand on him, lead him to truth, because he is a criminal, a killer, savage. You know what he can do. . . .*

Ivan and his cameraman drove up and down the wet streets doing interviews with frustrated searchers. The cat hunters were covering most of the city now. The drunks and the easily bored had gotten tired and gone home, but now there were worshipful pilgrims alongside the tough and hungry men turning over the garbage cans. There was a report that an American billionaire had offered a reward of ten million dollars for the cat's skin, which would be the centrepiece of a jacket for his wife. Another that a group of sorcerers would pay fifteen million to use the cat's hide, teeth, blood, claws and eyes in their spells. Ivan put them all on the air, carefully identifying them as rumours and unconfirmed, but nonetheless, as the drunken producer in the control room pointed out, sexy as hell.

Judd cruised the south end of 17, the wasted half-deserted shabby bottom, past the warehouses where runaways squatted in dark rough lofts, past the factories and the rotting houses along the beach. He used to know most of the people inside. He could summon up their pictures beside their addresses, along with the records of their offences as he drove by: 17 Porter Street, Hudson, counterfeiter, mediocre twenties turned out on a press in the basement; 19, nothing known; 21, nothing known, 23 Porter, incest suspected but never proved; 25, always complaining about 23's basset hound, who hallooed in the middle of the night, dreaming of buried fox kittens; 31, break and enter, second-storey guy, agile, rubbery, adept at getting through tiny gaps in steel bars, sometimes so tiny he couldn't get the stuff out—they'd find paintings slashed and china smashed and a frustrated pool of piss on the wooden floor by the window.

Or was that 25? The faces merged and blended. His files were jumbled, mental pages stuck together. Who had died? Whose child had grown up, gone to law school, taken up arguing for the wise guys?

He parked by the library beside the dental school. He liked to sit in one of the damp leather chairs and look at the lines of books with their black-and-white certainties. Shelves of facts and people captured for all time. The inside of his head was fading and failing.

The librarians liked him and let him drink his coffee in the chair and watch the students, along with the old people filling up their days, the puzzled immigrants poking around for books they could make sense of. The library was a place of pause and truce. The smell of unwashed bodies, the polite poor.

The evening light was fading, the puddles in the street shining with gasoline colours, oily greens and pinks.

There was a staircase that led up to the library's reference section; he looked up and caught a movement, a flick of a cylindrical body, a reptilian tail disappearing up the steps. It didn't fit. The certainties of the library faded. Another mystery.

Judd heaved himself out of the chair, trudged to the staircase and up the steps. He felt like an old bobby on the beat, rattling doorknobs. It was dark in the reference section, with pools of dim yellow light on the oak tables where students looked up the population of Suriname and the atomic weight of lead. Heads with eyeglasses swivelled to look at him and swivelled back.

A sound, a rasp of skin on concrete, near the back, past the stacks of encyclopedias and collected political debates. A slither and a choking sound. He moved forward.

Gracie was sitting in a straight chair, her head held still with clamps. It looked as if someone was torturing her, and his hand went to his holster, but then he saw the big bearded man talking to her gently. The bearded man was peering into Gracie's open mouth, then turning to a screen and spinning through yards and miles of open-mouthed images, framed in skin, black, white, olive and sometimes fringed with hair, but mouths and teeth, some striped with fillings, others unimproved, some with gaping cavities, some split or shattered, some quite well shaped but with some trivial imperfection, none, the bearded man was saying, "none like yours, Gracie. None as good as you. You're the best I've seen in forty years, the very best." He was reviewing slides of every known mouth in the dental school's database, making absolutely sure that at the end of decades of searching he'd found the only truly perfect mouth on the planet. It would be a sensation in the dental journals.

The corners of her clamped mouth twitched. She was trying to smile.

Judd turned and walked down the stairs, the blood pounding in his head. Everything he thought he knew it seemed he didn't know at all. The world was strange and he hadn't explored it at all. He knew nothing. He was a sap, a sucker. And Gracie was in another world, her pretty mouth opened for the bearded man. She'd kissed Judd and given him comfort. But the bearded man called her perfect, and Judd could see her eyes wet with loving tears. The street was misty, fog trailing along the concrete, hiding the houses, hiding everything.

When he got home in the morning he said to his wife, "Fuck it, I'm moving to the basement."

"What do you mean? Why?" His daughters behind her shoulder.

"I'm just moving." He felt as though there was a slimy, smoky stink coming from him; if he let them get too close they'd smell it. He threw his clothes, toothbrush and shaving kit into some cardboard boxes and carried them downstairs, where he set up the folding camp bed he used when he went travelling with his daughters. The basement was unfinished. He dressed by the pale light of a naked bulb and washed in the laundry tub. He could hear his family moving around above his head and he yearned for them, but after a couple of days of hearing parts of phrases through the wooden beams he suspected they were laughing up there and probably at him, the big stumping stupid gorilla in the basement.

On the third morning when he woke up he heard nothing from above. They had gone out early, and after an hour he figured out why. It was the old woman's funeral. They hadn't even woken him, just let him snore away in his basement. He reached the cemetery late, half shaved, misbuttoned, and watched them lower his aunt into the long hole. His daughters looked sweet, and his wife looked faded and angry. A cop from 17, a kid on traffic detail, regarded him with what seemed like suspicion: why did he seem so seedy? Most criminals made stupid mistakes, and this was one, this tardy, slovenly appearance. Now they'd keep an eye on him, looking for mysteries and out-of-character behaviour. Maybe they'd talk to his wife. If the will came in with his name as beneficiary there would be a further check. Maybe they'd find the ashes of the gloves he'd used and extract the remnants of his fingerprints or his DNA. Maybe some drifting bum had seen him crouch and fire the match. Maybe they were all watching him, waiting to make their case.

The cat's hip was worse than it had ever been, and now there was a new intrusion, a slight thickening of the outer surface of his left eye. He shook his head to clear his sight, but the slight coarsening of his vision remained. He was limping through the rain, the moisture clotting his fur, using the minimal cover of the gutter. He could still feel the pull of the healing plant, but it was wavering, as though the plant itself was ill.

Suddenly he felt a strong tug from inside an open door

to his right. The same kind of healing call, slightly changed, less pure but still promising, and much closer than the plant he had been searching for. He opened his mouth and used the taste/smell organ at the base of his tongue to lap and winnow the air. The pull grew stronger. He edged around the doorway, encountered a steel gate with four inches of space at the bottom and squeezed underneath it.

There were rows of plants on high wooden counters around the large room. The one he wanted was at the near end, beside the wall. The jump was much too great, but there was a wooden box beside the counter. He lunged up heavily, missed his footing, slumped sideways, clung with his front claws and pulled himself up on the crate. Then he gathered himself and leapt onto the counter.

One of the plants toppled and fell to the floor. Its pot cracked. He froze at the noise and then moved on, picking his way heavily through the dense rows of foliage. Just before he reached the end of the row, he began to detect something strange in the smell from the plant that was calling him. It wasn't the one that could save him but something close, a cousin, a harsh and primitive relative with some helpful properties but no cure. He felt a sudden blackness inside, a sad hungry disappointment, but he gathered the strength to move forward, to reach out for the tough leaves before him and begin to chew.

It made him feel a little better. The hip had started to throb after the misstep on the box, and he could feel the juice of the plant smoothing out the twists in his flesh. The mist in front of his eye began to clear a little.

There was a moving figure on the other side of the

room, far enough away that it posed no threat. He watched it without curiosity, continuing to chew the leaves and feeling the pain recede. He could hear faint music, a piano and a violin, and the fall of water.

Levering was tending his plants, misting and pruning. He hated the synthetic fluids used for freezing tissue; he was on the track of a new, natural poultice that would numb the ache in dental nerves when they were being attacked by caries. He'd used a little of a primitive version on Gracie's wound, and it had reduced the pain but left a little residual redness that he disliked. He was finishing the smaller collections on the table when the pot crashed to the ground. He looked up briefly and went back to his myrtle, hyssop and walnut shoots.

The plant room was next to the dental classroom; the great skylight swept over both. The man and the woman with the camera returned for four days, documenting the lectures with the sleeping animals and the routines with the plants on the great benches below the glass. Their lens caught the image of the cat as it sucked the leaves.

A squad of cat hunters had picked up the raccoon near the racer's house and brought it to Ivan Teuti. There was no reward, but since the raccoon or one a lot like it had been seen with the cat, the capture got them on television. The camera swung across the line of intent faces as Ivan asked them about the animal in the cage.

"Dirty bugger, excuse me, hard to catch, a biter—"

"Real mean. Ernie here got a gash on his thumb, from the claws, I think–"

"Hissing and stamping, vicious."

The raccoon sat on her haunches in the steel cage and rubbed her little hands together.

Ivan Teuti spoke to the camera. "Is it right, do you think, to believe that animals have friendships? Is it possible this raccoon is a comrade, an associate or protector of the missing Jones? And if you think, as many people do, that Jones has secret or magical powers, do you also think our raccoon shares them or has powers of its own? Certainly there are many parts of this story that just . . . defy . . . explanation. We'll be taking calls about that, right after this."

The television station's phone number flashed up on the screen briefly. Ivan was visible in the control room on three cameras at the same time, his face, his body and the view over his shoulder. He looked equally graceful in each one. He had no bad side. His clear, clean skin shone on the screen. His smile was perfect. He was more real on the screen than off it.

Nineteen

THE RAIN STARTED the day after the fire at the Massie house and continued, sometimes light and sometimes gushing from the sky. The man who drove the backhoe at the graveyard cursed; hard to see through the plastic windshield and hard to keep the holes tidy in weather like this.

Donalda Massie had left instructions that her body be placed in a cardboard box for the convenience of the handlers and committed to the ground in that temporary casing. Then the grave should be filled in loosely and watered so that the organisms in the earth would be encouraged to begin their work. She believed she would be released and forwarded for union with the moons of Jupiter only when her physical body was consumed. When her last molecule entered the last worm, her spirit would rise out of the mud, through the smoke and rain, up with increasing, eager speed through the thin air of the outer atmosphere, along the dust-pocked corridors of space, scorched by the sun and finally, in serenity, combine with Europa, the sweetest moon of all.

Her will proceeded to the distribution of her estate. Judd and his family got nothing. The money went to Barney the botanist for services rendered. Donalda had laughed to herself as she wrote that, imagining stammering Barney explaining this sudden good fortune to his wife. There was also a donation to the society for the protection of animals, which was to use it to care for her cats until the last one died, and to use the residue for other good works. There were no surviving cats.

Judd was half angry and half relieved. He didn't have to deal with increased suspicion in the division house, although he thought he already saw raised eyebrows and narrowed eyes when he passed, and there was still the stench of fuel he thought the others could smell on him. But he was furious at the dead woman. He remembered the hundreds of lost hours sitting in her living room smiling and paying attention to her animal and astronomical fancies. Either her mind was so skunked that she forgot about him and the girls when she came to make her will or she had been malicious for years, laughing at him while he sat dutifully in that old stinky house staring at the stained wallpaper. And again and again there came back to him the image of the dodging cat, with its one white foreleg, his redemption flicking around the corner and away. Two million dollars to buy his family out of the city, or at least fifteen thousand to fill up the snitch fund. Gone, just gone. So close, and gone.

His wife's footsteps sounded over him at night as he lay under the bare lightbulb, an irritated clicking that drove needles into his head. His two girls laughed together, their voices coming faintly through the ceiling. The sounds would come back to him from time to time as he drove the city's alleys looking for the cat.

A huge oval pool of low-pressure air had settled over the city, and at night the rain was constant. It spattered on his windshield, so heavily at times that the wipers couldn't clear it and he was driving blind. He didn't slow down. His car sent out its own message of authority, enough to make any pedestrian or driver keep his distance. Under the streetlights the young prostitutes ambled and posed. He was on the Baby Stroll, where children from the outer suburbs and far-off towns came to earn their livings in the big city. They walked like the models they watched on television, one foot swinging in front of the other, hips curving out, their faces blank and their eyes staring.

For a moment he thought he saw his older daughter with her elbows cocked in the rain, her little breasts thrust out, but it was another girl, a skinny redhead with padding in her shirt. The car's fan blew damp air over his forehead. He realized the girl on the street looked like his wife when they first met. He had loved her proud, demanding manner. This girl would be the same way: teasing her guy, cutting him down, then making it up to him with a little pat on the top of the head.

He came into the strip bar, looking for his usual place at the back, but this time the head waiter intercepted him, showed him to a place beside the runway. A girl with intense pink hair on her head and between her legs was finishing her third dance, her rosy body a yard from his face. He knew he was at the goofs' table, reserved for visiting conventioneers and crazy fat boys from the suburbs with rolls in their pockets, the suckers who would buy the house champagne. He had crossed another line now, from cop to rube, but he felt too weak to move, and suddenly there was Gracie, stripping off her robe and looking at him.

The deep bass line and the drum thump banged on his breastbone and shook the belted flab under his shirt. He could feel his revolver near his armpit, sitting on a pulse point, throbbing. The orange and green lights spun.

Gracie turned and dropped her G-string. There was no snake. She was back to working alone.

Julia found a sodden newspaper with the headline announcing the reward for her. She sat in the bush and tried to figure out what it meant to be worth four million dollars. How should she feel? She pulled out the cellular phone and switched it on.

Ivan Teuti saw the identifying label on the phone screen and answered on the first ring. "Where are you, Mrs. Will?"

"In the woods."

"Can I come and see you?"

"I don't know."

"I'll come without a camera, if you want. Just me. We can talk. Where are you exactly?"

She looked up at the buildings that towered over the trees. "By a big place with an insurance sign on it—V and P? On the path in from there."

"I'll be right there."

It took him fifteen minutes. She watched him from a screen of leaves, walking back and forth, peering into the forest. "Miss? Ma'am?" He was alone.

Suddenly she was overcome by a convulsion of sadness. He found her on the ground, dirty, disconsolate.

"What is it? Why did you run?"

"I lost my cat." Weeping again.

There was a sudden rustle of wet leaves. Three small dogs broke into the little clearing, stopped and stared at them. Two cocker spaniels and a corgi, their brown eyes rolling, showing the whites, their lips parted to expose their teeth, their heads low like hyenas. Three treble growls.

"I think we'd better move along now," said Ivan, and she stood up, staring at the little dogs.

Ivan picked up a stick and swept it ahead of them as they moved. The dogs yelped and dodged. The border collie approached in a flash of brown and white, his cold eye fixed on Julia's leg. Ivan caught him with the blunt end of the stick. He shrieked. The two spaniels moved back.

"Fucking little dogs have gone crazy all of a sudden," said Ivan. The collie tried again, jumping this time. Ivan caught it again with the stick, forcing the ragged end down the animal's throat. He had a sudden flashing memory of the little mouse. The dog choked and howled and then ran. The spaniels followed, looking back once or twice in fear and hunger.

"You can't stay here," said Ivan. "There are these things and then there is the money. If the gangs get on to you, there could be a big fight."

"I'll go with you."

They got into his car. Ivan pulled out onto the wide boulevard beside the park. The vendors were closing down; too much rain. A gang of hunters with bags and nets passed by, peering into the park. He smelled the earth of the park on her and the sour scent of her clothes.

"Listen. Where do you want to go? Home?"

"No."

"He's really sad, you know, and shaken up; he's put out the reward for you."

"No, I don't want to go there."

"Family?"

"Not for this."

"I can take you to my place. I mean—"

"We could go there."

The big store windows with the fat statues, the great white-and-blue china bowls and wooden boxes. A mad terrier paced down the middle of the road, its tongue falling out of its mouth. Ivan's insides were jumping with his good luck. He draped his overcoat over her head and ran her into the apartment building like a criminal avoiding the cameras.

François's lawyers got an injunction to clear a path at the Fesnos plant. The workers ignored it. There was an intermittent sound of splintering glass and tearing metal from inside the factory and shouts at the security guards who walked the fence. Anti-meat activists collided at the fence with union pickets. A squad of evangelical Christians marched the perimeter, proclaiming that only Jesus could settle the matter. A police camera crew recorded the movements of a camera crew from the anarchist media group. The watery-eyed man leapt constantly at the barricade, shouting, "Fuck you! Fuck you!"

François gave interviews. The reporters only wanted to know about his wife and his cat.

Lillian watched him on the little television set in the kitchen. Her jaw moved constantly. She was worried about her daughter and angry at the insane reward put up by her son-in-law, but those emotions now seemed to have moved away from her and were kept at a bearable distance by the rough slick taste of peanut butter, the sweet tang of cola and more than anything else the greasy, firm savour of Friendly Pig sausages, which she ate directly from the packaging, right out of the refrigerator. The thick meaty paste seemed to be a solid token of the fortune that protected her.

There was an arrangement of mirrors in the plant room that caught sunlight from a recessed window and diffused it around the space. The cat woke up early in the morning in the developing glow. It brought out the tiny lattices of veins in the young leaves and slowly drew apart the petals of the flowers.

The cat felt better than he had in days. There were still intrusions in his haunch and eye, but the temporary plant cure had made them supple and drained their heat.

He jumped all the way from the counter to the concrete floor. He felt strong. He walked slowly to the end of the room.

Two big hands reached out from a line of shrubs and seized him. He yowled. Levering picked him up, brought him to shoulder height, held him in his left hand and pushed back his lips. The cat's white teeth shone. Levering smiled.

Twenty

THE FAT MAN with the lungs full of water had managed to heave himself up from his log and trudge out of the park to the street. He was heading for the hospital, even though the place pissed him off; they were always on him about diet, exercise, taking his medicine. He could feel the rain and the wind picking up. The air was cool, and his big face began to sting.

He weighed as much as a large calf, and much of the weight was fluid. He had only two little pockets of lung tissue to breathe with; the rest was submerged. He was panting. He felt a kind of undertow, as if the air and the street were dragging at him, trying to bring him down.

The water inside him moved up again, and his heart began to break its rhythm. He saw a sudden ragged flash of light and whatever was pulling him strengthened and yanked, and he lost his footing and toppled dreamily like an ocean liner upending and slipping into the deep sea.

Five miles up and thousands of miles north there was a sudden skew in the river of air that flowed east from the storms of the Pacific. The cold stream pierced the bulkhead of temperate gas and lanced south, drawing millions of tons of heavy freezing air after it.

The arctic front rolled down the great eared bay and spread out across the forests, dropping the temperature a sudden, shocking thirty degrees, raising flocks of birds that screamed at the sudden pressure inside their heads and flapped off toward the south. Animals that had crouched for two weeks in the rain suddenly sprang out into the new snow that fell in clots and swaths, filling up gullies and burying young trees.

The fat man died two hours after the leading edge of the cold front passed through the city. The seasons were dislocated. Early September and the temperature kept falling. The pools of stagnant water in the street rimed over and froze through. Lights dimmed as a hundred thousand furnaces kicked into flame. Cars slewed and glided, rotating at high speed on frozen highways, tapping and slamming into each other; in the dusk the light and heat from the collisions glowed on the traffic as it moved by. Hospital lobbies filled up. Bodies were jammed together with arms hanging strangely, jaws crooked and twisted, blue patches around their eyes.

The little dogs ran on, snapping at ankles, their claws tapping on the ice. In the sewers the musty waters slowed and turned to slush and the vast armies of germs began to die; their tiny bodies floated to the surface and formed a deep tan sludge that moved heavily toward the lake.

Julia stayed in Ivan Teuti's apartment for three days. The small rooms comforted her. During the afternoon she lay in the living room, and a regular glowing beat of red and green from a neon sign far down the block seemed to fall in step with her pulse. She felt synchronized with the city, floating twenty feet above the street. She could feel its cooling stone and steel in her bones.

The first night she slept alone in the living room. She tried to remember her bedroom in the big house. The sight and feel of it were fading. Glass, tile and François' round, big-shouldered body pressing down. He had chased her with furious intensity. She remembered his flushed face in the restaurant. He had cut off her exits, corralled her, checkmated her. She'd yielded without passion on the implicit condition that the courtship would continue forever. Then he'd put her in his pocket and turned his burning desires back to his business. She'd sold herself to a man who took his payment back.

Ivan and Julia did not touch. She walked around the apartment, sniffing his light odour. It was strong in his closet and in the bed, very strong in the soiled laundry hamper, mild and elusive in the kitchen but present all the same. She was trying to decide. She tried on his clothes and underwear, took an inventory of the scents and lotions in his bathroom, wrote out a list of the books and music he owned.

He watched her as she hunted his life through the apartment and waited for her to make up her mind. He kept no letters that she could find. He had no business files. His computer was almost blank. He had no pets, no hobbies, no correspondents, no pictures.

The Buddha finally decided the question of Ivan. She found the little red-brown wooden statue in a pile of coins beside his bed. It was out of place, a little token of his interior life. It was double faceted, sentimental but a symbol of yearning—emotional, even spiritual. He was the kind of man, she thought, who would keep this dimension of himself cooped up in a little carved figure, private and even furtive. She picked up the little statue. It shone in her hand.

She tried to imagine him in her previous life. She'd keep

him upstairs in a tiny wooden room secretly constructed in the rafters of the big house. She'd wait until François fell asleep, his fleshy lips parted, air whistling through his throat, and then she'd creep upstairs and open the little iron-bound door to the little priest's garret where she kept Ivan. But the two lives wouldn't come together. When she opened the little door his bed would be empty.

He had no serviceable memories to tell her and had to make some up. "My father was a doctor, a pathologist. I got a love of bodies from him. I used to come to the dissecting room and watch him work—"

"You didn't."

"They use little vacuum rods for the eyes: pluck them out of the sockets, pop."

She knew he was lying and she didn't care. "And my dad was a flier," she said, "a parachute jumper with a parachute embroidered in red and silver. He used to jump out ten thousand feet in the air and ride on the air. . . ."

"I know how to speak to worms and snakes. I can talk them out of the ground."

"So can I."

She watched on the apartment's television set as he reported on the hunt for the cat and its owner, his pale eyes glistening as he talked about the pain of her family.

The cat hunters ranged the frozen streets under dark skies and struck out angrily at the unwanted small animals. The gutters were lined with dead squirrels and pigeons. There were more rumours. François had found the cat, taken it home and refused to pay the reward. His wife had taken the cat and run to Brazil to get her face changed. The cat had appeared to a church congregation in a vision and healed all the sick. The cat was dead, killed by the police.

Certainly Judd might have killed it if he'd found it. He carried a golf club in the back seat of his car, and he could imagine bringing it down on the cat's head in payback for his fortune slipping away, the picture that came back to him constantly, the cat's back twisting away from him and the fur slipping out of his fingers. All the same he could picture himself grinning in a newspaper photograph with the cat and the woman and the cheque and his children in the background looking at him respectfully.

He was sleeping in the unmarked car now and sneaking back into the basement only to wash and change his clothes. He booked off sick. He was on his own patrol now, roaming around 17.

He was drinking more. He tried to get to a perfect state in which the buzzing of his life would die down and the images would recede. He usually overbalanced. One glass over the line and he'd be hunched over some bar with tears in his eyes. Pain would begin to lift the top of his head and run from behind his forehead all the way inside the shell of his skull and down through his jaw. His hands stung, his body felt dirty, his feet were heavy as they plodded on the sidewalk, and the fire was starting to burn through his flesh. He could feel the camp fuel catch in his belly and run up the inside of his skin, inside his arms and legs, scorching.

The bank machine wouldn't give him any money. His wife had moved the account somewhere. He leaned on the street people for more. Late one afternoon Lukey came by, looked in his bleary face and threw a five-dollar bill on the car seat beside him.

"Get yourself something to eat, man, you look wiped," he said, and the snake stared at him with tiny mournful eyes.

As he moved through 17 the dealers and hustlers watched him, calling each other on their phones, keeping tabs: a bull on the loose, a sergeant going crazy. He figured stories would be getting back to the station, and he started keeping a lookout for patrol cars, driving on side streets. He walked up and down the alleys, shining his floodlight up onto the fire escapes, peering in the ice and grime for the yellow-green glow of the cat's eyes. Rats ran behind heaps of garbage as he passed. Once he met a cat patrol and beat its leader with his flashlight. Word got around and the cat hunters avoided him.

François brought in a security company to deal with the workers' occupation at Fesnos Meats, and it used a rein-forced truck to crash through the plant's front door. The workers retreated as the guards began to occupy the rooms around them. They used clubs and flexible leather staffs, and the Fesnos workers began to limp onto the killing floor with broken arms and bruises.

"We should set the fucking place on fire," said the watery-eyed slaughterman.

"Burn it down and piss on the ashes," said a maintenance engineer.

"Six million dollars—*six* million dollars—for his cat and his piece."

"Not a dime for us."

"Asshole."

"We got wives and kids."

"My kids got a cat."

"Well, fuck this," said the chief slaughterman and led his troops out into the parking lot, into their trucks and cars and into a caravan that made its way through the icy streets toward François Will's house.

It was late afternoon. The feeble sun reflected off the chrome of the cavalcade. The packing house workers drove slowly, their arms out the windows in the cold air, slamming the metal of the car bodies with hands and clubs, making a low booming sound as they moved through the city. The television stations picked up the parade and followed it through 17 Division. Judd looked at it blankly as it went by. Two hundred cars, then two hundred and fifty. Cat patrols joined. The city's frustrations and anger were converging, focusing on the caravan. Hans saw the image in his living room, ran to the closet for his heavy coat and jumped downstairs in time to climb up the side of a dump truck as the parade passed. Nobody spoke, but as the parade lengthened, the thundering of the metal increased. Hans began to beat on the side of the freezing truck with his bare hand. The drumming went through his body. He looked around and grinned. The parade grew as idle, angry, curious people joined in. Ivan's mother found a place at the back, marching to Hans's drumbeat and calling on Jesus to come out from hiding. From the front of the parade came a shimmering, slithering noise as the slaughtermen sharpened their knives.

Julia was using her tongue on Ivan, moving from the soles of his feet to the tops of his feet, alternating right and left, her tongue making tiny circles and swooping patterns on his ankles, his calves, lingering behind his knees, his body lurching with pleasure, feeling the heavy flesh on the backs of his thighs, jiggling it, making it sway, moving to the front, the muscled pad over the leg bone, then inside to the hollows near the juncture of the groin, bringing him almost to tears, tasting every shade of salt and sweetness and bristles and soft hair, touching his cock with her left ear as she dug her tongue into the corded surface below his balls, when the parade began to pass underneath the front window of the apartment, the smooth scraping of the knives and the boom of the clubs ringing off the walls. He pushed her away and got up and, holding a pillow to his dick, walked to the glass and looked out and smiled and said he'd have to go. She lay in the bed feeling the strain of the muscles in her jaw and the slippery texture of his skin on her tongue.

Kessler the driver figured out where the parade was going from the television coverage and stumped out in his thigh-high cast; he stood beneath the withered trees beside the gates and waited for it to arrive. He could hear the boom and clatter from a couple of miles away. There were five hundred cars now. Every disappointed soul, amateur commando and sorehead in the city was out to even the score. When the parade got to the steel gates, the chief slaughterman started to honk his horn rhythmically, two long, three short, and the other horns began to join in.

François watched from the top-floor parlour as Kessler limped over to the steel gates on his crutches and spoke to the chief slaughterman through the bars. Kessler felt a burst of power. He could make a decision now that would pivot events. He could stand as a brave protector of his employer's property, maybe get hurt, maybe get killed, have his image flashed around the world. Or he could open the gates and limp away to the dark northern forests. He lit a cigarette. The smoke rippled in the cold wind.

Julia watched the television set in the apartment as Ivan's camera van got to the gates of her husband's house. Ivan tried to interview the chief slaughterman, who waved a metal appliance in the air and pulled the trigger at its base. Curved metal shears met and sprang apart.

"What is that?"

"An aitch bone cutter. Severs the carcass. Portable power, stainless steel, fourteen hundred pounds of force, it can go through a main hog bone in under a second. State of the art."

"Take your fucking head right off your neck," said the man beside him.

François looked at the picture on his parlour screen. The shears met in the air again.

Some of the people in the cavalcade had left their cars and started walking forward to the gates. A moving mass of the discontented and disappointed: ring-nosed punks, pissed-off teaching assistants, accountants whose ledgers did not balance, police officers with rusted handcuffs, fishermen with empty creels, anti-vivisectionists with their animal companions. Hans was one of the first to get to the gates. He stood on the verge of the frozen lawn, unzipped his fly and took a piss in the flower beds, his stream shifting and warming the stems of a withered rose bush.

"We want to talk to Mr. Friendly Pig," said the slaughter-man. An icy brick flew by, launched from beyond the gates, landing and shattering on an ornamental birdbath on the snow-covered lawn. The marble of the birdbath broke and fell. There was a cheer from the column outside the gates. Another brick flew, landed and bounced. A rock got farther and smashed one of the small round windows beside the front door of the house. François heard the thin sound from his television set as an echo of the sharper real sound of the glass breaking from two floors below him.

There were already police spread thinly along the col-umn. Suddenly there were more of them, several squads arriving in a rush, some in thick shells of ceramic materi-al to deflect bricks and bullets, and helmets with thick plastic that protected the faces inside.

Every few minutes a stone came flying from some-where in the crowd into the grounds, and a wedge of police would make a run for its launch point. The rest of the time the police and the parade stared at each other. François kept watch from his parlour. Kessler limped up and down the line of five hundred cars looking at the frozen mud on the bumpers, trying to use woodcraft to figure out where they'd come from. After the sun went down, the police turned on big electric lamps that lit the fence and the gate. People slept in cars or stamped up and down the barrier, but nobody left.

Lukey fell into an old habit, boosted six pairs of pants from a department store, got caught, taken to the station and booked. He explained he had an animal to take care of, that his pet would be frightened and lonely. Aw, said the booking officer: you really should have thought of that before you took the pants.

The snake was hungry. It could feel emptiness all along its bony ribs. It moved along the floorboards of Lukey's seedy little squat looking for rats. It found a hole in the drywall beside a door; a protruding nail scraped its skin as it passed through the channel. The hallway was dark, and a passing freak stepped on the snake, sending it whipping into a leathery circle. She screamed, and the snake slid off through an open door and out into the frozen street.

It was terrifying. Dark bad-smelling boots rushed at the snake and rushed away making sharp noises. The surface of the street was slippery and numbingly cold. The snake could feel its insides cooling and slowing down. A few minutes of this and it would lose its ability to move and then fall asleep and die in this noisy, frightening place.

There was the hum of an engine from around a corner and a suggestion of warmth. The snake turned into the alley and saw a rectangle of blackness above him, an open door into the back seat of a waiting car. With a great effort it raised itself and heaved its way into the blackness, underneath a layer of dryly sliding newspapers on the car floor. After a moment the door closed behind him, another door closed on the other side of the seat and the car began to move. The snake could feel a little sensation coming back into its body, but it was hungrier than before, and weaker. It fell asleep under the papers on the dark humming floor of the car.

Ivan came back to the apartment at two o'clock in the morning to change his clothes. Julia was watching the independent channel's news signal, moving video tucked away in the corner of the screen beside weather symbols, stock market reports and advertisements. Her house loomed in the corner of the screen with the silent, still file of protesters in front of it. The grey light from the screen glowed on her face. A tiny Ivan spoke to both of them from a spotlight inside the screen.

"What are they there for?" she asked. "What are they doing?"

"Oh," he said, "they're just raising hell. Something in the air these days."

"What do they say?"

He sat beside her. "They don't say much, they don't know much, but they'd love to be here right now, I can tell you that." He stroked her hair. "A woman worth four million dollars." He began to touch her lightly. "A hundred thousand for each eye, ten thousand for the elbow, the bones inside the arm five thousand each, a thousand for each finger, twenty thousand for this—" his lips were moving against her breasts "—twenty thousand for this, fifty for that, a bag of gold for this, a king's ransom for this, a chest of diamonds for this, a trip to Venice. . . ."

She lay back. She felt full as a topped-up vessel, a vase bearing heavy flowers, full everywhere, head, body, limbs. She wanted to seal him up inside her. She'd carry him around the way an organ grinder carries his monkey, hanging from his waist. She'd tote him into the grocery store and sit him in her lap in the church pew. They could wear masks.

Levering was always falling in love with an animal or person or plant because of the exceptional, sensational architecture of a mouth or eyes or the perfection of the juncture of a stem and leaf. He loved the cat's claw as it dug into his hand, the passive weight of the animal's body and its eyes as it hung in the air, waiting for something to change, for the appearance of an escape route.

The cat suddenly twisted in his arms, thrust out with its back feet and shrieked. Levering felt something strange in the area of the right rear leg. Something about the animal was off balance, out of line. He pressed down with his thumb on the top of the cat's right hip. The cat groaned and wrenched away. The camera above the skylight jerked a little and its microphone picked up a hiss of sympathy from the woman on the roof.

Levering kept a small cage with solid walls in the corner of the lab for special therapeutic challenges. He had a theory that the body concentrated better on healing itself when all distractions were eliminated. He lowered the cat into the cage, checked the supply of dry food and water and carefully lifted the lid into place. The cat was in darkness. Spots drifted in front of his eyes. He began to limp slowly along the walls of the cage, feeling for an opening, a weakness or a hidden passage to the outside.

In a few hours the cat knew every scent and seam of the wood that made up the crate. He paced the floor of the box in the dark and stood on his back paws reaching up as far as he could, patting for some change in the smoothness that would mark a way out. There was none.

Levering lifted the lid once or twice, splashed fresh water into the cat's bowl and dropped leaves and herbs into the box. The floor of the box became thick with drying grass and brown seeds and husks. At first the cat ate nothing, his stomach contracting, his fur turning dull, but then he began to chew on some stalks. Levering was delighted. He knew the cat could be turned from a meat eater to a happy animal on a vegetable diet. He wanted the entire world to live in harmony, its perfect teeth chewing only food that grew from the ground. The cat would eat nothing that had ever had a face, and he would grow strong, vibrant, sinuous, healthy, a super-cat that lived on carrots and oats. And from his stunning example the news of the meatless and murderless society would spread.

The cat drifted in and out of sleep. Sometimes he'd hear the fall of water outside his box or the low rumble of Levering's voice. Sometimes there was a snap or a thud, or the sound of something dragging on the concrete floor. He dreamed of his old room and the fall of the light on the white couch, the flash of bronze and steel, the firm touch of the woman's hand and the meat she gave him. The inside of his mouth grew dry. He could hardly chew the tough leaves. The dreams grew vaguer and more difficult to wake from, full of savage animals, the feeling of sharpness up and down his side, a growing cramp that seized his flesh.

The cat paced the box again and again, trying to keep his leg from dying altogether, brushing his muzzle whiskers against the walls; there was a tiny scoop near one corner that reminded him of a space in the tree trunk he'd used to leave the estate. He cried all one day and then stopped.

The servants trooped out of the Will estate holding white handkerchiefs above their heads and were allowed to squeeze through the narrow door set in the big steel gates. The parade had been parked outside for a week. The street was grimy and strewn with papers, half-eaten food and plastic bags. Canteen trucks stopped to sell soup, coffee and sandwiches. Lillian stayed in the kitchen and ate crackers, rolled oats and dry linguine straight from the package. François heated up cans of beans and made toast from old dried bread. They didn't talk but chewed in comradely consideration. Each of them was furious with Julia. Lillian could feel her place in life falling into bits. She'd given up the lease on the apartment over the dental school and thrown away all her old furniture. If this house came down, where would she live? Every time François heard a shout from the road outside he felt his wife's betrayal. She'd buggered off and left him to fight alone.

It was something in the air, something about the image of the hulking silent picket, the clear and frustrating fact that the woman and the cat and the money had gone, as well as the brutal cold that seared your flesh and made the insides of your lungs feel like sheaths of paper. The city was pissed off. It didn't even like looking at television anymore. The warm smiles of the newscaster and the cheery jokes of the sports people rang false. You had to keep an eye on it, in case the search turned hot again, but that was a duty, not a pleasure. People slouched in the bars with one eye on the screen and told each other what a dopey jerk the anchorman was. Only Ivan was immune. He still seemed like an ordinary guy. He was everywhere, still loved, warm and sociable, frustrated like everyone else but living through the story with the people, one day on the picket line, the next in the missing persons squad room, speculating with the chief constable.

The wind from the north grew stronger, shiftier, picking up scraps of paper and hurling them into walls or keeping them balanced above the ground, rotating and flapping above the frozen soil. Icicles gathered on gutters and eaves and then snapped in the wind and blew along the streets, landing on heads and cutting faces. Fingers froze inside woollen mittens, feeling only the nagging scratch of the fibre. Faces went red and then white, waxy to the touch, smooth with dead cells.

The commanders of the animal brigades reviewed the videotape from the roof of the dental college. It was clear there were outrages inside. Levering was a renegade; he talked about a meatless world but put animals through hell for his own profit. It was hideous to think their teeth were being drilled, filled, scraped and pulled for no good purpose.

"Meatheads," said the girl in charge of propaganda and media strategy. It was the movement's most powerful insult.

There was complete silence when the squad reviewed the video of Levering putting the cat in the box. Three of the five people in the room recognized the cat from the flash of white on his front left paw, but nobody said anything. There were sideways glances at impassive faces but absolute silence on the subject. Each of the three thought perhaps he was the only one to make the connection. Each began to think about what he might do with two million dollars for the cat—six million dollars, if the sausage-maker's wife was in the neighbourhood as well. Most of the money would go to the movement, of course—half, at least, or some substantial sum. And a million and a quarter, a million and a half would make quite a change in anyone's life. It was a lot to think about.

Each of the three volunteered to go along on the liberation raid, along with two of the other senior commanders. The explosives engineer was already thinking about early retirement in the South Seas. He put a little extra oomph in the charge designed for the security door. He wanted to be certain.

Twenty-One

A HUNDRED SMALL dogs had gathered at the fence of François Will's estate. They were led by a miniature pinscher, his small sharp face lifted into the cold air, his muzzle full of the scent of the spoiling food in the kitchen beyond the barrier. The pinscher ran up and down the wire fence, stopped and stepped back; two corgis moved past him and began to scrabble at a small depression at the midway point between two steel posts. The earth flew back in a plume. The dogs at the front of the pack yipped and whined. The space below the sharp points of the wire grew deeper as the dogs scratched and bit at the half-frozen earth, the heat of their breath turning the ground into mud that smeared their muzzles.

Kessler was using his observational powers to examine the fading sky; faint high cloud, he thought, meant a warming trend for the morning. He felt a sudden sharp pain in his thigh and shouted, then looked down at a carpet of small rough bodies pushing against him. He fell onto the cold earth of the flower bed. A trail of blood shot up and then began to spread beneath the small dogs' bellies. He couldn't believe it; he was a man of nature and a pioneer, and these idiotic little city animals had bitten through an artery. He pressed his hands to his leg and howled. The police beyond the fence battered the locked door.

There was a treble cry from the pack that carried out beyond the barrier. Little dogs leapt from their beds, raised their hungry heads from their bowls and stopped in their patrols of their backyards. Those who were free began to run to the field and the break in the fence. Others strained at their leashes, snarling, or began to jump against the barriers that kept them from the street, clawing at the doors, whining and yapping. Bigger dogs watched the groups of smaller ones passing in the road and cowered.

Kessler shouted again. He felt the sudden stab of a hundred needles and then a nipping at his windpipe. It was completely astonishing. The man of the wilderness was being devoured by tiny domestic pets. His throat was full of blood, and blackness fell onto him from the sky.

The little dogs beside him sniffed and licked the blood on the earth. The television cameras swung around and pointed through the gate.

The man with the aitch bone cutter pointed it at the sky and pressed the trigger. The steel blades clapped together twice. Engines started firing up and down the line of cars. The police squads by the gate moved into a close line.

"Son of a bitch," said the slaughterman, firing the cutter a third time.

"You got that right," said a cameraman, moving in on a tight frame of the dogs lapping and nipping away at Kessler. A tiny bichon stopped beside the lead truck and snarled. The camera followed a white streak closing in on the slaughterman, who held out the aitch bone cutter with both hands, protecting his groin. The cutters clapped together on the dog's body, severing it behind the shoulders. The bisected carcass fell to the floor of the flatbed.

There were a hundred dogs in the pack now. Their eyes glistened in the floodlights. The police were jumping out of the way to let them get by. They surged through the opening beneath the fence.

"Shit!" cried the watery-eyed man. "What about the money?"

The money; it seemed very clear suddenly in the cold darkness that the little dogs were headed for the money. They were going to eat François, and if that happened the jobs were gone and the reward was gone. The driver of the flatbed gunned his engine and smashed the truck past the wedge of police into the fence. It bent, buckled and fell.

Judd drove in the twilight past the station house down toward the television studio. His body was awash with vodka. He could feel it swaying back and forth inside him like a large rubbery shape, overbalancing him as he sat behind the wheel. It smelled bitter, like fuel. He could imagine its real colours, the rose and pale green of spilled gasoline, drenching the inside of his head. The car engine missed and died.

He abandoned it in the middle of the street, leaving the door open behind him. He stumbled and half fell over the hood and then looked up at the crowd gathered at the studio door, staring at the huge screen on the top of the studio building. The picture of the cat strolling through the lion field was playing again. Then the image changed to the amateur video of the cat lounging on the roof of the garage. Then the live shot from the big house up north with men running through a breach in the security fence, the police firing shots into the air, small dogs at work on feet and knees.

Judd began to walk to the studio. The crowd in the street became thicker, the air white with breath suspended in the cold; men stood inside restaurants watching the screen through the windows. The screen suddenly was showing pictures of the missing woman. When they saw Julia's face, the cat hunters grumbled and swore.

Street vendors were selling images of the cat pressed on metal discs and hung on cheap chains.

Ivan's recorded voice came from the huge speakers hung beside the screens: "The alleged redemptive power of the cat, an increasing focus of controversy in the Church, has now split the scientific community as well. Dr. Herbert Bean, dean of . . ." And Bean's little head and shoulders flashed onto the screen. Judd groaned.

The image of the cat leapt suddenly into the upper air. Judd craned his head up until the vodka almost pulled him over. He could feel the cat far above him in the darkening sky.

There was a sudden smooth glistening presence on the surface of the street. Judd looked along the curb and saw fluid coming out of a grating. The fluid was the colour of tea and carried with it coils, scraps, shreds and lumps like strange floating paramecia.

Every grating along the street was gushing. He saw a manhole cover a few feet from him nudging upward with the power of the stream. Something huge had obviously happened. The city's hydraulic gates had failed. The sewage had broken through. The city's hidden river was coming for him, for his wife and his girls.

Judd was at the back of the television studio now. He saw the bottom end of the black-painted fire escape. It ended ten feet in the air, but there was an empty car parked in the space below it. He put one foot on the car's bumper and climbed up the hood onto the car roof, grabbed the freezing iron and pulled his heavy body up onto the slats of the platform. He looked down and saw people in the street walking through the cold brown sludge as if it didn't exist.

The starving snake felt Judd's car stop and then a thin cold breeze from the open door. It hated the cold, but there was no food in the space around it. The snake slid under the seat and out the door and down beneath the floor of the vehicle. There was a stamping, crashing sound from behind, and it began to hurry along the street underneath the parked cars, feeling its blood slowing down. It had to find another warm place and it had to eat. There were more feet running beside the cars. It came to an open trash can with a fire inside and slithered closer, feeling the heat in its blood. The smoke drifted across its flat face.

There was a crowd of men beside the car. It parted slightly and the snake could suddenly see a route downward, a black square that should lead to cover and warmth and safety; it could smell the sewer pipe, could sense the narrow, hot, stinking security of the place. And there was food as well. A ravenous beagle was dancing at the feet of the crowd, snapping at the cat hunters. The snake was already halfway across the open space in the centre of the crowd at the studio door. It took the beagle in its mouth and bore it screaming through the narrow gap that led to the sewer, safety, warmth and a meal.

Judd looked down. The dark sludge was three feet high

in the street now and rising silently. The people at the door
of the station still seemed completely unaware of it. They
were about to drown in their own waste, and they talked
and shouted to each other without noticing it. His home
was two miles east and downhill from the town centre; the
sewage must have engulfed his house already. Perhaps his
wife and children had escaped to higher ground somewhere, but more likely they were caught in the house,
treading the tainted gluey stuff, holding their breath as
they were nudged by floating unspeakable debris, gasping
in the diminishing layer of air at the top of the living room,
weakening, finally failing, relaxing into the clammy por-
ridge as it infiltrated their mouths, noses and lungs.

He looked out over the city. A tide of bubbling syrupy
fluid as far as he could see, creeping up the sides of the
buildings. Below the rising surface, dappled with garbage,
people on the street were still moving, unconcerned, as
though they could breathe the sewage. He shook his head
as he climbed; was his head making this up? The tide
seemed so real, so full of sins and ugliness. He even heard
a growing sucking sound as it rose.

He climbed the five floors to the roof, up a calm progression of flat brick and to the painted image of Ivan Teuti
with his microphone in his hand, the station trademark
flashing above his fist. He climbed past Ivan's pale eyes.
The crowd on the street below began to murmur. He
could hear them through the muddy water, and he saw
their eyes turned upward.

He reached the roof and stood on the edge of the
screen. There was a faint smell of burning electrical cable

and a low note of power from a transformer box. He could see the moving dots that composed the picture of the cat, each as big as a fingernail, moving in waves across the immense screen. Ivan's voice was thundering, too loud now to be understood, the words rumbling over Judd and making the bones in his body buzz. There was a mesh cage behind the screen that surrounded the base of the transmission tower.

The cat's image was on the big screen, straight up in the sky, somewhere at the top of the tower. He could feel the cat's being in waves pouring through his body. There was a padlocked gate in the cage. He pulled out his revolver, lurched and shot three times. The third bullet smashed the hasp of the lock. There was a shout from the crowd. The water had reached the roof of the building. His hatred of the cat above him kept him climbing. The sound of the tide had gotten louder, mixing with the huge bass voice from the speakers, and now the smell filled his head—rusted iron and wood, rot, dirt and sweet decay.

The ladder up the tower was narrow, with barely enough space on each thin pipe for his foot. He felt all his unsteady weight as his arms pulled and his legs pushed. He panted and sweated. The waves from the cat became stronger; the radiation was coursing through his body now, defining each nerve and muscle. He could feel the cat's purr in the air, the huge powerful vibration lifting him. The shouts from the submerged street grew fainter. A steel door opened below him, and two security men ran out through the brown tide onto the roof; he looked down, and saliva rolled from his mouth, falling through the air to land at their feet.

The metal pipe was beginning to freeze his hands through his gloves. Once or twice he missed his hold and swung out into the open air, hearing a faint breath from the crowd far below. The sound from the cat drew him back each time. He felt as though he were curled against the cat's warm fur. The brightness of the cat's presence intensified. He was climbing into the light. It took his breath away. The sewage was lapping at his boots. He stopped and laid his face against the leather of his glove, the high wind whirling through his hair, feeling the low drone from the cat's huge body spilling out from the top of the tower, through him and beyond him into the sky and the city.

Two poodles and a Maltese found their way into the house first, through a broken window in the basement. François heard them scrabbling around down there, snapping at each other, bounding up the stairs to the kitchen door and bouncing off. Then he heard a brick smashing the living room window, and then more little dogs scrambling and snarling through the opening.

It was Julia's fault, clearly her fault. He'd loved her so much that he'd offered to pay for her and her cat, and that had inflamed the city, and she had run away and stayed away as though the money didn't matter, as though no amount of money he could put his hands on would make any difference to her. They'd had a deal, unspoken but binding. He would keep her in comfort and adore her, and she would accept the adoration. He was in her bedroom, his heart beating hard. He could hear a group of men crawling through the living room window and stepping down onto the thick carpet. There were shouts and the sound of splintering wood as the front door went down. Shots from outside as the police tried to protect themselves from the crowd.

He went to her closet and embraced an armful of her clothes. Her smell was still there, like a delicate powder that filled his nostrils. She was rustling next to his body. Her great mink coat hung richly on a wooden hanger.

The floor groaned. Lillian walked into the room, her thighs rubbing and the flesh under her jaw swaying.

"They're in the house," she said.

"I know."

"Do something about it."

"Nothing to be done."

She was at the dresser, fumbling through the jewellery box. "Take the furs," she said. "Take everything you can carry."

"It's useless."

"Give me the coat."

He threw the heavy golden fur across the room. She thrust her arms into it, smoothed it across her body and began to put rings on the ends of her fingers.

There was a sudden smash and gurgle and then the sound of running water. Someone had broken the main pipe. The water was rushing out from the wall in the stairwell, down the risers onto the soft floor.

"Fuck you! Fuck you!" It was coming from downstairs; maybe a dozen men, chanting as they smashed china in the dining room.

Lillian was jamming necklaces into her pockets. "It's survival now, sweetie," she said. "Take what you can and get going. We'll start all over again somewhere else."

François picked up one of his wife's shoetrees and peered out into the hallway. Two men had taken a painting from the wall and were manoeuvring it down the stairs, as careful as professional movers, backing a little now and then, easing it along.

He felt his strength collapse. He fell like a bag of meat on the heavy carpet. His skull bounced on the pile. He began to weep. To be deserted, stymied, stalled and now robbed, vandalized—everything he'd accomplished was washed away.

He felt her huge arms lift him from the floor. Lillian cradled him like a child, leaned forward and shrugged her shoulders. The great soft folds of the coat moved over him and sealed him inside. He closed his eyes. Her skin exuded the kitchen smells he remembered from his childhood, vinegar, cinnamon, olive oil, bacon and lard. He thought of his irritation at the sight of her gulping down the food he'd bought, but it seemed now he'd bought his salvation. He'd fattened up a mother to carry him away to safety.

He felt her lumber to the staircase on the opposite end of the hall. It led to the kitchen. He could hear the men with the picture swear as they stepped into the river on the descending carpet. She edged down the kitchen stairs, one heavy step at a time. Through a slim gap in the coat he caught glimpses of moving bodies, tilted doors and shattered windows. Three men bumped into Lillian as they ran by, their arms full of little sculptures and drapes. She roared at them. "Sorry, lady," they said as they ran out the front door.

The little dogs were struggling through the water on the main floor of the house, trying to find the delicious garbage. Lillian pushed open the door to the kitchen, and a herd of excited dogs ran past her. They seemed to think she was a bigger dog, a comrade, in her huge pelt. She opened the door to the walk-in freezer. It was filled with meat, boxes and crates of it, halves of beef hanging on steel hooks from the ceiling, cartons of ground sirloin, pig carcasses stacked on a table, a bin of turkeys. There was a high yelp of excitement from the dogs as they went past her into the cold room.

"All right in there?" she whispered to her chest.

"All right," murmured François.

She tiptoed to the back of the kitchen. Some of the protesters found their way to the freezer and shouted with pleasure, loading up with frozen slabs of lamb and filet, tearing smoked hams away from the famished dogs.

"I need the keys to the big car," she whispered.

"In the garage."

She eased down three wooden steps, found the keys on the hook beside the light switch and set François down gently on the concrete floor. He sat cross-legged on the cold surface. He wanted to go to sleep. She opened the door, scooped him up, set him down behind the front seat and covered him with a blue plastic tarpaulin from a rack on the garage wall.

"Stay down," she said, and got into the driver's seat. In his daze François imagined they were playing bandits and bank robbers. This was fun.

Lillian backed the big black car out into the courtyard and navigated through the line of vans and cars. The police had pulled back from the estate; they were trying to stop people going in, but they let the looters out, their cars full of carpets, clothes, wine and steaks.

Under the tarpaulin François felt comforted and peaceful. Lillian drove hard, loving the limousine's heavy graceful carriage around the corners and its confident acceleration on straight roads. It wasn't so bad. She had the coat, the car and the jewellery, her little pension and her savings. Even if he was wiped out, they had enough to live in a little apartment somewhere. Maybe Julia would come back, maybe not.

"Mother McCoy?" His voice tiny.

"What?"

"I love you."

"I love you, too, François."

In the grey winter dawn Julia was in Ivan's car, which was moving west from Chinatown toward the station. The collar of her coat was pulled up to hide her face. Ivan Teuti whistled without a melody as he drove. He had no idea what he wanted to do or what he was going to do. He looked at his pale hairless hands on the wheel.

She drew her legs together; the cloth of the coat whispered on the seat. "What are we doing?" she asked. He turned his pale eyes to her. He looked like something made of porcelain, as though he would chip and smash if you hit him. A big man with a sack and a flashlight held up his hand to stop the car, then jumped out of the way as Ivan sped up and drove past. The man spat.

More and more people, all facing the television station, moving forward, some edging out into the street. A line of cars formed behind an abandoned vehicle. The way was blocked. She drew the coat up farther and looked at him. He stopped the car, opened the door.

"Leave me the keys," she said.

He put the keys on the driver's seat and stepped out into the street. She closed her eyes and leaned forward, touching the dashboard of the car with her cheek. His voice came from outside the car: "Remember me."

His taped face was on the screen and his voice was in the air: "Impossible to calculate the stress on the city's emergency services. And the response—" He began to force his way through the crowd.

"Hey, you're—"

"Hey, it's the guy—"

Hands on him, friendly, petting him as though he were a child. "Love your work!" Smiles above the scarves, below the hats, and guards forcing their way into the crowd, calling out in an official manner for a clearing—"News coming! News coming through here!" He smiled. He felt completely empty, balanced, drained.

The explosives engineer had been quite lavish with his supply of powder. When the charge went off at two o'clock in the morning, it knocked down the central door of the dentistry faculty and blew a hole in the wall behind it. Flying concrete crushed three cages in the animal annex, along with their occupants, two guinea pigs and a lop-eared rabbit with a full set of braces. The liberation squad with its blackened faces and bandanas sprinted down the line of animal pens, smashing locks and throwing open doors. Three of them ran to the end of the great room, toward the dark cage with the cat in it.

As they ran they looked at each other. Two million dollars, and permanent financial security for the animal liberation movement, or for any one of them, or even a more modest foundation for all three, if they cooperated. The tallest raider raised his pry bar in the air and brought it down hard on the black-cowled head of the smallest, who fell unconscious to the floor. The man in the middle swore and swerved. They reached the box at the same time.

The tall raider raised his metal bar again and swiped in the air. The bar glanced off the shoulder of the other man and landed hard on the wooden top of the box. The sliding lock on the box lid shifted. The smaller man struck out with his pry bar twice. The second blow knocked the box on its side.

The other raiders had begun to move up and down the lines of pens, flinging open doors. The dogs began to chase the cats; the ape with the flashing steel teeth climbed the steel wire of the open cages and crouched on top, hooting in fear.

Gracie and Levering had been working late in the big dental classroom, filing and polishing a slightly buckled plane on the inside of her left bicuspid that he agreed might give an unwanted nuance to her reading of the dialogue when she appeared before the camera. He was working without anaesthetic, gently probing and cleaning the irregularity.

When the explosion knocked down the door in the next room, Levering dropped his drill and ran toward the sound. Gracie yanked the drain from her mouth and ran after him, dropping the plastic cape on the floor.

The cat crawled awkwardly from the fallen box. The two raiders looked at it. Jones began to swell and growl; his fur stood on end; he backed away from them howling like a siren, his tail thick and stiff. The smaller raider made a sudden jump for him. The tall man brought his bar down hard on the smaller man's head, stumbled with the effort and fell. Jones turned and ran, shrieking, through the liberated zone, his wails disappearing into the frenzy of howling, barking and screaming.

Gracie was standing beside the door, watching Levering run toward the tall raider. She saw the little black cat with the white leg run out of the big laboratory and slow down and stop outside the door. His sides were heaving. She could see he was hurt and sad, and he reminded her of the barn cats at home. She reached out to him and he limped over to her; he hung from her hands as she picked him up. There were sirens outside. She found her coat, put it on over the cat and moved carefully along the wall and out through the shattered hallway to the street. The raiders were escaping. The cats in the laboratory were pouncing on the white mice and sinking their steel-braced teeth into the backs of their necks.

Judd had shoved his right arm through the rungs of the ladder and wedged himself tight, caught his breath, looked down at the crowd and up toward the top of the transmission tower. He felt the deep drone of the cat in his gut. He closed his eyes and tried to think of his little girls, but he'd lost their images now. They were drowned and at peace; there was room for nothing in his mind except Jones. The cat's great yellow green eyes scorched through him. He gave a shout, waved his left arm, slapped his thigh like a rider slapping his horse. The crowd below shouted with him, their voices carrying clearly through the discoloured water.

Gracie had reached the fringe of the crowd. She'd run as far as she could, down past the long row of hospitals and insurance companies that lined the boulevard near the university, past City Hall, where patrols of cat hunters met at the end of a night of searching. She was at the edge of the crowd near the television station, and the press of people made her afraid, but then she saw that everyone was intent on something above—a big man almost all the way up a spidery tower, hanging in the air.

Gracie had a stitch in her side. She stopped and leaned against a building to catch her breath. Her left arm was stiff from the weight of the cat. Suddenly she felt the prick of something sharp in her side, a set of claws digging into her ribs. She opened her coat. The cat was looking at her calmly. She turned to her left, and the cat eased the claws; when she turned back to the right again the cat dug into her skin again. The cat's head moved. He was looking toward the south and the lake.

Gracie felt the cat's body vibrating against her.

She began to walk south. She turned once or twice and

felt the cat's claws guiding her. She moved away from the crowd, toward the wide highway at the bottom of the city.

Ivan reached the gate. The security guards inside unlocked it and let him squeeze through. One or two people were still yelling: "News guy! What's new?" But most of them had moved back from the fence to focus on the man climbing the tower. Ivan felt a slight resentment. He moved to the studio.

Julia smelled him still in the car, the pale aroma of his skin. The memory of him suddenly broke her; she didn't know whether she resented him or cherished him or both. She pulled up her scarf and stepped into the freezing street.

Ivan knew exactly what he was going to do. The last barrier was going down.

Judd was climbing again up to the cat in the sky. He was graceful. He remembered his childhood, marching in his aunt's living room in the old uniform. Her face in youth came into his mind, almost displacing the cat for a moment; it was scornful. He could see she had been planning to humiliate him for years. Then the buzzing cat came back into his mind, and he jiggled with sudden joy, his hands warm now in the rays from the tower, a substitute sun. The cat had disappeared behind it. The sun got nearer, and he could hear rumbling from inside it as though huge rocks were crashing together in caves. There was an overpowering smell of gasoline, and the sun's corona began to sear his face. He turned his head away. The sun's orbit took it lower and lower and finally it took up all the space above him, touched him and pushed him gravely off the ladder, out into the cold and falling shouting through the dry air to the street.

The screen cleared. Ivan was looking out over the city. His face was as big as a house. His expression was grave and disappointed.

He had come striding into the station, throwing down his coat, shouting that he had a flash, a bulletin. He loosened his necktie and ran his fingers through his hair. The producer on the evening shift tried to ask him what the news was, but he brushed him off—no time; the opposition had it; we have to be first to air; give me air!

He sat down on a black stool facing the camera. The floor director gave him a time signal: ten fingers, five, two, go. The red light clicked on.

"I have terrible news," said Ivan. "Terrible, terrible news."

He could feel the city slowing down, the heads turning to the sets, his face drawing them in a million times, stacks of him in appliance sections in the department stores, tiny rows of him in the electronics shops, transfixing the shoplifters in mid-boost. He was on at City Hall. He loomed over bars. He was rising and falling inside elevators.

"I have terrible news," he said again.

In cable-company control rooms he repeated himself a thousand times. The technicians flashed his name on a card and plastered it below him, with the title "Bulletin—Live."

"It's the worst news of all. I can't imagine anything worse," said the Ivans. The city leaned in to the screens.

"All the lies they've told you, everyone who has lied to you, all through your life? This is worse. This is the most evil lie of all. The most . . . the most squalid. The most diabolical." He stopped to catch his breath. Outside, in the street, across the city, people were starting to shout. He leaned forward again, put his finger to his lips, shushed them.

"It's gone on for months."

Another shout.

"We've all been looking—all of us, as a city, as a society, because we are honest, because we care, we have been looking, out of love, for a little cat. Just an ordinary alley cat. Just a regular cat. To return him, out of love, to the arms of the people who love him."

He leaned into the camera again.

"It spoke well of us, I think. It was the character of the city, coming out in a, well, a kind of citizens' crusade for kindness and love.

"And I have terrible, terrible news."

The camera was focused closely on his candid, friendly, sorrowful face.

"It was a trick," he said.

There was a low moan from the crowd.

There was a tear in his eye. Tiny muscles tightened in his throat. He seemed to be fighting off collapse, but his character was so strong that it blazed out over the city, and the audience was moved by his courage.

He opened his lips to speak again, closed them, finally

whispered, the sounds almost too faint for the microphone, "It was a trick."

Julia stood in the street, listening, straining to hear what Ivan was saying.

"I'm not an educated guy," said Ivan. "You all know me. I'm just one of you, no more, no less, just a guy."

"That's right!" shouted some men in the crowd below the station.

"They thought they could trick me the way they trick all of us," said Ivan. "They thought they could get me to go along with this con of theirs. This swindle. This big hustle."

"Fuck the rich!" yelled a kid in the crowd. There were murmurs around him.

"This little cat. This cute little cat. This little cat that made his way into all our hearts. There is no cat."

A gasp of fury from the city.

"It's a hired cat. A little actor cat. They got him from an advertising agency. The whole idea was to sell sausages. Friendly Pig sausages."

The president of the station glared at his television screen. News was news, but this was going a bit far.

Ivan smiled a brave smile. "You are good people. Look into your hearts and find there—no, not anger! No, not hatred! No, not resentment! Compassion. For people who tried to make free with our good nature! Who tried to turn our dearest hopes into . . . cold cash!"

"Sons of bitches," said the switcher at the control console.

"Ladies and gentlemen, boys and girls, friends, it's hard for me to bring you this news. But let me ask one thing. Don't let this make you mean. They have stolen your hopes, but you can find other hopes. Just go on with your lives. Try to find comfort in each other. Try to be kind. This is Ivan Teuti. Good night and good luck."

He turned away. For the first time in his life he felt clean, pure and past the wall.

Julia understood what he had done to her and began to move back through the crowd, holding her purse over her face. If they recognized her they would kill her.

A bottle curved high over the crowd, falling toward the police line, flashing in the light. It crashed on a car roof and spattered shards of glass in a circle. A motorcycle cop reached up to his face, stared at the blood that came away on his leather glove, swore and raised his club. The people in the crowd nearest him lurched back. The crowd behind them pressed forward again, and the line fell over the motorcycle cop, who started swinging at heads and legs as he went down.

There was a sudden rasping sound, a splay of colour and then a pop of blackness. Judd's body had fallen off the power housing, hit the main cables to the tower and put the station off the air.

"The motherfuckers took him off the air," said a slouching man, and threw his own bottle high in the air.

The window at the front of the station fell. The perimeter fence began to ripple. There was a crunch behind the security line as a guard's leg gave way. The crowd began to push in toward the doors of the darkened station.

Julia reached the edge of the highway. Gracie had one leg over the guardrail. The traffic was racing by her, whipping her open jacket into the air. Julia could see fur in Gracie's folded arms—black, with a white blaze on a dangling leg. She shouted. Gracie's turned to her, then turned back and stumbled into the highway. Julia screamed. A taxi brushed Gracie's sleeve, and Jones scrambled out into the open, climbing her jacket in panic. Julia crawled over the barrier and started running toward him. Gracie lurched forward, and the cat reached the guardrail on the far side of the highway.

Lillian saw the cat flying toward the side of the road and stamped on the brake. The furniture truck that was following her rammed the car into the barrier. When it bounced back, the truck's bumper knocked it onto its side and shoved it, trailing sparks, out into the middle lane of traffic. François sat up as he felt the edge of the car lift into the air; he saw his wife standing by the side of the highway, ten feet away, as he rode helplessly toward a concrete abutment. Gracie jumped and slid under the protective wires. Lillian was shouting. The car smashed into the guardrail on the opposite side, and the furniture truck rammed it again, lifting it directly into the concrete pillar. A construction transport carrying steel girders braked hard. Its load came away from the back of the vehicle and scythed over the railing at the side of the road, missing the cat's head by a foot.

There was a sound of brakes, metal colliding with metal and with concrete, the scraping slide of cars on their sides, brassy music from radios through shattered windshields. The oil from François' car caught fire. The paint began to smoke and peel. His arm was jammed in folded metal. Lillian was lying on the front seat, a motionless furry mound. He felt his blood begin to drain. His head filled with warmth. He saw his faithless wife staring at him across the railing.

The sound alerted the people who lived in the hanging steel beneath the upper highway and they began to climb down the struts to see what they could see. The traffic travelling in the other direction on the lower highway had already begun to slow down. A radio station's helicopter began an approach at low altitude over the lake. Its beating engine thudded in Julia's ears. She saw Gracie turn and run back toward the center of the city.

There were sirens now, coming to the highway from the north. The crowd had begun to break windows and television sets, jamming into bars to get at the big screens that showed sports highlights. Everyone suddenly felt a rage at the glass, at being smiled at, nagged and ordered around by processions of images. Whenever a Friendly Pig commercial appeared, the crowd threw ashtrays, rocks and glasses.

A plainclothes policeman took up a stubborn position in front of an electronics store to defend its monitors from the approaching crowd. He pulled out his gun and shot a waitress in the chest above her name tag. The crowd clubbed him to the ground, and one man pulled the gun away and began to fire it into the air. Other policemen reached for their weapons.

The wind increased, driving pellets of ice into the faces of the crowd. Fires started.

Highway rescue crews were at work on bent and broken cars with huge wrenches and pliers. Scavengers threw open car doors and grabbed purses, bags and coats. The cat bounded down the shoulder of the hill from the highway to the lake. He reached a patch of grass underneath a narrow office building beside the dock. Some of the ground was sectioned into eighteen tiny golf holes, and the cat could smell an entire cluster of his healing plants in the rough beside the seventeenth tee.

The crowd from the television station was starting to move in the direction of the highway to look at the accident. The police held back. A group of men found the big car with the bodies of Lillian and François inside and began to smash in the windows. They were furious at the butcher, his wife and his cat, furious at the cold and sleet and the piercing, rasping suspicion that they had been screwed again. They had always been screwed and would be screwed forever. Now they had the butcher in a bent steel can; sadly, he was already dead, but they were going to pry him out, strip him down and yank him apart.

Julia picked her way between wrecks and reached the guardrail. She could see Jones down the hill. He was thin, limping, lonely. She climbed over the guardrail and moved down the hill toward him.

The stalks of the healing plant had thickened to protect its interior from the wind. The cat barely had the strength to chew through the outer fibrous coating, but his teeth released a heavy, nurturing liquid that began to lift the heaviness in his body.

The power died across the city. The stars emerged above the black buildings.

The cat lay in the oily smoke rolling down from the highway and let the juices from the grass begin to heal him.

Acknowledgments

My thanks to Froma Harrop and to Robin and David Craig, who provided refuge and comfort; to my friends Ian Porter and David Kirk, who read early drafts of early chapters and told me how they might be improved; to Suzanne DePoe and to Jackie Kaiser, who saw artistic and commercial possibilities in my cat; to John Pearce, for early encouragement; to my parents and children, who provided puzzled support; and above all to Anne Collins, my editor and collaborator, who wisely and gently extracted a book from a muddle.

Toronto
September 2002

BILL CAMERON is no stranger to media or the city. A former news anchor for Citytv and CBC in Toronto, he has also written and produced numerous documentaries from such places as Rwanda, the West Bank and Nicaragua for CBC-TV's *The Journal*. A Gemini Award nominee and playwright, Bill Cameron is now a writer, independent broadcaster and host of the I Channel's *On the Record*. He lives in Toronto. *Cat's Crossing* is his first novel.

ABOUT THE TYPE

The body text of *Cat's Crossing* has been set in 'Perpetua,' a typeface designed by the English artist Eric Gill, and cut by the Monotype Corporation between 1928 and 1930. Perpetua (together with its italic partner 'Felicity') constitutes a contemporary face of original design, without historical antecedents. The shapes of the roman characters are derived from the techniques of stonecutting. Originally intended as a book face, Perpetua is unique amongst its peers in that its larger display characters retain the elegance and form so characteristic of its book sizes.

ABOUT THE "LEAPING CAT"

The feline icon featured throughout *Cat's Crossing* references the animal motion studies of Eadweard Muybridge, who in 1887 developed a pioneering 24-camera stop-motion method of photographing animal movement. His work is generally regarded as a pivotal stage in the early development of motion pictures.

To see the cat leap, flip pages quickly from front to back.